Troubles Won't Last Always

MAR 2008

CH

Troubles Won't Last Always

A *novel*

Michelle Caple Taylor

URBAN
CHRISTIAN

www.urbanchristianonline.net

Urban Books
1199 Straight Path
West Babylon, NY 11704

ISBN-13: 978-1-60162-957-9
ISBN-10: 1-60162-957-5

First Printing March 2008
Printed in the United States of America

10 9 8 7 6 5 4 3 2 1

This is a work of fiction. Any references or similarities to actual events, real people, living, or dead, or to real locales are intended to give the novel a sense of reality. Any similarity in other names, characters, places, and incidents is entirely coincidental.

Submit Wholesale Orders to:
Kensington Publishing Corp.
C/O Penguin Group (USA) Inc.
Attention: Order Processing
405 Murray Hill Parkway
East Rutherford, NJ 07073-2316
Phone: 1-800-526-0275
Fax: 1-800-227-9604

Dedication

This book is dedicated to the women who inspired me to write this novel; my mother, Gracie M. Caple, my sister, Vanessa E. Jordan, and my sister-in-law, Jennifer B. Caple. I thank God for each one of them individually, in their own right, for who they are in my life. I love you, ladies.

Acknowledgments

I acknowledge Jesus Christ for the ability to write this novel. I would like to thank my husband, Marvin C. Taylor, for his continuing love and patience through this trying process. I thank my children, Malik, Maliah and Quentin for respecting Mama's time to create. I thank my father, Joe H. Caple, for his support system, and I thank my twin brother, Michael A. Caple, for his belief in me.

I'd like to thank Joylynn Jossel-Ross, my editor, for her honesty, her commitment and dedication to making this novel all God would have it be. Thank you, Joylynn, for not giving up on me.

I would like to thank Reverend Joseph Simmons for his ability to hear from God, move with God and afford me this opportunity to be with the Urban Christian family. Thank you, Reverend Simmons, and Carl Weber, for this beautiful beginning.

Prologue

Mia was a strong woman whose character was made and modeled by life's trials and tribulations. Mostly one woman in Mia's life inspired her, and that was her mother, Imani. She called her Mani, which was Mia's word for "Mommy." Imani was the one person Mia admired most in her life.

Imani had a giant of a spirit. Her faith in Jesus Christ was her strength. She was not big in stature, though—she was five feet seven inches and weighed 120 pounds easy. She was high yellow in color, which most blacks would classify as light-skinned. Her hair was as nappy as a rooster's tail, red and short. She wore it in this little bob with short bangs.

Mia's mother, at the age of fourteen, married her father, Jamal. He was a husky, black, small fellow. He had a big afro and a smile to die for. Jamal came from a religious family and he was very much into the church. About four years into their marriage, Jamal accepted his calling to the ministry and became a preacher.

Three children were a result of Imani and Jamal's union. Jasmine was the first of two girls. Jasmine was so pretty.

She was light brown and stood about five feet and seven inches tall. She was slender and never seemed to get over 125 pounds. The child could pass for a model any day. Jasmine's personality and her looks fit her perfectly. She was happy, to say the least, and showered with love from both sides of the family.

Then there were Mia and Mike; they were twins, but not identical. They came along approximately seven years behind Jasmine. Mia was only five feet and four inches tall. No one could ever tell, though, because she wore high-heeled shoes every day. She never gained over 130 pounds before committing herself to a crash diet. It was partly Mia's low self-esteem that caused her to be extra attentive to her appearance. Mia would sometimes take her black skin and shine it up, brush her wavy, shoulder-length hair, then smile in the mirror at herself and say, "You're beautiful and you matter." Mia had adopted this routine to encourage herself when there was nobody else to encourage her.

Mike had low self-esteem as a child too. He was short and extra skinny, almost sickly looking. He had inherited Imani's red hair with brown skin. Like his mother, he also had nappy hair that made it look like BB pellets on his head. Thank God for change, because Mike had a growth spurt in the eleventh grade and grew to be six feet tall and developed some muscle and weight. He even shaved off all his hair. He looked like a different person and girls finally started to notice him. People swore he was the famous Tupac's twin or Tupac raised from the dead.

Mia loved intensely for the sake of not loving at all. She undercommitted herself to anyone for fear of neglecting herself. She didn't want to be neglected anymore. She worked, but on her own terms. Mia believed she had inherited her mother's strength, which would influence her later in life.

As a woman of twenty-nine, loneliness caused Mia to settle for less. She accepted men who meant her no good. She remained in friendships that didn't bring out the best in her. Subconsciously, Mia believed that she didn't deserve but bits and pieces of love. Whatever love could be mustered up out of pity, Mia believed that was good enough. It was better than no love at all as far as she was concerned.

Mia absorbed the words of her mother when she shared words of wisdom with her. Imani often spoke on God and His love. She would tell Mia things like God was watching her, and not to sleep with anybody before she was married or He'd see. She told her it was wrong for a man to touch a woman before marriage. She also told her that a liar was the worst thing she could be, and according to the Bible, it was a sin. Mia's perception of life was based on those words of the Lord, and this forced Mia to search for her purpose in life.

Mia's character included wisdom and the deepness of a woman and all her complexities. Her complexities held the traits of honesty and a real spirit of kindness to all whom she would meet.

No matter what Mia was going through, she always tried to be there for her sister. Jasmine was forced to deal with dark secrets of betrayal and a stolen virtue, but she seemed to pushed on. Generational curses caused her to be molested by uncles who obviously saw no wrong in their behavior. It took something away from her, but Jasmine was so much like Jamal in character that it seemed like it never fazed her at all. Mia learned as years passed by that smiling people were usually the ones in the most pain—hiding tears behind their smiles.

Jasmine held a very clear perception of life. The trueness of pain and pleasure compelled the necessary components within Jasmine to be a whole woman in all her senses. Mia admired who Jasmine was and who she had become. Mia remembered the nights Jasmine rocked her to sleep well above the age of eleven. She recalled how Jasmine let her sleep closely under her. When things at home seemed at their worst, with Imani and Jamal not speaking for days, Jasmine would smile and let Mia have a portion of her childhood happiness. The sisterly love filled the void of a friend Mia needed as she grew into a woman herself. Jasmine would forever be Mia's closest friend who would be there for life.

Like Imani, Mia admired Jasmine, who would become a woman of all trades—businesswoman, student, wife, mother and friend to many. She loved all who were close to her unconditionally. For all the love she gave completely would be returned to her unconditionally as well.

In the process of Mia evolving into a complete woman, her sister-in-law, Summer, brought a breath of fresh air into her life. She was a down to earth woman full of emotion. Even though Summer had four sisters of her own, she was drawn to Mia, Imani and Jasmine. Mia, Jasmine and Summer were all only one year apart in age, and Summer was the baby girl. Mia felt especially close to her and clung to her every word. She seemed to bring some normalcy to a nontraditional and unfeeling family.

Summer often looked at Mia and immediately saw the innocence and carefree spirit of yet another broken woman. It was only as time went on that Summer would be that common ground between Mia and Mike that established their worth to be loved and love one another openly. Her foreseen love for Mia's twin brother would open up a well of welcomed love for Summer, making her a much needed and much appreciated addition to the family. She and Mike looked like opposites, but they hit if off. Summer was short and cute. She was only four feet and seven inches tall. She had short, dark hair that she wore with little spikes. She was light brown and was a little muscular.

The appreciation of God's gift opened the door for womanly bonding and caused these women to grow more in love as the years rolled on.

The closer Mia got to Summer, the more she was able to see into Summer's soul. She knew, without a doubt, that Summer had experienced some bumps along the road in her journey through life. Her mother had raised Summer and her sisters as a single parent. The struggle of sharing everything and missing out on so many things caused Summer to grow up quickly. She saw the world for what it was at an early age. Her perception of it was that it stank.

Soon after Mia met Summer, Mike made Summer his wife. The sanity of marriage and the walk of a Godly woman brought back sweet memories of Mia's innocence—it seemed so long ago. Summer brought forth Mia's self-worth by evolving into a woman completely taken back by love by her twin brother. These actions caused Mia to take a different look at who she allowed inside her circle of life and through the love of the Father, she would learn that although she seemed troubled at the time, those troubles won't last always.

Chapter One

Mia reflected on her life and her broken marriage. She and Mitchell had been married for eight years. It seemed like eight long, miserable years because Mitchell was selfish and conceited. Mitchell used to make Mia weak in her knees. He was tall, brown-skinned and built. He was so fine. He had short, thick, curly hair and long sideburns with a thin moustache. He was six feet tall and weighed about 230 of solid muscle.

Mia wondered what had made her fall in love with him in the first place. She considered it may have been her past thoughts and perception of settling for love. Mitchell would talk down to Mia; he would criticize her personal taste and call her names. Still, Mia had three kids by Mitchell and kept believing that as long as she had a man, she should be happy.

Tashema, their first born, was four when they divorced. Next, there was their little boy named Tarel, who was two years old, and a little girl name Bridgett, who was barely pushing one year old. Mia came to her senses when after eight years, Mitchell still stayed out all night long and refused to tell her his whereabouts. Painful memories of her mother pretending it was all right pushed her over the edge. She didn't become numb and cold and pretend it was okay. She had to demonstrate she was somebody and she deserved to be loved and respected.

Soon after the divorce, Mia pursued her degree to get her doctorate, and in two years she had obtained it. She thought about all the time she wasted being a housewife and being only a few credits from her doctorate because Mitchell wanted her to have a baby, then another and another. He never encouraged her to go back to school, so she finally realized that if she wanted anything out of life, she had to do it herself.

The hardest part of the transition was the expense of doing it alone. Her first home was the most exciting purchase of her life. It made her appreciate all she had gone through to get to that point. She remembered a conversation she had with her mother.

"Mia, now see how good God is. You moved on and life has been better for you ever since."

"Mani, it hasn't been easy. Sometimes I would lay awake at night wondering how I was going to pay these bills, much less afford my own place."

"Well, if you're going to invest in something, it might as well be something worth investing in. Not no deadbeat man."

"Mani, he's still the kids' daddy." Mia spoke dryly, as if trying to convince herself Mitchell was worth speaking up for.

Imani sighed. "He ain't my daddy."

"Okay, Where is this conversation getting us? Dag, Mani, do you always have to say everything you think?" Mani didn't respond.

They both stood in silence inside Mia's new house. It was a sweet moment for the both of them. The feelings were indescribable for Mia, but they were all joyful.

* * *

Now another era had arrived in Mia's life. She contemplated going on a date with a coworker. Should she open herself up to more pain and hurt? She was aware that every relationship would carry its own tribulations. Yes, she understood that perhaps love could come out of this, but she also had to face reality. Was she ready for simple disappointments? Simple disappointments could be deadly at different intervals in her life.

There were days Mia remembered simple disappointment meant the difference between living and dying—like the days that her food stamps were declined when her job only paid the rent for the roof over her family's head. It wasn't about pride those days, but staying alive. The hardest part was breaking down and taking from strangers. But one never knows who God has put in their paths to bless them. Embarrassment was no longer an issue. It was about survival. It was those days when Mia was forced to grow up and see the sadness in life. That the rain fell upon the just as well as the unjust. It was a struggle.

Thinking back over those times, she asked herself, why did she go on? Why did she keep pushing? Then it came to her; it was because of her children. They were the reason she lived instead of dying.

At that instant, Mia decided to go on her date. In all her experiences, she had forgotten one of the purest and best emotions of living, and that was loving. It was worth the chance because she had nothing to lose, but everything to gain, including love.

Mia walked the halls of her new home. It took some getting used to, but she knew she would get here one day. A gynecologist/pediatrician, single mother and divorced woman, her life left her little time for herself, except this weekend.

"Mia, go ahead and go out. I will watch the kids," Imani spoke insistently.

"For what?" Mia exclaimed. "You'll be fussing tomorrow about how bad they worried you and don't bring them back no time soon."

"What difference does it make? You still going," Imani spoke sarcastically.

"All right, I will bring them on over."

"Okay. See y'all in a few."

"All right, but one thing, Mani. What if he turns out to be a jerk? I can't go through another bad relationship."

"Stop saying what you can't do," Mani scolded her daughter. "You always worrying about what you can't do. Just do it. God got your back."

"I guess you're right," Mia said, undoubtedly speaking with questions in her statement.

"I know I'm right. Can't tell you young girls nothing. If you had waited and heard from God before getting married in the first place, you wouldn't be in this mess. Instead of trying to find a man, you would have been old enough and got married and still had a man."

"Mitchell and I were twenty-two. That is old enough, and I don't think I'm trying to find a man. I was simply asked to go out on a date." Mia's voice was raising. She then said, "Okay, Mom. Look, I will drop the kids off in a minute."

Mia did drop the kids off, but instead of going out on the date, she went back home. Mia took the Friday night to soak in a candlelit bubble bath in her designer bathroom. She had dreamed of this bathroom along with her four-bedroom condo for years. She used to imagine relaxing in a warm bath before going into their lavish bedroom to join Mitchell. She had accomplished part of her dream.

Besides Mitchell staying out all night, she believed the episode preceding that event was what put the icing on the cake. Memories of the past played out slowly in Mia's mind . . .

* * *

"Mitchell, I don't want to hear another story about Denise. Every day you got a story. You make it sound like you two are more than just coworkers, and I am beginning to smell something fishy."

"I was just saying she said they got drunk and she hadn't been to bed yet."

Mia rudely cut off Mitchell. "Blah, blah, blah. I mean, Denise is cute. She is a woman. She may be a little on the big side in my opinion, and she does cute little things with her short haircut, but overall, I am not insecure. She is a woman just like me. She is a little on the short side if you ask me, but that has nothing to do with nothing. My point is, you shouldn't be spending all this extra time talking to another woman. You looking for trouble."

"How I'm looking for trouble? She told me she was pregnant with another man's baby and the man is married. She was crying and all that stuff. She just needed someone to talk to."

"She don't have friends? I mean, why do you think she keep telling you all this personal stuff?" Mia tossed her hands in the air as if to throw the question out to whomever would answer it. "Furthermore, black women have enough trouble holding their marriage down without another black woman stabbing them in the back. I don't like her for that alone."

"Why you tripping?" Mitchell looked at Mia like she was weird.

"Mitchell, I don't think it's a good idea to keep talking to her like that. Any woman who tells a man all her business is out for something more. And since your car been broke down, you always calling me at the last minute, with, 'You don't have to pick me up, Denise can drop me off.' I don't think so!" Mia snapped at Mitchell like she wanted to snap his head off.

"You the silliest woman on God's earth. You always trying to make something out of nothing."

"I mean, it's true; I know women. And why I got to be silly? I'm just telling you I know how they play the game. Why you think she run over to the car looking me up and down every day?" Mia exclaimed.

Mitchell continued to have his talks with Denise. She was not an ugly girl; she just didn't seem like someone Mitchell would have any interest in. However, Mia had an uncomfortable feeling about their entire relationship. When Mia came to pick Mitchell up from work, Denise broke her neck to get over to the car and speak to her. Denise and Mitchell always walked out together. The hurtful part was that Mitchell didn't spend three minutes a day talking to Mia, but it was quite obvious he spent every day at lunch talking to Denise.

Upon first sight, Mia didn't see Denise as a threat; she was an average girl. On a scale of one to ten, she was a five and a half. However, the more Mia talked about Denise to Mitchell, the more Mia could see he was finding a friend in her that he should have been finding in Mia. Mia asked and pretended to be interested in their conversations at lunch to see exactly what Denise was up to—just like in the book of Daniel, she was reading the writing on the wall; Mitchell was heading for an affair, and there was nothing she could do to stop him.

Even sitting in her tub, Mia felt her heart breaking all over again. Just the memories cut deep. A tear fell from her eyes. Maybe she should turn her thoughts to something else; even put on some comforting sounds of gospel, but Mia decided that she needed to remember . . .

"Mitchell, where are you going?" Mia asked annoyingly.

"Why it always got to be the third degree every time I'm stepping out the door?"

"For one, you never take me with you. And the other is

wherever you are going, you can't seem to get home before the wee hours of the morning."

"Whatever. I'm a grown man, and if I want to stay out all night, I will," Mitchell said demandingly.

"I mean, what have I done to you? You act like I did something to you. You are all mean to me for no reason, and you walk around like I did something to you. Don't be fooled; if Ms. Denise whispering in your ear, remember she known for breaking up marriages."

"Whatever. I'm gone."

Mia was devastated. Her marriage was going downhill and she had no idea why. She lay in the bed after Mitchell left. A few hours passed, and Mia looked at the clock. Two o'clock came, then four o'clock. Finally, Mia heard the key turn in the lock. Mitchell walked in, but never came to the bedroom. Soon after, Mia heard him snoring. She got up and walked into the den. Mitchell had made himself a bed on the couch. She felt like her heart was about to break. Why was Mitchell acting this way? she asked herself. Mitchell continued this routine for several weeks in a row.

"Mitchell, what the heck are you doing?" Mia asked angrily.

"Girl, what you talking about now?"

"Who are you sleeping with? How do you just start sleeping on the couch? Do you realize you're hurting me, and I haven't a clue what I've done to you?"

"You here is the problem," Mitchell snapped.

"I'm here? Negro, what you talking about?"

"I can be your Negro, but what does that make you?"

"Stupid, plain stupid for putting up with you this long. We've been together for seven years and you walk around and act like everyone in the world is your friend. You believe that everyone has your best interests at heart but me. Yet, I cook for you, I clean for you, I have sex with you, and do all sorts of things for you. You sleeping on the couch and having sex with me in the middle of the day on the same bed you don't sleep in. I buy you things and when you need someone, I'm the one who has your back. But people don't see the real Mitchell; the one who has an attitude most of the time. You're moody and you act like I owe you something. If you're so miserable being with me, then go on about your business. I don't see any chains holding you," Mia yelled with her hands placed firmly on her hips.

"And I don't see anything holding you back," Mitchell shot back.

"You're exactly right," Mia said. She rolled her eyes and snapped her neck before turning away. Mia turned around almost like a soldier in formation and went into the bedroom. She went to her closet and pulled out her suitcases and then went to open her dresser drawers. Mia began throwing her stuff in the suitcases.

"Mia, what you doing?" Mitchell asked, entering the room.

"What does it look like I'm doing?" She spoke dryly.

"Look, sit down; you're not going anywhere."

"I'm not?" Mia exclaimed.

"You know how we have a few words sometimes and it gets out of hand. Tomorrow we won't even remember this. Come on, we can make up. The kids are at your mom's house. Sit down."

"Maybe you won't remember tomorrow, but I don't deserve this. I will remember you sleeping on the couch and coming in all hours of the morning. You talking with your little girlfriend and giving her an hour of your time, but my hour is for sex and sex only. What is it that I won't remember tomorrow?"

"Don't go, Mia."

"Bye," Mia spoke with authority and walked out. When Mia closed the door, Mitchell opened it and walked behind her and down the apartment steps.

"Mia, you don't want to do this." Mitchell spoke softly.

"I don't want to be treated like no second class whore anymore either."

"Who treating you like that?" Mitchell exclaimed.

"You are, and the sad part about it is that you won't even acknowledge it."

Mia threw her suitcases in the trunk of her car. She brushed sternly past Mitchell, got in the car and closed the door. Mia pulled off while Mitchell was still pleading with her to stay.

Mia thought to herself, *Where will I go?* Her mother was so firm on staying, no matter what a man does, she would never let Mia come home. Mia didn't need to feel unwanted anywhere else, so she decided to go to Mike's. Mia felt like her heart lay on her breasts. Tears streamed down her face because she already knew Mitchell had been unfaithful. Their intimacy felt different, and deep down inside she had begun to feel dirty afterward.

Even to this day, Mia prayed for continued strength. The verbal abuse and terrible behavior had been too much for Mia. She breathed a big sigh of relief that part of her life was over with, and she decided to get up and make the most of her life now.

After draining the water from her bath, Mia fixed herself a glass of wine and went out onto her balcony. It was a warm night out and as she sat in her lawn chair, she could see the city lights down below. Beyond the city lights she could see the mountaintops that the sun slowly set behind. It was beautiful. But the best part of it all was below her condo lay the ocean and the sand. How extradionary was that? A city view from afar but the winds and waters beneath her feet.

Mia relaxed in her Victoria's Secret nightgown. The long

sleeveless satin gown felt good against her body; and it was her favorite color, midnight misty red.

Mia finally tried to make sense of things in her life. What was a complete life without someone to love? She had been through so much when it came to love. Mia's energy seemed to slowly drain from her body. Dating seemed like a tremendous task. The more Mia thought, the more she contemplated this dating thing. *Perhaps I will go tomorrow night,* she thought. Mia drifted off to sleep and needless to say, stood up her date.

She awoke in the middle of the night, reflecting over the beautiful ensemble God had given her. It beat living in a shelter any day, she thought. Even then, Mia found contentment in the walls of a shelter home. She had grown tired and weary of being in other people's houses; having to borrow other people's things and sometimes being in the way. The toll had grown heavy on her shoulders. In the shelter, she didn't feel isolated, and her burdens were at rest. Other women in the shelter had found themselves in a similar situation, but for different reasons. Mia felt the same as she did when she was in college and lived in a dormitory. It wasn't home, but it was housing. Mia was at peace, but it was hard for Imani to understand. Imani pleaded with Mia to come home. Against Mia's better judgment, she did just that.

Mia missed the company of her loyal sisters in the shelter. They used to sit in the den, watching television and sharing stories of their experiences. The shelter, for many of them, was a transition period as well as a resting period. It was an unspoken truth for abused women that no matter how they came out of the situation, they needed some time to just be alone. There was that need to just put the pieces back together mentally before they could put the tangible parts of their lives back together. Mia understood this without counseling. She was there because she needed to be where she would be understood the most. Mia also wanted God to have complete control of her life, and what better way than to give it all to Jesus and rest in his arms.

She needed to sleep without someone expecting anything in return; to rest without wondering whose space she was invading. She needed to eat without starving for fear of what she consumed could be for someone else. Mia didn't want to worry about how she would eat, sleep or make it through tomorrow. She knew she wouldn't have to explain her choices to anyone but God. For the first time in months, Mia was at peace and it was at the most unlikely place anyone would expect—a shelter. She and her kids were fed, warm and clothed.

Leaving the shelter seemed premature to Mia because she needed healing, but she pushed on in order to maintain the dignity others felt she had to maintain. Mia felt she was simply living beneath her means, because her Father, Jesus Christ, owned everything on Earth and in Heaven.

Mia had made up her mind that anything was better than being with Mitchell. Mia believed Imani wanted her to take Mitchell's abusive and cheating ways. Imani knew her daughter's struggles wouldn't be easy. Her mother was even unsure if Mia was strong enough to make it on her own.

Just the same, Mia still didn't regret leaving Mitchell. All she kept remembering is how she almost lost her mind.

Summer, a new era woman, had become Mia's strength in a silent way. She often told Mia, "You can do bad all by yourself. Many women raise children alone and make it. It won't be easy, but, Mia, you can do it. You're smart and beautiful and don't let anyone tell you different."

Summer had been raised by her mother. She saw the strength of one woman raise many children. Her experience was her proof. If put to the test, Mia knew Summer could pass this test. It was herself she had the doubts about every now and then. She knew she was extremely strong, but sometimes she felt like she couldn't do it on her own.

Mia's household always had two parents. For that reason, Mia could never envision her family without a daddy. How could she? Why would she tear her family apart until all that was left was her sanity? She had a choice to live life or die trying to live life. Mia decided to live life, so Mitchell had to go, but she realized that he was still her children's father forever.

Jasmine, who was a realist and a survivor of life's circumstances, often coached Mia through trying times. She helped Mia walk through the changes happening in her life. Jasmine felt her pain and offered her support emotionally, and sometimes bought her things to cheer her up. She wanted to see her sister get through this and succeed. Imani, Summer and Jasmine all encouraged Mia, for they knew the different walks of being a woman. They each shared their lives with Mia, and without them, Mia would be incomplete.

"Mani, I won't get the kids today," Mia told her mother through the phone receiver. "I think I will go out tonight. Will you watch them again, please?"

"Okay, but come get your busy bodies tomorrow."

"Thanks, Mani."

Eventually, Mia got up and got dressed.

She put on a pair of jean shorts, a white strapless shirt and soft brown sandals. She threw on a baseball cap and headed out. She spent the day window shopping. She then bought a sandwich and pulled a book from her bag and picked a spot in the park. Before Mia knew it, the sun was setting and it was 7:00 in the evening. Mia grabbed her things and headed toward home. She thought as she strolled along, *maybe I will do another bubble bath. No, maybe tonight I'll actually go out. What should I do?* Mia looked to the sky for an answer. It was a beautiful night with a slight breeze blowing.

"Thank you, Lord, I will."

After arriving back home, Mia showered and dressed in a white sleeveless dress that hung comfortably over her frame. She threw on some three-inch sandals with tie straps that went up her legs. Her white dress hung a little bit below her thighs. She pulled her hair up in a bun with a few strands hanging on the sides and in the front. Mia thought she didn't look half bad. She threw on some simple earrings and a soft necklace to accentuate her look.

A little while later, Mia walked into the Chow Spot. It was a poetry place. She chose a table near the center, right in front of the stage. She held her poetry book close. The rhythm of the club was flowing. Soft jazz played in the background for each poet.

"Are you having a drink?" The waiter approached her.

"Yes, soda please. Make it a Pepsi."

"Yes, madam."

"Do I look that old?" Mia never looked up.

The waiter responded. "No, you look that good."

Mia looked up. His smile was breathtaking. He had long dreads that looked shiny and soft. His face was like midnight, and smooth to the naked eye. She smiled back finally.

"Thank you."

"I'll be right back with your Pepsi."

Mia felt flustered. *Don't even go there, Mia,* she thought. *Besides, what can he offer me as a waiter?* When the waiter returned, Mia said thank you, gave him the money and never looked up again.

"You're welcome." The waiter walked off briskly.

The line was down to no one to read, so Mia made her way on stage.

"Hi, my name is Mia Reese." The musician began to play. "No music, please." Mia rolled the words off her tongue slowly and gently, as if the words were a prelude to her poem.

"The title of this poem is, 'IS'." She opened her poetry book, cleared her throat and began to read:

His eyes were like murky waters,
visible but unseen.
His features like mountaintops,
defined and bold,
strong in its own structure.
I felt the earth shake beneath me.
My heart trembled,
And . . .
I became lost in the moment.
Now I sit,
Unable to regain my composure,
Or understand
What has taken a part of me.
It seems as if I was hit from behind,
Unprepared, unexpecting or capable of seeing his face
     again.
He was BAD . . .

Mia continued to speak softly and sensually:

Never had I envisioned what
I saw on that moonlit night.
It was God before me,
In all His awesome power.
His exquisite taste and beauty
It was love all over again.
My soul aches,
And I wallow in my pity as I wonder could He love me
Just the same . . .
It was MAN
In all his glory . . .

The crowd stood to their feet and clapped vigorously as Mia made her way off the stage.

She sat and exhaled.

"Nice poem," spoke the waiter.

"Full of compliments, aren't you?" responded Mia.

"Yeah, and it's been too long, huh?" The waiter lifted his eyebrows in exclamation.

"Too long for what?" Mia asked sternly.

"Since you had a good man."

Mia sighed. "I apologize. I guess I have been a little rude to you."

"Apology accepted. My name is Braxton Hamilton." Braxton held out his hand.

"Hi, Braxton, my name is Mia. Nice to meet you." Mia spoke with a gentle smile on her face.

"Look, I'm ready to get off. Do you mind if I sit and have a drink with you?"

"I don't see why not."

Braxton returned with two more Pepsi's. "I took the liberty of getting you another drink."

Mia smiled. "Thanks."

"So, do you come out much, Mia?"

"No, not really. I'm a pediatrician and a single mother. I don't have much time."

"Well, you're out tonight."

"Yeah. It's pathetic when your mother feels it's time for you to go out. I guess she is feeling sorry for me."

"Sounds like a considerate mother." Braxton smiled and he and Mia continued to talk a while longer.

"Well, looks like everyone is gone except us. Should I walk you out?"

Mia looked around, for the first time noticing the emptiness of the room. "I guess so. Yes."

Braxton walked Mia to her car. Her Jaguar was parked right out front.

"Well, here I am." Mia swirled around in front of her car.

"Mia, may I call you sometime?" Braxton didn't hesitate to ask.

"Hum, I don't think so."

"Why not?"

"Well, I guess you can call if you're looking for a friend."

"Okay, friend. I can deal with that."

Mia wrote her home number on the back of her business card. "Here you go."

Braxton grabbed her hand and kissed it. "Thank you. Good night, Mia."

She watched him walk away. She got in her car, pulled out her cell phone and dialed Jasmine before pulling off. "Hey, bat," Mia playfully called her sister. "I just met this fine man. Girl, he is fine!"

"Where you meet him at?"

"This place called the Chow Spot. Remember the little poetry place?"

"Oh yeah. Well, good. I was afraid cobwebs were going to grow on your thang."

"Real funny. Anyway, I'm driving, so I'll call you back."

"Bye."

Mia drove home and changed out of her clothes and into her silk gown. This one was a fuchsia red, also Victoria's Secret. She went outside and lay on her lawn chair. She looked at the blue and orange lights that lit up the night sky. She grabbed her comforter and a glass of wine and snuggled up under the stars. It was nice and quiet. Then her phone rang. It was 12:00 A.M.

"Hello," Mia answered.

"Mia?"

"Braxton?"

"Yes. This is Braxton. I was wondering if I can see you."

This is definitely a bootie call, Mia thought.

Chapter Two

As a result of Braxton's late-night call, they agreed to meet-up for a date. Braxton's intention had only been to check to see if Mia had made it home okay, and to secretly make sure she had given him the correct phone number.

The very next day, Mia dressed in a pink floral print dress in preparation for their date. She wore her pink lace-up sandals and a small necklace with a diamond piece hung from her neck. She put on matching earrings and let her hair hang. Simple but elegant, casual yet dressy; she had accomplished her goal. She wondered if she had let herself get a little too excited about her first real date in ages. Mia fixed herself a small glass of wine and ate a few crackers with tuna.

"Can't be all hungry on the first date; need to eat like a lady."

Mia kicked off her sandals and tried to rest her nerves. When eight o'clock approached, she drifted off to sleep. When she awoke, it was ten o'clock. Her heart immediately sank. "What in the world? I know this guy didn't ask me out and then stand me up." Mia felt disgusted, and her self-esteem dropped by the second. In the midst of her ranting, the phone rang.

"Hello," Mia answered both sheepishly and with a little attitude.

"Hi, Mia, it's Braxton."

"Oh, hi. What can I help you with? I mean obviously you have an issue with time." Mia smacked her lips in frustration after speaking.

"Look, I apologize about tonight. I guess I should have explained that I'm also into construction."

"And being into construction mean you don't call? So explaining it doesn't change anything. You should have called, like I said," Mia exclaimed.

"We were working on a project on the bridge on Fifth Avenue. It ran late. It was an emergency. But if it isn't too late, we can still go out."

"No. You messed up on the first date. I think I should take that as a sign."

"Can I make it up to you? I mean, signs can be misinterpreted. I really don't believe in them anyhow."

"I don't know. I'll call you."

Mia hung up, wondering why she had decided to put herself through the twist and turns of a relationship. It always ended up opening up her heart to disappointment.

The phone rang again. Mia looked at the caller ID, clicked to answer, and then hung up. Braxton didn't call anymore that night. However, the next day, he was calling bright and early.

"Man he act like we been dating for years and I just broke his heart. He's probably a crazy man, a prowler or something like that."

Braxton called over the course of the next few days. Mia finally gave in to him and accepted another date.

Mia decided this time to just throw on some slacks, a halter top and a slight two-inch sandal with her hair hanging.

She put on a little makeup because she wanted to be the best looking woman Braxton would see tonight.

The doorbell rang. Mia opened the door and there he stood, all six feet of him, smelling good and looking good. He stood with peach roses in his hand.

"Hi, Mia. I brought a peace offering."

"Hi, Braxton, and thank you. They are lovely." Mia reached over and gave Braxton a distant and soft hug. She patted him on his shoulder gently as she moved aside to let him inside the door. "So, what's the plan?"

"I thought we would go to dinner and then dancing. You know, the normal for a first date."

"I'm not much of a dancer these days. It's been a while."

"Well, let's take it as it comes." Braxton grabbed Mia by the hand and proceeded toward the door.

"Sounds good to me."

Dinner was at a five star restaurant. The conversation was good, and Mia was falling for this man all too quickly. She liked the way he talked, the way he smelled, the way he looked and the way he walked. They went dancing, and it turned out that she liked the way he danced too. They clicked like Ben and Jerry. It must have become clear that they had pretty strong chemistry because they decided to go for ice cream. Everything was smooth. It didn't seem like they had just met. The laughter came easily and the time flowed by quickly. Before they knew it, the night had drifted into the morning hours. It was 3:30 A.M. when they decided to go back to Mia's condo. They walked hand-in-hand to Mia's door.

"Mia, may I kiss you good night?" Braxton asked, almost bashfully.

"Is it still night?" She eluded his request.

"From the looks of it, it's morning." Braxton looked up in the sky and then looked back at Mia seriously. "Well, may I kiss you good morning?"

"If you have to ask, perhaps this date wasn't all I thought was." Mia took a step closer to Braxton.

"It was more," Braxton whispered.

Mia stood in her doorway, looking up at Braxton. Braxton, with a settled smile, approached her and grabbed her elbows gently. He pulled her slightly to him and stooped down to kiss her. His kiss was as soft as his lips. Mia met his kiss, and for a moment, she drifted away. It was one of those kisses that immediately made her feel like she was being lifted to another place. Her head spun, and for a moment, she imagined she was away to some other place. Minutes later, their eyes met in a stare.

"Are you sure I can't treat you to breakfast?" Braxton asked Mia hesitantly.

"I'm not sure, but I'm going to say good night now."

"Good night? Mia, I thought we established it was morning."

"All right, how about have a good day." Mia smiled.

"Okay, I'll call you later today."

"Okay, good day." Mia gently closed her door while watching Braxton stand there like a dazed puppy.

Mia leaned up against her door. She felt like a silly teenager. "Wooooo-weeeee! He's fine and he kisses good."

Mia danced down the hallway to her bedroom, stepping like a model, doing the robot and all sorts of crazy stuff as she finally fell across her bed and held her pillow. "Life is not so bad after all."

Mia woke up a few hours later, feeling refreshed. She went to her bathroom and began her shower. Mia stood in her shower, letting the warm water run across her body. How wonderful it felt to be the center of a man's attention once again. Mitchell had rarely kissed her, let alone made her the center of his attention. Imani said she required too much attention, but it was the same attention any woman would have longed for. It was a sore subject between Imani and Mia, so Mia stayed safely away from the conversation with her.

Jasmine felt just the opposite and suggested perhaps Mitchell could have been a little more loving. What is too much attention? Every woman needs a man and every woman needs to know that a man loves her above all else. If that wasn't the case, God would have made man alone.

Meanwhile, the sun had gone down and Mia looked at her clock. It was 8:30 P.M. later that evening, and no call from Braxton. The day had flown past very quickly. She wouldn't admit it, but she had waited for his call. She constantly checked to see if her cell phone was on, and to see if a dial tone was on the regular house phone.

"Oh God, here I go, acting like some crazed woman waiting by the phone. Let me find something to do."

Mia began baking cookies. Once they were done, she pulled a blanket out of the closet and turned to Lifetime. Once she was engrossed in a movie, the phone rang.

"Hi, it's Braxton." His voice sounded like rushing waters. Her stomach immediately churned and the butterflies felt like they were wrestling for space.

"Hi, Braxton. How you doing?"

"Missing you. Can I come over?"

Mia's stomach flipped again. "Sure you can."

Braxton came by, and he and Mia watched Lifetime together. After the movie, Braxton spoke. "You can exhale now."

"Shut up, crazy!"

The two of them laughed, and then kissed. It was something all too powerful as their lips met.

As the months rolled on, Mia realized she had found a best friend. They had so much in common. They were both very gentle spirits. There was nothing she couldn't ask of

Braxton; there was nothing he wouldn't do for her. She was, however, having a problem with him constantly breaking dates. She understood that he was a construction worker and had to take work as it came along; however, he rarely answered his phone! Mia decided not to let any bad thoughts control her actions. It was obvious he loved her and only her. How could something so right be wrong? It couldn't. One thing was certain: real love couldn't be mistaken for anything else. And it felt real good.

Chapter Three

The phone rang at about 1:00 A.M.

Mia hated these types of calls in the wee hours of the morning. She looked at the phone as it rang for the third time, contemplating whether to answer it. It usually meant something was wrong. Her heart went pitter patter. Finally, on the fifth ring, she answered.

"Hello."

"Hello." The voice of an unfamiliar woman asked, "Is Braxton there?"

"No, he isn't. Who is this?"

The woman hung up.

Who was that? Mia asked herself. Mia dialed Braxton's cell phone. He answered on the first ring.

"Braxton, where are you?" Mia asked directly, and feelings of nervousness came upon her.

"I'm just getting off work. Why?" Braxton wondered why Mia sounded so weird.

"A lady just called here for you, and when I asked who she was, she hung up."

"I don't know who that could have been."

"No idea?" Mia exclaimed.

"No idea. What are you doing?"

"I was asleep."

"Can I come over and stay with you tonight?"

"I don't know. Looks like someone else is expecting you. For someone who has no idea, someone knew where to call and find you."

"Come on. I don't know what that was about. Besides, whoever it was knows we are a couple."

"Okay." Mia smiled. "I like the sound of that, 'couple.'"

"Good, I'll be over shortly."

Mia jumped up and put on her perfume and one of her favorite gowns. This one was short, sexy and red. When the doorbell rang, Mia sashayed to the door and stood with her hands holding the door open. After opening the door with a big smile, she said "Since no one else was expecting you, then I guess my expectations for tonight are good."

"Dag, you're darn right they good. You look good, girl." Braxton rushed over and bear-hugged Mia. She embraced his hug and placed her arms around his shoulder while standing on the tips of her toes. She looked Braxton in the eyes. "Thank you." Mia spoke sheepishly.

Braxton had on jeans and a T-shirt with sneakers, and his boyish look turned Mia on. "You don't look so bad yourself," he replied.

"Yeah?"

"Yeah."

Braxton picked up Mia and took her to the bedroom and for the first time—months after their initial encounter—Mia gave herself to Braxton. Although God might not have approved, she needed what Braxton had to offer; it had been far too long.

The next day, Summer came over to visit. "Leave the door open and let some fresh air come through the screen door."

"What's going on, Mia?"

"Nothing much."

"How are things going with Braxton?"

"Fine, I guess. Someone called last night about 1:00 A.M. looking for him."

"What? Did he say what that was about?" Summer exclaimed.

"Said he didn't know." Mia spoke slowly.

"And you believed him?" Summer remarked.

"For now," Mia answered.

A gentle knock came from the door. Summer looked through the screen door and saw that it was Jasmine.

"Jasmine is at the door," said Summer.

"Can you get it please, Summer?"

Summer strolled over to the door and answered it. "Hey, Jasmine."

"What you bats doing?" Jasmine smiled as she waited for a response.

"Nothing, but it looks like you're getting ready to work the streets dressed in that short skirt." Mia looked Jasmine up and down as she spoke.

Summer laughed. "Well, I just dropped by to say hey. I got to go, girl."

"Summer, I just got here. Where you going?" Jasmine asked her.

"I'm going out. Bye." Summer walked out the door without another word, twitching her tail and flicking her fingers as if to say, "toot-a-loo."

"Bye then." Jasmine respond after the door closed. "What's up, Mia?"

"Nothing, girl. I was just telling Summer that Braxton received a call this morning around one o'clock from some woman. She hung up when I asked who she was. He said he doesn't know anything about it."

"Well, just give him the benefit of the doubt for now; he might not know what it was about. I like Braxton. He seems to keep a smile on your face, so give him a chance, Mia."

"Okay." Mia agreed.

"What are you doing today?"

"Nothing. I just swung by because I was at the mall. I'm not staying either. I have to go pick up the kids. Love you, girl. Just came by to check on you." Jasmine headed toward the door.

"Okay. See ya."

Mia told herself to be prepared. Braxton was probably just like any typical male and was up to something. She had bypassed the "it's me" syndrome and had come to accept that men were like dogs with two legs. Not to say they weren't worth a dime, but she didn't know one who had ever been completely faithful to one woman. It required a mature woman to accept an affair. More than likely, it would happen once. After that, she decided she would get rid of his butt. No one needs a love like that.

Imani used to tell Mia to give it to God when she was married to Mitchell. But to Mia, it sounded like she was saying give him his space to cheat.

The phone rang.

"Hello," Mia answered.

"You know Braxton has a woman, right?" The strange woman spoke convincingly.

"Excuse me," Mia said.

"You didn't actually think a man like Braxton was alone. I mean, be realistic."

"Whoever this is, if you can't identify yourself, this conversation is over."

"I just identified myself. Didn't you hear me say, you don't actually think Braxton didn't have a woman?" The stranger spoke with a snobbish tone.

"Who is this?" Mia frowned. "Maybe Braxton has a girl, because any real woman would identify herself."

"Funny, I see you got a sense of humor. Maybe you will laugh when he leaves you cold and dry, 'cause he's coming home."

The phone went dead and so did Mia's heart.

Chapter Four

Mia paced back and forth, angry over the phone call she had just received. Minutes later, the phone rang again.

"Hello!" Mia exclaimed, her previous anger still evident.

"Hello, is Braxton there?" It was the same woman's voice.

"Oh, so now you trying to be funny. Who is this?"

"This is his wife," the woman said matter-of-factly.

Mia lost her breath. "Excuse me?"

"Well, his fiancée anyway."

"First his wife, then fiancée. Who are you?"

"My name is Tracie. Braxton and I were engaged. We separated when he started to see you."

"Well, then that means it's over between you two."

"I wouldn't say so. He was over here the other night," she bragged.

"And for what reason? You can't be telling the entire story."

"To see the kids." Tracie spoke sincerely.

"You all have kids together?" Mia couldn't believe what she was hearing.

"No. They're my kids, but he loves them dearly."

"It looks like you don't want to let go. I had nothing to do with your separation or break-up, so what in the world are you calling me for?"

"Because you finalized it."

"How about I tell Braxton you called when he gets in?" This time Mia hung up the phone. "The nerve of that woman calling my house," Mia spoke angrily.

Speak of the devil, Braxton walked in.

"Mia, where you at, girl?" Braxton spoke enthusiastically.

"I'm back here in the bedroom, Braxton!"

"What's up, lovely?"

"Well, Tracie just called."

"Tracie?" Braxton said, surprised to hear her name.

"She obviously feels things aren't settled between the two of you. Do you care to share with me? She said you two were engaged."

"Silly girl, that was a long time ago. It's over between us. She shouldn't be calling. I don't even know how she got your number."

"A long time ago? How long before we met?"

"Maybe a month and a half."

"Not so long ago, Braxton!"

"Long enough, Mia. It's the past. What does it matter how long anyway? I'm happy, aren't you?"

"Yes."

"Well, okay then, enough of that. Can we talk about something else now?"

"How do you know it's over with? A month and a half is no time at all. You didn't give yourself time. You were going to marry her."

"I had been thinking about leaving for a long time, and when I finally left, it was already over in my heart. My God, we were engaged for three years. Shouldn't that tell you something? She was good to me, but my heart wasn't there."

"How do I know your heart is here? I mean, you were getting ready to get married."

"I'm here, Mia. That says it all. Trust me."

"You were there for three years. It proved to be a mistake. You realized it and left. That says so much for commitment and security after a three-year relationship. How do you expect me not to feel a little insecure?"

"Something has me here with you now. I don't play games, Mia." He walked up to her, put his arms around her and began kissing her neck. "It's not me. I'm a man."

"Indeed you are." Mia smiled, being taken in by Braxton's touch.

"That is what I'm talking about. Now come to your man and let me show you what I'm working with."

Mia giggled like a little girl as she snuggled a little closer to Braxton.

Braxton squeezed Mia in his arms. Mia felt safe and secure. Maybe now Mia would finally understand what Imani had told her for years: *When you have a man in your life that makes you priority over all things, you experience the trueness of real love and the worth of that love.* Mia thought her mother could be right.

The next day, however, something deep down inside of Mia told her to let it go before things turned ugly. Her mind told her she wasn't ready to deal with such a conflicting situation, but her heart told her she needed love, and she needed it now, no matter what the cost.

"Maybe I will call Mani to get some direction. I'm desperate." Mia sighed. Mia dialed the phone number. "Mani, hey. It's me."

"Uh-huh. How you doing?" Imani replied.

"Running wild."

"The kids want to stay the summer. What do you think?"

"It's fine with me."

"What's the matter? You sound like you got something else on your mind."

"Nothing. Just called to say hey, but I have to go. Someone

is at the door," Mia lied. She had changed her mind about talking to her mother. She didn't tell her mother about the drama with Tracie for fear her mother might judge and dismiss Braxton as a no-good liar. She really liked Braxton and wanted to give the relationship a fair chance.

"Okay. Goodbye."

After hanging up the phone, to Mia's surprise, her lie manifested. Someone tapped on her door, but they were gone when she opened it. Mia stepped out and peeped down the street. Before she could close the door, she noticed an envelope on the ground.

"Wait, what is this?" Mia opened the envelope, pulled out the enclosed letter and read it.

Dear "Other Woman",

    I know you don't know me, but I know you. You're the one who took my love away. Braxton is hurt, maybe even confused, because of the rough times between us. If you've ever been in love, then you know how I feel and you will let him go.

                                      Sincerely,
                                 "The Woman"

Mia knew the letter was from Tracie, and she almost felt sorry for her. *What am I supposed to do? Neglect myself for her?* Mia thought. *She had her chance with him. Just the same, I know how she feels to know another woman is with the man she loves.*

Mia knew how heartwrenching and painful Tracie's nights could be. How long they could drag on and on. *Do I believe in love, or do I believe in chosen beliefs? I have my morals,* Mia confirmed in her thoughts.

Summer came to mind as Mia wondered how to face this obstacle. Summer was a young woman whose strength lay in her commitment to her husband. It was an undying love.

It wasn't easy being the denied wife in times of tribulations, the times when Summer needed Mike and he wasn't there due to the barriers of his childhood. He would shut down and be unresponsive and distant. He was in his own world, alone. It hurt Summer, but she chose to handle it. It was a matter of running or standing through the storm. But Mia knew that storms seem to last forever when your heart is broken.

Mia was sitting alone in her den when Braxton came out of the bedroom. He was smiling. "Last night together was nice, right?"

"Yeah, I enjoyed your company." Mia wasn't smiling.

"Mia, what's wrong?" Braxton asked.

"Braxton, I think we should move on with our lives. You know, each go our own way."

"What? What are you talking about?" Mia's comment had caught Braxton off guard.

Mia passed the letter to Braxton. "Read this letter."

Braxton read it in silence. "Where did you get this from?" he asked, handing it back to Mia.

"It was left at my door."

"Look, Mia, Tracie can't understand that it's over between us," Braxton explained.

"Have you made it clear to her that it's over?"

"I'm here with you all the time. How much more clear can I make it?"

"How about making sure she understands that it's over between you two?"

"I've tried. She knows how I feel about you. I haven't lied to anyone. Come on, let's go out or something. Don't let her get to you. Let me take you shopping," Braxton said seductively.

"That isn't the answer."

"I know. I just don't want to argue. I don't want you to doubt my love. How else can I show you?"

"That's for you to decide."

"Well, you know I want us to get married one day."

"No, I didn't know."

"Well, now you know; so let's go somewhere, okay?"

"I want to talk about this marriage thing some more."

Braxton's cell phone rang before he could reply. "Hello," he answered and then listened intensely to the caller. A few seconds later, he hung up.

"Let's put that dinner on hold. I have to run out."

"It's nine o'clock at night. Where you going?"

"That was Tracie. She said she was going to kill herself. I have to go." Braxton raced out the door, leaving Mia alone.

Braxton knocked once on Tracie's door, and when she didn't answer, he turned the knob. It was unlocked, so he let himself in. He was afraid of what he would see. He wasn't in love with her anymore, but he still had love for her. He didn't want to see anything bad happen to her. When he got inside, she was on the chair crying, holding a bottle of pills.

"Tracie, what are you doing? Why are you doing this?"

"You know how you left me wasn't right, and now you with someone else like we never existed," Tracie cried.

"Tracie, things didn't work out between us; you know that."

"But how are you with someone so soon?" Tracie asked.

"I need to go on with my life. I didn't choose when that someone new would come into my life, but she did and that's that."

"Braxton, you know I still love you. You know I'm the right one for you."

"So what you going to do, kill yourself? Is that going to make anything better?"

"No, but if I can't have you, I'd rather not live."

"What about the kids?"

"They have their daddy and the rest of their family."

"But they need their mama."

"I know, but I need you. If you say we can be friends and just try to make things work, I will put these pills down and I will never mention killing myself again."

"You're going to put the pills down and never mention it anyway. You're just trying to have your way."

"You're right, and that should show you how much I love you."

Tracie leaned over and kissed Braxton.

"You know we can't go there." He gently pushed her away.

"Just one last time."

"For what? For you to go and tell Mia?"

"I promise I won't. Just one last time."

"Promise?" Braxton asked reluctantly.

"Promise."

"Okay. I miss the way you do that thing. You know . . . when you turn and, you know . . ." Braxton blushed.

"Yeah, I know." Tracie spoke leisurely. She grabbed Braxton by the hand and led him to her bedroom. Braxton seemed to forget all about his relationship with Mia; at least for the next couple of hours anyway.

Chapter Five

How much is too much for the sake of love? I feel like the other woman. Well, no, I feel like a woman hanging on to something that won't last. I wish I had inherited Jasmine's wisdom for life. I have her carefree spirit deep inside of me. I hope it will release itself in time, Mia thought.

Mia picked up her cell phone. "Jasmine, want to go out?"

"Where's Braxton?"

"Girl, drama."

"Not Tracie?"

"Yes, Tracie."

"Okay, I'll be over in a short while. I was dressed to do something anyway."

A little later, Jasmine walked in with her three-inch heels, ready to go out.

"Ready to roll, girl?" asked Jasmine.

"Yeah, I'm ready."

"So, what are you going to do about this situation, Mia?"

"I don't know. I'm not sure I'm up for the battle."

"Mia, don't put yourself through nothing else with no man. Mitchell took you through enough for a lifetime."

"Don't start, Jasmine."

"It's true."

"Well, what about you? I mean, what is going on with you and Evan?"

"Change the subject, please."

"That is what I thought."

Jasmine was not any better off than Mia. Her love life was a mess.

"You would think that women our age would have a life by now." Jasmine changed the subject. "Let's go to the G-Strap."

The G-Strap was a popular night club. It played mostly reggae, and the crowd was mixed with people from all cultures. The atmosphere was upbeat, but the setting was very laid back. It had a large dance floor with elegant glass tables and booths surrounding the dance floor. The seats were cushioned and the bartender was up on a stage area across the room from the DJ.

When Jasmine and Mia arrived, people were in the streets, waiting to get in. It was a cool night for the middle of the summer. Jasmine and Mia stood in the street looking very in-style, wearing the latest fashion. A man walked by smelling all good, and Mia looked at the gorgeous man.

"Oh my God, Drake, is that you?" Mia squealed.

The man turned and looked around. "Hey, Mia. What's up?" Drake said.

"Nothing. How are you doing?"

"I'm okay." Drake looked Mia up and down, taking careful observation of her appearance and physical stature. He spoke.

"You look good."

"You do too."

Drake was with a few friends. "We're getting ready to go downtown." Want to come?" Drake invited Mia.

"I can't tonight," she replied.

"All right, but give me a call sometime. I'm listed." Drake winked and walked off.

"Mia, who was that?" Jasmine asked.

"Some guy I used to talk to a little after Mitchell and I split."

"He was fine," Jasmine squealed.

"He looked better than I remember."

The rest of the night, all Mia could do was think about Drake as she penned a poem in her heart.

How do you let go of what seems so real
What seems to be the reason for the beat of your heart?
You inspired me
You strengthened me
In a way no other can.
The simple nature of your being is what captured me
Mind, body, and soul.
To be with you for eternity
Is to live my life
To its full capacity.
How can I go on if I didn't
Exchange those vows with you
Today, tomorrow and always?
Its up to you and me to know that
It's real.

"You thinking about Braxton?" Jasmine asked her sister.

"No. I believe that is a done deal."

"Then what's on your mind?"

"Drake. He was good to me. No drama either."

"Then what happened? I know there is a story behind letting that fine man go."

"I flipped out on him one day. Then I was back and forth with Mitchell. I messed up."

"Looks like some heavy chemistry is still there."

"I know. I feel like I've been hit with a Mac truck. It caught me off guard, you know, seeing him."

"Yeah, I know."

"You ready to call it a night?"

"Yeah, I'm ready."

On the ride home, Jasmine and Mia were basically quiet.

Jasmine pulled up into Mia's driveway. "Well, here we are."

"Okay. Thanks, Jasmine, for going out with me. I know the club scene isn't really your thing."

"For you, sis, anytime."

Jasmine sounded distracted. Mia looked at Jasmine's somber expression. "You okay?"

"Yeah. Just thinking about moving into my own place this week. Maybe if I move, things will be better between Evan and me."

"Who knows, but don't go making any decisions based on Evan. You know I think he acting funny anyway. Things can change in no time."

"I know, but maybe it is time for me to be on my own."

"It's your choice. See you later."

"Bye."

Mia watched her sister drive off and then headed in the house only to find Braxton on the couch. She wondered if he got the note she wrote earlier, telling him she would be going out with Jasmine.

"Braxton, hey," Mia said dryly.

"I got your note. You have a good time?"

"Yeah. It was cool."

"You okay? You sound out of it."

"Yeah, I'm fine. Is everything okay with Tracie?"

"Mm-hmm, we talked."

"Oh."

"You're not going to ask about what?"

"Don't really want to know." Mia looked at Braxton with a look of complete disregard.

"What does that mean?"

"I don't know. Just don't care, I guess."

"Maybe it means you met someone else tonight."

"No, I didn't meet anyone."

"You ate yet?"

"Nope."

"Let's go get something to eat."

"Perhaps I should eat something before I go to bed."

"I am starving. It has to be breakfast this time of the morning, though. It's almost 2:30 A.M."

"Whatever is fine with me."

Mia and Braxton left. They went to a little breakfast spot not far from Mia's condo. Mia picked over her food, feeling traumatized.

Is my heart open for any lover or is Drake my true love? Something happened when I saw him. Do other women go through this? Who do I love and who loves me? The Word says God put Adam to sleep and created Eve from his rib. I wonder whose rib I came from. Who is my husband? Mia was so frustrated. She looked over at Braxton, who was eating like he hadn't eaten in days.

"Mia, you didn't hardly touch your food," Braxton said to her.

"I wasn't as hungry as I thought."

"Okay, we can get a doggie bag."

"You sure you don't want anything else? You practically licked your plate clean."

"Funny, girl. No, I'm good. Let's go."

When Braxton and Mia arrived home, she went straight to bed. Braxton showered and then joined Mia. Mia cried with her back to Braxton.

All I want is to be sure I'm with the right man. Otherwise, I can never be happy.

"Braxton, are you awake?" Mia spoke softly.

"What is it?" Braxton answered nervously. His conscience from sleeping with Tracie had gotten the best of him already, and he was waiting for the bomb to drop anytime. He lay still, waiting for Mia to speak.

"I think we need to slow things down."

"You mean break up?" Braxton looked over at Mia. She didn't turn around to face him.

"No, just you stay at your place and I stay here at mines. At least until things are settled with Tracie."

"Okay, and you want me to believe that's all there is to it?"

"That's all there is to it. I mean, unless you know something I don't."

"Unbelievable, just like that." Braxton sat up, looking over at Mia. He couldn't believe his bad luck came back to bite him in the butt that quick. Mia was breaking up with him and she didn't even know he deserved it.

Mia still didn't move from her position in the bed. A tear rolled down her face because she could feel Braxton looking over at her. Braxton lay back down with his back to Mia, and they didn't speak another word throughout the night.

Braxton packed up most of his things and left the next morning before Mia had even gotten out of bed. She heard him shuffling around, but she figured it was easier to just let him leave without a discussion. She didn't want him to know she wasn't sure why she had made the decision so abruptly to end things; she just felt in her heart it was the right thing to do.

"I'll call you tonight," Braxton said, even though he wasn't sure Mia was awake.

Right after Braxton left, Mia got out of the bed and sat on her couch and cried. *This is why I didn't want to get back in this dating game. Nothing but heartaches.* The doorbell rang.

"Who is it?"

"Drake."

"Drake?" Mia peeped through her peephole. She straightened herself out and brushed her hair back from her face. She opened the door.

"What are you doing here?"

"I'm sorry for surprising you. You've been on my mind ever since I saw you."

Mia looked past Drake outside her door. She was wondering if Braxton had time to pack his things in the car and leave before Drake had walked up to her door.

"Come on in," Mia said slowly. "I'm glad to see you."

The moment turned quiet and then still.

"Mia, do you remember the last time we made love?"

Before Mia could respond, Drake kissed her. All the feelings she thought were gone rushed to the surface stronger than ever.

Mia pushed Drake back. "I mean, how do you just show up? How do you know I don't have a man?"

"I showed up. That should tell you that I don't care about another man."

"You shouldn't assume anything."

"Then where is the other man?"

"You just missed him. He left. We needed a little time apart." Mia spoke quietly.

"Then the door is open as far as I see."

"I don't know, Drake. The back and forth thing; I'm over it."

"It's only back and forth if you refuse to hold on to love."

"Dag, what was that? Some line out of a book?"

"No, it's true. Sounds corny, but it's up to you whether you allow love in your life. I mean, what are you looking for, Mia? No one is perfect. We are humans; let's be realistic about things."

"I didn't say I was looking for perfection. I'm just not trying to tread the same ground twice, maybe three times. I want to get a little further than I did the last time. At least have a lasting relationship."

"I'm trying right here," Drake responded.

"You should have tried harder the first time."

Chapter Six

"Morning, Mia," Drake said. "Last night went by fast."
"Good morning, Drake."

Mia cuddled into Drake's arms and just thought. . . .

Stuff happens. I feel like these emotions have been caged in forever and a day. I knew there were some precautions to be taken, but in the heat of the moment, I didn't take any. I know that Mani has always talked to me about sex before marriage, fornication and adultery. I tried so hard to avoid all three. It was hard to turn off my desires and I grew weary of the fight.

In spite of being promiscuous, my sexual partners can be counted on two hands at the most. Still, I can't help but feel like religion takes the best out of my life. If I had just had the chance to enjoy life when I was young, maybe I would be more grounded, a little happier and not so emotional as an adult. Trying not to smoke weed, drink, party and do all the other stuff teenagers do made my younger years boring. I eventually let all of my frustrations out in other ways. My curiosity for life and a thrill had me running to do any activity I could possibly do. I think religion kept me alive and grace spared me from AIDS or other STDs.

What if I had chosen to do drugs or smoke a little weed? No, that would have led to heavier drugs. Scratch that. I would have had more sex. No, that would have classified me as a whore, and that's not me. I would have partied more, but was it really in my heart to? Okay, maybe I got it backwards. I feel like I would have concentrated on life more, got more serious about my future and God's will for me. Could Drake had been part of God's will for me?

Drake is a strong man. He never minded working and then making time for his lady. He would work and come home, shower, eat and cuddle with me. He had dreams that he talked about. He did things in life. His love for life was passionate and his love ran deep. Drake was raised well. He was the protector of his family. He valued a woman's perspective.

His weakness, however, was his mother. It seems to me that his single mother made him her man. She was all in his business, putting stuff in his head. When something needed to be done, she would call on her "man." When a holiday came around, she would call on her man to make plans. Pretty messed up, if you ask me.

Yeah, I tripped on Drake but it was his loss. If his mother hadn't been running his life, he would have realized that when he took his eyes off me, he took them off the prize.

The phone rang.

"Nothing beats this darn phone around here," Mia said sarcastically as she answered it. "Hello."

"Who is this?" Mia asked.

"It's Braxton. What's up with you?"

"What's up with you? Didn't expect your call." Mia spoke politely.

Braxton noticed that Mia sounded bubbly, and considering the state of their relationship, it didn't seem right. He hesitated and spoke, "Mia, I know like heck you don't have company."

"No, I just woke up like a second ago."

"So, you still feel the same way about needing that space?"

"Have you settled things with Tracie?" Mia looked over at Drake, who had fallen soundly back to sleep.

"Darn it, Mia, I told you there was nothing to settle."

"Okay. Well, I have to go. I have a lot to do today." On that note, Mia hung up the phone.

Drake rolled over. *Drake wasn't 'sleep at all*, Mia thought to herself. Her stomach suddenly felt nervous. *Please don't let him trip.*

"Hey, who was that?"

"Braxton."

"Braxton. That's the dude you used to talk to back in the day, right?"

"Drake, you're funny. It was yesterday. His spot isn't even cold. You got me acting like a slut."

"All I want to know is that it's over. It's over, right?"

"Yes." Mia responded very slowly and reluctantly.

"You still messing with him?" Drake sat up and looked at Mia with his arms folded over his muscular chest.

"No. Not really. Kind of thinking about him a little, though. I mean, just out of habit. Things just ended."

Drake became agitated. "You sure about that?"

"Well, we have some unfinished business that we need to deal with."

"So, you want to be with him?" Drake threw his hand out, waiting for a reply.

"No. I just need to tell him that I'm involved with someone else now, if that's even the case." Mia looked to Drake.

Drake nodded his head in agreement, "That is the case," he assured her.

"Yeah?"

"Yeah!" Drake leaned over and kissed Mia again, again and again.

After a couple of months of talking to Braxton on the phone and occasionally meeting him for lunch, Mia made plans to go over to Braxton's place and tell him it was officially over. After her visit, Mia was so messed up in the head, she couldn't even concentrate when talking to Drake. So, she told him that she thought they had moved too fast and that she needed time to herself. Needless to say, Drake didn't put up a fight. Perhaps he had gotten what he wanted. This entire ordeal compelled Mia to spend some quiet time with herself. She frequently visited Imani so she could take the kids out but other than that, it was her and God. A couple of months later, Mia found out she was pregnant.

"Summer, this is Mia," She sobbed into the receiver.

"Mia, are you crying? What's the matter?"

"I just took a pregnancy test."

"Mia, are you pregnant?"

"Yes."

"Who's the daddy?"

"I don't know. I believe its Drake's. Or it could be Braxton's. I'm close to three months. With the stress that I've been under, I hadn't even noticed because I'm always irregular."

"Girl, didn't I tell you to tell them men to keep it wrapped? Your brother is going to flip."

"Neither one of them are around now and I'm pregnant. I already have three small children of my own. What am I going to do? I can't even think straight."

"Have you told anyone?" asked Summer.

"No. Just you."

"Okay. I'll be over in a minute. Mia, I'm sorry. Don't cry."

"Summer, don't call Jasmine and tell her. You know she will flip."

"Ha! Girl, don't I know it."

About thirty minutes later, Summer arrived at Mia's.

"You not still crying, are you?" Summer said after Mia let her in the door.

"No. I'm fine.

"Let's call Braxton and then Drake." Summer suggested.

"No, I'm only calling the one I think is the daddy."

"Which would be?"

"I don't have a clue!"

Summer and Mia laughed hysterically. Mia had to laugh to keep from crying.

"You ready?" Summer asked.

"Yeah."

"Get to dialing then."

Mia began to dial Drake's number.

"Hello, Mia, what's up?" Drake answered after seeing her number on his caller ID.

"No surprises with caller ID, huh?"

"Something like that. What's up?"

"Well, uh," Mia stammered until Summer shoved her shoulder, knocking the truth right out of her. "I'm pregnant."

"What?" Drake said in shock.

"I'm, um, pregnant."

Drake became silent.

"Drake, you there?"

"When did you find this out?"

"Well, I started feeling sick last week during the morning. I took a home pregnancy test last night. I didn't have a clue."

"Did you go to the doctor to make sure?"

"I'm going tomorrow."

"Well, go and make sure before we get excited. I will call you tomorrow night."

"Drake, what am I going to do?" Mia was worried.

"Don't worry. It will be all right. Okay?"

"Okay."

"All right. Bye."

Mia hung up.

"So, he took it pretty well?" Summer asked, rubbing her sister-in-law's back for support.

"Mm-hmm. He seemed a little shocked, of course."

"Sista girl, you going into work today?" Summer looked at Mia for an answer.

"I think I will to keep my mind occupied."

"Well, then I will call you tonight. Keep your head up." Summer grabbed her purse and headed toward the door.

"I don't have a choice," Mia said.

"Talk to you later then. I will let myself out."

"Bye," Mia said, wishing she could let herself out of her troubles.

Chapter Seven

Should I or shouldn't I call Mani? Mia played that song in her head the last hour in her office before she started dialing.

"Hey, Mani."

"Hey, Mia. How are you doing?"

"Okay. How about you and the kids?" Mia asked curiously.

"I'm doing all right, I guess. The kids are good; enjoying summer with their grandmother."

"You don't sound all right. What's going on?"

"I think your father may be seeing someone."

"Mani, why you say that?"

"He been coming in late at night, and having to make more trips out than usual. He doesn't want me to go anywhere with him anymore."

"How long has this been going on?"

"A few months now."

"Why you didn't say something earlier?"

" 'Cause I ain't really worried about it. I know God will bring him in."

"Well, you're right. Prayer changes things. The Bible says where two come together and agree, anything you ask in His name shall come to pass. So, we come in agreement now that if anyone is in between you and Daddy, she got to move. In Jesus' name."

"Amen." Imani chuckled.

"Didn't think I was listening all those years, did you?" Mia said. She could tell her mother was smiling through the phone.

"Well, call me if you need to talk later. I have a patient in a few minutes, so I have to go."

"Okay. I will talk to you later then."

Mia hung up and then began to think to herself.

Men; it doesn't matter who they are. All these years Mani and Daddy have been together and still a woman has to look forward to this as the years roll on. Let me call Jasmine. I know she can cheer me up.

"Hey, Jasmine, what you doing, bat?"

"I ain't doing nothing. What you doing?"

"At work."

"Why aren't you working then? Since you at work, try and do some work."

"I'm waiting on a patient who hasn't arrived yet. You know it's slow on Friday."

"Oh well."

"What are you doing today? Anything exciting?"

"Trying to keep from killing Evan."

"What you talking about?"

"He's back on that stuff again."

"No, Jasmine!"

"Yep. I mean it's been years, and I can't understand why he went back to fooling with those drugs. But I told him it's the crack or me. He is high night and day now."

"I'm sorry to hear that," Mia replied.

"Evan gets up and goes to work every day. He's a hardworking man. But the drugs and trying to be a hardworking man don't mix."

"I feel you. Life is a trip, isn't it? But just trust in God. I know it's hard now, but give it to Him. You stay focused and He will turn this thing around for you. And if He doesn't, it's not because He couldn't, but you have some decisions to make yourself. He might be telling you that Evan is not the one for you. But you don't know that until you hear from God. Matter of fact, we don't know anything until we hear from God," Mia said, wondering why everything was easier said than done, and why she couldn't follow her own advice.

"I know God's real and all, but He's really testing me," Jasmine responded.

"He won't put more on you than you can bear. If it becomes more than you can bear, remember who made you and Evan, then give it to Him. Jasmine, you talk to Summer?"

"Yea, uh, she, um, stopped by this morning," Jasmine stuttered.

"What did she want?" Mia asked, although she could tell that Summer had run her trap to Jasmine.

"Uh, nothing."

"You're a terrible liar. I guess you know I'm pregnant."

"What? Did you say you were pregnant?"

"No need to play stupid, sis."

"So, who do you think the father is?"

"I'm certain it's by Drake, but Braxton is a possibility, just because I slept with him before I got with Drake. But I'm going to the doctor today after my last patient, and she will tell me exactly how far along I am."

"You're a doctor. Why don't you do all that yourself?"

"I can only be my own doctor up to a certain point."

"I guess you're right," Jasmine agreed.

"Mia, have you told Mommy?"

"Nope, and don't you tell her either. I haven't decided if I'm going to keep it."

"What do you mean? You laid your butt down and conceived it. You can't have no abortion."

"I have three small kids. I can't afford another one. You act like money grow on trees."

"You should have thought about that sooner, sister girl."

"Well, I didn't, Jasmine, but I'm thinking now; and what is done is done."

"That is what I'm saying. How are you just going to undo a human life?"

"Look, I'll talk to you tonight. My patient just walked in."

"All right. Bye."

Mia's new patient sat on the examination table. Mia extended her hand to make her acquaintance. "Hello, I'm Dr. Mia Reese."

"I know exactly who you are, Mia."

"Have we met before?"

"Well, not in person. Only over the phone."

"What are you doing here?" Mia asked, after figuring out the "new patient" was Tracie.

"You're a doctor, right? I need your medical attention. I need a pregnancy test."

Chapter Eight

Although Tracie had come into her office merely to taunt her and really wasn't pregnant, Mia still had bigger things to concentrate on—herself and her unborn baby.

Later that night, Drake called. "Well, what did the doctor say?" he asked Mia.

"It's confirmed. I'm two months," Mia said slowly.

"Dag, for real? I was thinking it was just a scare."

"Nope, it's the real thing."

"So, what's going on in that head of yours?" Drake asked Mia.

"I don't have to keep it, you know. I mean, if you're feeling some pressure to step up and do the right thing, don't. I have options."

"Hold up. First, you're not getting rid of my baby. Second, I don't believe in abortion."

"I can't do this again. I'm already a single mother," Mia blurted out.

"Don't worry about all that. I wouldn't leave you alone in this."

"If you say so. I heard that before," Mia stated.

"I just said I wouldn't, right?" Drake insisted.

"Right."

"Well, Mia I got a lot of things to sort out and get straight, so I will call you later. I need to digest all this. We have some decisions to make."

"Call me later, Drake." They each hung up the phone. Mia sighed.

A few days passed and strangely enough, Drake didn't call. Mia was on pins and needles wondering what he was thinking about. Then finally, he called.

"Hey, Mia, I been thinking."

"Thinking what, Drake?" Mia almost cut him off in mid-statement, she was so anxious to know what he was thinking about.

"Did you sleep with someone else around the time you got pregnant? Like Braxton? I was just wondering." Drake asked as politely as he could, trying not to offend Mia.

"No, not around the time I got pregnant. I slept with him a little bit before I got back with you. Why?"

"So, you're telling me you slept with that dude?" Drake exclaimed.

"Yeah, before we got together. You sound surprised, like I only slept with you in my entire lifetime."

"How do I know it is my baby? You could have been with someone else too."

"You can get a blood test to see that it is your baby!" Mia snapped.

"I can't believe you slept with Braxton. The first time we hooked up, it took you a year to let me sleep with you."

"I can't believe you're tripping!" Mia felt her blood rushing to her head.

"You could never let him go, could you? What he got, gold around his thang? What gives?"

"I can't even believe you're bringing up Braxton now. What does he have to do with you being the baby daddy? I mean, whatever, do you have gold around yours?"

"Apparently not, or we wouldn't be having this discussion. He was an issue then and it seems he's an issue now."

"We having this discussion because you're a jerk!" Mia shouted.

"Maybe you want my money?" Drake said in a cool fashion.

"Drake, what money? If you got some, I don't know about it. What do I need with your money? Everything I have, I got on my own. I don't need anything from you!"

"Look, I will talk to you later before I say something I'll regret."

"You've already said something you should regret. Bye!" Mia slammed the receiver down.

She was devastated. She ran into her bedroom and lay on her bed. Her heart felt like it was ripped from her chest; and she felt so lonely. Never had she felt loneliness like this. She refused to answer her phone that night. She cried all night long and her stomach hurt. She made a decision that night that she would not keep the baby.

The night was warm and Mia was miserable. She lay outside on her chair on her balcony. She hadn't been feeling all that well, either, and she was beginning to get a small stomach bulge. Mia knew her time was limited. She had waited as long as possible for Drake to call back, but a week or two had passed and there was no word from him. Mia was a wreck. Her whole appearance was rough, and she was sickly because she wasn't eating right. Her appointment for her abortion was the next day. She was a nervous wreck. She had taken some calls from Jasmine and Summer, and of course, Imani knew.

Imani wanted her to keep the baby. "God will supply," she

told Mia. But Mia knew she didn't have the energy or the strength to deal with a broken heart, a pregnancy and three other small kids. The few weeks that had already passed seemed like years.

Mia couldn't remember going through something that had such an emotional impact on her as she rubbed her stomach. The fetus would have to return back to Heaven with Jesus and be deposited into another woman's womb.

Mia was at the lowest point in her life. "Why, Jesus? All I wanted was his love." A turn of events had so suddenly changed her life. Once again, she felt herself regretting opening up to love. It was only for a moment that she tasted its sweetness. It seemed love never stood the test of time.

Chapter Nine

"Hey, Mitchell. It's Mia."

"What's up, Mia? The kids okay?"

"Yes, but I got myself into a little mess. Could you come and get the kids and take them back to Imani's?"

"Why can't you do it?" Mitchell asked, obviously bothered by Mia's request.

"I'm not feeling well," Mia said calmly.

"Mm-hmm, bye." Mitchell hung up before she could respond.

"Okay." The words fell to a dial tone on the other end of the line.

Mitchell always was a smart alec. That was one of the many reasons why Mia had divorced him. That and his tendency to treat her like dog poop. Yet she often felt like Mitchell understood her need for love; he just didn't feel the need to provide it to her.

Mitchell walked up to the door and rang the doorbell. Mia opened the door. There he stood, looking as evil as ever.

"Come on in, Mitchell. Thanks for coming to drop the kids

off," Mia said as she walked back into the kitchen where she was fixing a cup of coffee.

"No problem. I guess I needed to see the little ones anyway."

"You gained weight or what? You look kind of chubby," Mitchell observed.

"Pregnant," Mia said casually.

Mitchell sighed. "By who, Mia?"

"You wouldn't know if I told you."

"Are you going to have it?" Mitchell asked his ex-wife.

"Probably not. I have an appointment with the doctor tomorrow morning."

"How far along are you?"

"Sixteen weeks."

"A little too late to get an abortion, isn't it? That's murder."

"No, I am not going to a clinic. I'm going to the hospital."

"Wait, you said probably not, but your appointment is tomorrow? I thought you were undecided just a minute ago."

"No, I'm going tomorrow. Seeing our kids reminded me I had made up my mind. I can't do this all over again, especially alone."

"Should have kept your legs closed. If you say you're a lady, act like one."

"Should have kept your mouth shut." Mia looked up at Mitchell and rolled her eyes.

"I should take you to court to get custody of the kids. Look at you. You're an unfit mother, whoring around in the streets with men who don't give a darn about you."

"A judge will never give you custody of my kids. And mind your own business. If there's anyone whoring around in the streets, it's you. Why am I arguing with you? Get out!" Mia yelled while peeping down the hall to make sure she didn't startle the kids.

"At least my girl ain't got no kids."

"If she hadn't gotten rid of the last six from you and every Tom, Dick and Harry, she would have plenty," Mia snarled at Mitchell.

"Forget you, chicken head."

"Get out, stupid."

"Gladly. Come on, y'all!" Mitchell yelled to the kids.

Tashema with her long plaits came running from the back with all her teeth showing. "Hey, Daddy!" she yelled. She jumped into Mitchell's arms.

"Hey, baby!" Mitchell met her hug.

Tarel wasn't far behind her, and he almost bombarded Tashema trying to get her away from Mitchell as she leaped for his arms. Tarel was just as tall as Tashema, even though she was the oldest. Both of them clambered on Mitchell. They both had jet black hair and brown complexions. Tarel's curls were large and sat atop his head.

Finally, Bridgett slowly crept from the back rooms. She looked with her big eyes and her twisted locks on her head. She favored Mia more than Mitchell. She was a little lighter than her brother and sister. Bridgett rubbed her eyes because she had just woken up. She moved slowly toward the chaos.

"Hey, Daddy's little princess."

Bridgett's somber faced turned into a grin. Mitchell picked up Bridgett, directed Tarel and Tashema out the door and walked out.

"Bye, babies," Mia said as Mitchell closed the door.

Mia shook her head and looked up to the sky. "God, thank You for letting me get rid of that man."

Chapter Ten

The next morning, Mitchell called bright and early. It never really mattered how much Mia and Mitchell fought, they had made up their minds a long time ago that no matter what, they would always be there when the other needed it most. They really did have love for one another; they just couldn't live together.

Mia answered on the first ring. "Hello."

"You need someone to go with you?" Mitchell offered.

"Will you?"

"I'll be there in a few minutes."

Fifteen minutes later, Mitchell was standing at Mia's door. He yelled through the open screen door. "Mia, can I come in?"

"Yes, come on in."

Mia was ready to go. She grabbed her purse and Mitchell did a U-turn, following Mia out the door.

Mitchell and Mia rode silently to the hospital. Mitchell played some soft music in his truck; a rare action for him, but Mia figured he was trying to calm her nerves. They pulled up in front of the hospital and got out.

Mia walked up to the reception desk feeling dizzy and nervous. "I have an eleven o'clock appointment. My name is Mia."

The receptionist cut her off before she could give her last name. "Fill out this paperwork and bring it back up to me when you're finished."

Mia took the paperwork and sat down. Mitchell sat beside her, looking almost as nervous as she felt. His face was uncomfortable. Mia finished the paperwork and the receptionist escorted her to the back.

"Please put this gown on. You will get an ultrasound before the procedure," she said.

"I don't want an ultrasound," Mia replied.

"It's only standard procedure to make sure you're not too far along to have the procedure done. You don't have to see the ultrasound if you don't want to."

"Oh, okay." Mia signed. She felt some of the guilt fall off her shoulder. She couldn't bear to see the pictures of her unborn child. It would make it all too real. Right now, she could pretend it was a simple procedure and perhaps not think about it anymore.

The doctor came in and said a simple hello, did the ultrasound and walked out. Mitchell stood by Mia's side. "He was a weird one," Mitchell said after the doctor walked out.

"Yeah," Mia replied.

The same doctor came back. "Did you know you're pregnant with twins?" he asked Mia.

Mia looked at Mitchell, stunned, "What?" Mia asked.

The doctor looked at Mia coldly and repeated himself. "You're pregnant with twins. Do you still want to go through with this?"

Mia hesitated before answering, and then spoke a resounding "yes," but without her soul. The doctor hooked an IV to Mia's arm. She didn't remember anything else until she came to and saw Mitchell sitting beside her.

Mitchell was affectionate and quiet. Mia believed he felt her pain. Mitchell held Mia's hand tightly. He rubbed her head gently like a father consoles his wounded child. Mitchell helped Mia to the car after recovery and took her home and helped her to her bedroom. He threw a blanket lightly over her.

"Do you need anything before I go?" he asked.

"Nope. You've done enough. I am going to just sleep. Imani, Jasmine and Summer will be over later."

"Okay. I will see myself out."

"Thanks, Mitchell."

"Not a problem, slut. Oh, darn, did I say that out loud?" Mitchell smiled.

"Not funny, Mitchell. Bye"

"Bye."

Mia heard the door close. She rolled over and wept.

The only good thing that came out of this ordeal for Mia was re-establishing a friendship with her ex-husband. After the abortion, though, Mia never looked at love quite the same. She resented Braxton for his part in her life. Mia hated Drake with everything inside of her. In the end, no one was to blame but herself. She lived with the guilt and constant pain. Mia always thought, what if she had given her babies their lives, and chosen other options? Yes, it was twins. Mia was beside herself with grief when the ultrasound revealed this on the abortion table. All she could do was cry.

Perhaps she should have considered adoption? Imani didn't agree with her choice, nor did Jasmine, and that is why she was going alone if Mitchell hadn't called. Summer was in agreement to a certain extent. Even though Mia had walked the road alone, they all came out of it together in the end. A temporary decision for a permanent hurt was the dumbest mistake of her life. Mia should have just made Drake responsible and that was that.

Mia couldn't seem to get herself together after the abortion and decided she needed to be alone. She asked Imani if she could take temporary custody of her kids. She was supposed to get them every weekend, but it didn't work out that way—she saw them when she felt up to it.

The phone rang. It scared Mia because she had finally fallen asleep from earlier that day when Mitchell left.

"Hey, Mia, how you feeling?" Summer asked.

"Crappy."

"That will pass. You okay emotionally?"

"I don't know yet. I am very sad."

"Well, do you need me to come sit with you?"

"Could you for a little while?"

"Okay, but not very long. I have some papers to read for work tomorrow."

"That's okay, then. Don't worry about me. You have to teach class tomorrow. I am just laying here sleeping. I won't be doing anything else tonight."

"Okay then. I will check on you later. And I'm praying for you. It will be okay."

Summer spoke sympathetically.

"Hold on, Summer. My phone beeping."

"Go ahead and get it. I'm gone."

"Okay, bye." Mia clicked over to the other line. "Hello."

"Hey, Mia, what you doing?" Jasmine asked.

"Just laying here. I actually just got off the phone with Summer when you beeped in."

"What she talking about?"

"Asking what I was doing," Mia replied.

"Oh, you feeling okay?" Jasmine asked with a concerned voice.

"Not really, but I guess I will be okay."

"You in pain?"

"I'm cramping. But that isn't what I meant. I mean I'm hurting in my heart."

"You didn't have to do it. I told you that."

"I know, but it's easier for someone else to say that looking in."

"None of your family would have let you go without, you or any of those babies."

"I know. But it's so much easier to see when it's not you."

"I was just calling to check on you. I am cramping myself, so I won't be coming out unless you

need me to bring you something."

"Naw, I'm good."

"All right, I will talk to you later."

"Later then." Mia hung up.

But at about ten o'clock P.M. Mia heard keys turning in her door. She thought maybe Jasmine decided to come over after all. She had her spare keys. A few minutes later, Imani walked in the bedroom.

"Mani, you usually don't come over this late. What's wrong?"

"Your daddy has been making calls to other women in the house."

"How do you know it's not church related?"

"He's been whispering on the phone late at night. I asked him to throw that cell phone away, but he said as soon as he gets another one and changes his number. I asked why he needed to get another one and change the number."

"What did he say?"

"He said Ms. Corlette from the church had been calling him."

"So he basically admitted there was someone else?"

"Yes, he said he cared about her."

"Care how?"

"I don't know."

"Just care, not love?"

"I guess. There is a difference, I figure. You can care about the dog."

"Okay. He doesn't realize it's okay to care, but there is a line to be drawn?"

"It seems like he doesn't."

Mia's heart felt like it was in her stomach and she felt nauseated. *Do men realize what real pain feels like?* she thought. *Mani has been nothing but a good wife, an exceptional wife.* Mia was angry.

"Mani, it will be all right."

"I know it will. I just needed to talk."

"Let's pray, Mani. You have the right of way. The other woman had to go by God's word and the authority and power He gave you."

Mia began to pray. "Father in Heaven, Mani is hurt and feeling a little weak now. You said You would be our comforter, and if we ask, we shall receive according to Your covenant promises. Jesus, I ask that You restore what was lost between Mani and Daddy. I thank You for Your Word that says what God put together let no man put asunder. We consider it done. We decree that the adulteress or woman used by Satan move out of the way and we claim it in Jesus' name. Amen."

Mia looked at her mother. "I believe He heard us."

"Amen," Imani said.

"Okay, good night, boo. I also just needed to see if you were okay." Imani kissed Mia on the head. "I will see you later."

"All right. Good night, Mani."

Mia held her tears back as she hugged Imani and gave her a weak smile as she walked out her bedroom door. She settled back comfortably in her bed. Mia cried until her head felt stuffy as if she had a bad head cold. When she stopped enough to talk clearly, she decided to call her brother.

"Mike, what are you doing?" Mia said with a stuffy nose.

"Nothing. What's up? Sound like you been crying."

"Mani came by. She's upset. She thinks that Daddy is having an affair."

"Why would she think that? She caught him in something?"

"It seems he somewhat admitted talking to someone else that he says he cares about."

"She was crying?"

"I could tell she had been. Although, I'm not just crying because of that. I had my abortion today."

"Yeah, Summer told me that was today. You okay?"

"Yeah, I'm okay. Just a little worried about Mani. You know if she said something, she's stressed about it."

"Does Daddy know that she told you?"

"No, she doesn't want anyone to know. But it's time she started saying something because he let them church floozies come between the two of them. Either he's going to preach for God, or be a hypocrite and be left behind when Jesus comes. That is the way I see it."

"I will talk to him."

"Okay. Let me speak to Summer."

"Hold on." Mike handed the phone to Summer, who was sitting next to him.

Summer didn't even say hello. She just picked up the conversation where Mike and Mia had left off.

"Jamal is fooling around on Mani? Where you get that from?"

"I believe so. Well, Mani seems to think so. Anyway, call me once Mike talks to him."

"All right, I will. You be strong and hang in there."

"I will."

"Love you, Mia. Call us if you need something."

"Love you, too."

Mia decided to take things into her own hands. *Perhaps I will make a call and see for myself if Daddy is fooling*

*around. Ms. Crow, always smiling in his face. I'm tired of
it and I know it's her,* Mia thought.

"Hmm, let me see. The white pages will have her number."
Mia flipped through the white pages. "Debbie Crow, here it
is." Mia dialed the number.

"Hello, Ms. Crow, please."

"Hello. This is she."

"Ms. Crow, this is Mia. Jamal's daughter."

"Hi, Mia. What can I do for you?"

"You fooling around with my daddy?" Mia asked directly.

"Excuse me?"

"You heard me. Are you fooling around with my daddy?"

"Mia, I'm hanging up now."

Mia heard the sound of the dial tone before she could respond. "That probably was a yes. Homewrecker."

Chapter Eleven

"Hey, Mia. What's up?" Drake asked Mia like they had just spoken only a few hours ago.

"Who is this?" Mia asked.

"Drake."

"There is no reason for you to be calling. I got rid of the baby."

"What? When did this happen? I don't remember you leaving me a message or calling."

"Yesterday is when it happened. And I'm telling you now. There's your message."

"I need to get my stuff," Drake said before Mia could hang up.

"Your stuff! Are you serious? This is what you got to say? Look, let me make something clear to you. I got rid of all your stuff. I don't want your stuff."

"I need to get my stuff. You're holding onto my stuff."

"I don't need your stuff. I don't need anything from you. What do I need from you now, Drake? What about when I needed you to help with this baby, or just acknowledge there was a baby that you had fathered? What about that, Drake?"

"All I'm saying is—"

Mia interrupted. "And all I'm saying is 'click'." Mia hung up the phone. She was tired and weary and she had a terrible headache. She was too angry to cry and too tired to keep arguing about a point that was self-explanatory. He knew the baby was his and that was that. She also knew his stuff was only an excuse to come and see her face to face. "Regrets coming just a little too late," Mia said out loud. "Lord, why must life be this way?"

Over the course of the next few months, Mia only ached for a soothing heart. She didn't know if she hurt over the abortion or for lost love. She understood a single mother can maintain. Nevertheless, she longed for companionship, even though that could be a burden at times as well.

As she thought about the compromises of love, Mia finally knew, or had always known, there is no perfect love. She began to feel from lack of evidence the possibility of the existence of pure love with each passing day. All she knew was that she was hurt.

Something ran deep inside the pit of her stomach. The feeling seemed to live in Mia's rib cage, and she came to the conclusion that it must be pain—pain lingering from loneliness, disappointment and continuous broken hearts. It was hard for Mia to bounce back. It was okay, though. God woke Mia up again this morning. *He's not through with me yet.*

The phone rang and Mia figured it was Drake calling back.

"Hello." The caller hung up and ten minutes later, the phone rang again.

"Hello." Another hang-up call.

The same pattern occurred around the same time every evening, and Mia believed it was Drake calling. She figured he had something to say, and she had plenty to say if only he would identify himself. Mia was sick. She was feeling beneath the world. Part of her wanted to say to Drake that she was sorry. After all, they were his babies also. He had a right to have a say. But then part of her wanted to curse him out again because he didn't step up in the first place and do the right thing when it mattered the most.

"God, abortion is one of those things you do in life and you can't make it right." *How do I take a life when I don't have the power to give life? Mia thought. That messes up the whole plan to have another baby one day, or do the right thing next time because I can't bring back the life I took to begin with.* Mia began to cry. It was an aching and long, wrenching cry, like she was trying to get out all the hurt that was inside so she could breathe. After she had drained her eyes to the point of exhaustion, she literally felt like her eyes and her head would explode. She tried to gain her composure by taking a few sleeping pills to calm down.

Mia woke up five hours later. Her headache was gone and her eyes were basically swollen shut from the crying. She realized all the pain was still there. She decided she'd better try to live with it for a while, because change doesn't always come by the drop of a tear.

Over the course of the next few months, Mia was distant and lonely. It seemed like no one wanted to talk about things, so she had to ask herself, "Does anyone know I'm hurting?" Mitchell came around for a few days, made sure Mia was eating and the kids were cool when they were there and not at Imani's. Mia and Mitchell seemed like they could be cool, but then as usual, war broke out between them and Mia decided she would rather deal with the pain of her decision on her own.

Chapter Twelve

It was Christmastime already. Christmas seemed to come every other month for Mia's kids; always needing something and Mitchell not worth a dime when it came to shelling out cash. He has his own "single" life aside from the kids. When he had nothing better to do, then he could be Daddy. It was totally unfair to Mia.

Mia had the kids for the day, but she dropped them off at Jasmine's. She knew she was about to do something that was unfair, and probably a disgrace to herself and her family. But she didn't see the use in helping to save lives and cure people when she just took two little innocent lives. She had to quit her job. She was the biggest hypocrite alive. Her conscience wouldn't allow her to be a doctor anymore.

When she showed up to quit, instead, she received her walking papers along with a severance package that she could live off of. Mia went to human resources and asked to cash out her stocks and her retirement plan as well.

Mia's cell phone rang, but she didn't recognize the number. "Hello," she answered.

"Mia?"

"Yes, this is Mia. Who is this?"

"This is Braxton."

"Braxton? Hey, boy. How you get this number? I have a new cell phone number because my other cell totally crashed for no apparent reason."

"I called your mom. I couldn't get you at home all evening, so I asked for your cell phone number when I got tired of getting the home voice mail. Where you at, shorty?"

"Just coming in," Mia said as she drove, now only a couple of blocks from her house. "Where you at?" she asked.

"Around your way, looking for you."

"You mighty confident. How you know I don't have a man at home?"

"And your point would be what? If a man is there, he don't have a problem with you having friends, right? But that would strange considering almost a year ago, we separated, and I know you're not in love and married off that quick."

"Yeah, okay." Mia gave in. "I'm pulling up now."

Braxton walked up to the car. Mia jumped out of her car and ran into him arms.

"Hey," Mia said softly.

"Hey, shorty. You looking good." Braxton twirled Mia around like they were dancing.

"So, what's up with you? Why you looking for me? Tracie out of the picture now?"

"What is this, twenty questions?" Braxton asked with a crooked smile.

"I just want to know," Mia replied.

"Let's see, where do I start?"

"Wait." Mia grabbed Braxton by the hand, leading him toward the condo. "Come on in. Your timing is perfect."

Mia and Braxton walked into her condo. Mia cut her lights on and dropped her purse on the kitchen counter. "Have a seat. You're not a stranger," she said to Braxton while she walked to the fridge and grabbed a soda.

"Thanks." Braxton kept staring at Mia as he took a seat on the couch.

"You want something to drink?" Mia asked.

"Naw, I'm fine. Just sit down so we can talk," Braxton instructed Mia.

Mia went sat down Indian-style beside Braxton on the couch. She was smiling politely. She had mixed emotions about seeing Braxton.

"Okay, now to answer your questions. I have been working like a slave on a plantation. Second, I am looking for you because I haven't been able to get you off my mind since we split up, and lastly, Tracie was never really in the picture, so yes, she is out the picture."

"So, I don't understand. If I was on your mind so much, why are you showing up after so much time gone by?"

"I just got this strong urge the last couple of months that now was the right time to approach you. I had to wait until I felt it, you know. Then when I asked for your cell phone number, your mom told me you were going through some stuff. That confirmed my feelings. Maybe you need a friend?"

"Here we go with a 'friend' again. That is what got us into this in the first place, remember? You wanted to be just a friend."

"Hey, that's life. When two people grow to care about one another like we do, things happen. Regardless, whatever is going on with you, you can't go through it alone. Sometimes you need somebody on your side."

"What I went through was a long time ago." Mia felt uncomfortable talking to Braxton, because she never told him about her pregnancy, and he could have been the father. "I need somebody that understands me, that's it. Is that too much to ask?"

"I don't understand you? I know you're not implying that I, of all people, don't understand you."

"Do you understand me? I don't think so. If you understood me, tell me why my life is so crappy. All I've ever wanted was someone to love me. I felt like with love, everything else would be okay; you know, at least worth going through the trials of life."

"If you wait for a change, a change will come," Braxton responded.

"How long do you wait?"

"Until it comes is all I know."

"Braxton, I'm tired, so I'm going to bed." Mia stood up over Braxton.

"I'm out then." Braxton stood and walked toward the door. "I'll call you tomorrow. Let's do lunch, okay?"

"Sure," Mia said, walking behind Braxton to open the door. "Bye."

Mia closed the door gently. She leaned with her back against the door before proceeding down the hall to her bedroom. "Life is full of surprises."

Mia avoided Braxton over the course of the next few days. She didn't like unexpected pop-ups from old friends that could possibly penetrate her heart. She never told him that because she hadn't really admitted it to herself; it was just fear of falling in love again. That was the last thing she needed. She decided to save herself the trouble and avoid him altogether.

One day, Braxton dropped by her condo again, unannounced. She didn't answer the door. Mia peeped out her window and watched Braxton walk away. He was still fine as ever, but her heart could not afford it. He looked around quickly as if he realized someone was watching him, and Mia quickly moved from out of view. She had to laugh as she slowly peeped to see if he was still looking. He got in the car and drove off, while Jasmine drove up.

Jasmine walked into her sister's condo without knocking. She had seen Mia peeping out the window. "Mia, what on earth are you doing?"

"I am such a nut. It's like I draw these men and none of them are for me."

"What are you talking about?"

"You saw Braxton just leave, right?"

"I saw someone leaving, but I didn't know it was Braxton. You seeing him again?"

"He popped out of nowhere the other day, and I don't know what his deal is."

"Shucks, it don't matter what his deal is. You ain't got no deal, so what you hiding for?"

"I don't know."

"Life is too short, Mia, to keep running from love. Just take one day at a time. You will be all right."

"All right, but so far, not so good."

"Besides, those cobwebs getting thicker and thicker. You ain't getting no younger." Jasmine joked with her sister.

"Whatever, Jasmine." Mia laughed.

Chapter Thirteen

"Mani, can you have lunch with me today?" Mia asked.
"Yeah, I'm not doing anything. You talk to Jasmine and Summer?"

"Nope."

"I'll call them. We can all go," Imani suggested.

"Okay."

"Let's go to the Marriott for their lunch buffet."

"Okay. I'll meet y'all there."

An hour later, they all sat around the lunch table overlooking the city.

"This is nice," said Imani.

"What is going on, Mia?" asked Summer.

"I'm struggling. It seems that life is so messed up. It's depressing."

"It's depressing because of the choices you make," intervened Jasmine.

"What does that mean?" Mia asked.

"It means that you choose the path you walk, Mia," Imani answered for Jasmine. "I'm your mother, and I have told you time and time again that until you put God first in your life, nothing is going to work out."

"God *is* first in my life," Mia stated.

"Don't get Mommy started, Mia," Jasmine spoke again.

"Well, y'all, I don't think it's so much what she chooses to do. Sometimes I think it's what life deals us. Mia has not lived her life any worse than us. You just have to seek God's face in everything you do. We're guilty of not doing that ourselves. You don't beat someone up when they're already down," Summer added.

"No one is beating her up, Summer. It's just that Mani and I have been through these things—men, loneliness and needing a friend—with Mia more than once. She keep looking for something that we can't give her," Jasmine said.

"Which is what? What am I asking you all for? You have seen me go through some rough relationships. I haven't asked you, Mani, or Jasmine to go through it for me."

"Peace and happiness, Mia. Pick up your Bible and read it more and God will give you joy. The Bible speaks of peace that surpasses all understanding," Imani told her.

"I read my Bible, Mani, and I pray. You know that." Mia sighed.

"Well then, wait on God," Imani stated matter-of-factly.

"Let's change the subject. Jasmine, what is going on with you? Has Evan stopped smoking again?" Mia looked directly at Jasmine with a blank stare as she asked the question.

"He says he has. But the way he's acting, I believe he's just hiding it from me." Jasmine shook her head in frustration.

"What are you going to do? You been through this a few times with him and it doesn't look like he has changed," Summer stated.

"Mm-hmm, Summer. That is what I was thinking. You can't ever point fingers at someone else's situation because you're not in much of a different one yourself," Mia said.

"Shut up, Mia," Jasmine said with piercing eyes on her sister.

Imani began to speak. "We all going to be all right. As long as our anchor holds, which is Jesus Christ, we're all going to make it through all right. God does not ever leave you alone."

Mia replied, "Yeah, I know. I look at how he has blessed us to have one another in our time of need. It does not matter that we all have completely different lives. We manage to stay connected to one another and give a part of ourselves to one another. Especially to me. By me being the baby, I see a part of each one of you in me and that helped mold me into the woman I am. I know right now that does not seem like much, but I believe the end will tell the story."

"Well, all right then," spoke Summer.

"Amen, Reverend Ike," Jasmine joked.

"She always got to make a joke out of something." Imani smiled.

"What about Daddy? What is going on with y'all?" Jasmine asked Imani.

"Nothing. He said he threw away the cell phone. He hasn't been getting anymore midnight calls." Imani answered.

"So everything is okay then?" asked Jasmine.

"I gave it to God. It's quiet," Imani responded.

Chapter Fourteen

"Mia?"

Mia looked up from the table. It was Braxton. She had not been to the poetry spot since they stopped dating.

"Braxton. Hey, I came in for a soda. I didn't know you still worked here."

"I don't. I came here for a soda too and to just relax. Can I join you?"

"Look, Braxton, I know you been trying to reach me, but honestly, I'm not trying to go through no more drama, and I can bet Tracie is still in your life."

"She still in my life because of the connection I have with her kids. There is nothing between us. It's like you're trying to punish me for filling a void in some kids' lives that they wouldn't have filled otherwise."

"So, she can't get another man? Or as long as you're filling that void, she don't need another man? See, I don't have time for that."

"What is wrong with you?"

"Nothing is wrong with me. I have to go."

Mia stormed out of the poetry spot. She threw her stuff in her car and sped off. Braxton followed behind her. He drove so close, his lights blinded her. Mia went inside her condo and Braxton followed closely.

"What do you want, Braxton? I mean, you pop up and act like I owe you something. I don't owe you anything."

"This isn't like you. You're avoiding me."

"How do you know what's not like me?"

"Mia, tell me who hurt you."

"What?" Mia looked astonished by his question.

"Tell me who hurt you. This is the only thing that could make sense for the anger and hurt I see inside of you."

"How about every man who has ever been in my life, including you?"

"You asked me to leave, remember?"

"I was dealing with you and Tracie. What did you want me to do?"

"Look, I never meant to hurt you, ever, and I'm here now. Can't we try and put the pieces back together?"

Mia began to cry. It seemed the pain moved through the expression of her tears. "I'm scared to try. I mean, if we fail, I don't think I'll have the strength to get back up, not again."

"We won't fail, and I'll be there to catch you before you fall."

Mia collapsed on her bed in frustration.

Braxton walked over to Mia. He lay down beside her. He kissed her weeping eyes. Then he squeezed her shoulders and moved his hands down to her elbows and squeezed her gently. Then Braxton pulled Mia close to his body and never moved the entire night. Mia sobbed uncontrollably. It seemed as if the dam broke and the waters came rushing forward.

In the wee hours of the night, they lay wide awake and Braxton spoke quietly.

"Mia, can we try?" Braxton asked sincerely.

"We are trying right now." Mia never looked up or moved from her position in Braxton's arms.

Braxton looked down and tilted Mia's face towards his, kissing her softly.

Man, I can't explain the feeling here, Mia thought. *Fear is in my throat and it's hard to breathe. Should I try love again? I know I'm not strong enough. But funny how God gives you what you need when you need it. I think I will give it to God. Perhaps Braxton is the breath of air I need to just exhale for a moment and rest.*

When their lips parted, Braxton sighed. "Mia, you ready to tell me what's going on with you?"

"No. I apologize, but I'm not ready to discuss it."

"Okay, when you're ready, I'm here to listen."

"Thanks, but some things are better left in the past. I'm okay," Mia reassured him.

After that entire ordeal between Braxton, Mia took the time to rest. She curled up alone in her home. She felt blessed and fortunate. She slept a lot. She cried a lot and prayed throughout it all. She had a nervous breakdown; she needed it. She needed to cry over wrong decisions, confusion and pain. Seldom had she cried like she needed in order to restore her body and mind. Through her divorce, abortion and disappointments, she was always expected to look like she had a clue what to do next. She never had a clue; she just felt her way through.

But now she needed to rest. Mia thanked God for rest in His protective arms when in the end, nothing else stood like the anchor we hold close to our hearts—Jesus.

Several months passed by and things were good. Braxton had filled that void of a companion, best friend and lover. The stability did Mia good. Since she was feeling comfortable and stable, Mia decided to venture on her own and start her own practice. She brought up the subject while she and Braxton was relaxing at her condo, watching movies.

"Braxton, what do you think of me starting my own practice?"

"About time, letting all that talent go to waste."

"Seriously?"

"Yeah, seriously."

"Then it's settled. I will take out a small business loan and go for it!"

Braxton smiled and hugged Mia. "You can do it."

"Yeah, I been thinking about it for some time. I need something for me, something that defines me for where I am right now in my life. I need to take control."

"Yeah, there is no other way. Everyone needs to do their own thing, I mean so you won't always feel compelled to live for someone else. We all should have our own dreams."

"Well, my ultimate dream is not really to own this practice, but it's a start."

"What is your dream?"

"To be an author. I know it's far-fetched and crazy considering that out of all the millions of writers, very few ever make it to the bestsellers list, much less leave a legacy in society."

"I mean, you can do it if you put your mind to it. It sounds like you're full of doubt."

"It seems so childish and unrealistic when you have bills to pay and life goes on. Regardless of what you desire to do, life will go on and those bills will still be due."

"You should give it a go one day."

"Yeah, I guess, one day. But for right now, I'm going to work on my business plan for this doctor's office."

For the first time in a long time, Mia's troubles seemed to be outweighed by her dreams. Now if she could only make them come true.

Chapter Fifteen

"Braxton, I'm home!"

"I'm in here, Mia!" Braxton called from the bedroom.

"Oh my God! What is all of this?" Mia asked as she entered the bedroom.

Flowers were spread across the bed, candles were lit all over the house and a cooked dinner was on the balcony table.

"Braxton, the house smells so good."

"Is that all?" Braxton replied.

"No, I see the dinner and the rose petals all over the place. It's all so beautiful.

"What is the occasion?"

"Have a seat." Braxton extended the chair to her.

"Thank you, Braxton."

Soft music played in the background—"A Ribbon in the Sky" by Stevie Wonder. Two strangers walked in and set their dinner plates on the table.

"Braxton, who are these men?"

"Hired help."

"Hired help for what?"

"Just celebrating us. Things have been good lately, right?"

"Yes, they have been. But you shouldn't have gone through all this trouble."

"No trouble. Eat your dinner."

"You have all my favorites—steak, lobster, seasoned shrimp, and a baked potato!"

"Braxton, where in the world will I put all this food?"

"Eat as much as you can. It's okay if you don't eat much. I just wanted to have all your favorites."

The waiters brought out a bottle of wine.

"Let me guess, Spumante?" Mia smiled.

"You guessed it."

Mia dug into her food and Braxton laughed as she gulped down all her favorites. "Everything is delicious."

They shared small talk over dinner.

"Ready for dessert?" Braxton ask seductively.

"I don't have room for dessert, Braxton."

"Not even for your favorite desserts?"

"Not double chocolate cake with chocolate whipped cream icing?"

"Yes, and strawberries and pineapples if you want fruit. If neither one of them will do, how about some Häagen Dazs ice cream?"

"What? Man, you better bring me my dessert," Mia squealed.

Mia ate until she was stuffed. "Can I go take a quick nap?"

"You sleepy now, right? Understandable, but not yet."

Braxton called for the men standing, and they came and pulled Mia's chair back. They then led her to the bedroom.

"Uh, Braxton, I ain't into no freaky stuff."

"Girl, go 'head with that."

As they approached the bedroom, they stood and Braxton entered. He pulled out a Victoria's Secret olive green silk robe that had soft flowers printed on it. The robe was beautiful. He instructed Mia, "Put on this robe, and come back and lay down."

"Do we have to have company now, Braxton?"

"Yes, it's a surprise. Just put on a towel under your robe." Mia went into the bathroom to slip into the towel and the robe. It felt good against her skin. She exhaled.

Mia returned and Braxton asked her to lay across the bed. The bed was warm and the rose petals had been pushed around the bed. The two men approached Mia with scented oils of all kinds.

"Massage therapists and waiters?" Mia was overwhelmed with bewilderment.

"Yeah."

The massage felt wonderful and Mia felt relaxed as the jazz music played softly in the background. They massaged Mia for about an hour, and she slept peacefully while they did. After they left, Braxton motioned Mia to put on her robe and join him on the balcony again. The sun set over the horizon, and the sky was orange and blue. It was breathtaking.

"Thanks, Braxton, for such a wonderful evening. It was everything I could've imagined."

"The evening has just begun."

"There's more?"

Braxton began to sing. "Can we try . . . try and make it? You're everything I need and more."

Mia began to cry. Braxton stopped singing and dropped to his knees. "Mia, will you do me the honor of becoming my wife?" He pulled out a diamond ring and showed it to Mia.

"It's so beautiful." Mia was breathless, but she managed to say, "Yes, I will marry you!"

Mia laughed and cried simultaneously and Braxton jumped to his feet and lifted Mia in the air.

"Yeah! Yeah! That's what I'm talking about. You and me against the world!"

Mia laughed.

"Are you sure this is what you want?"

She kissed him softly on the lips and replied, "I'm sure."

Chapter Sixteen

Mia was determined to make all her dreams come true with the planning of her wedding. She couldn't wait to ask the women in her life for their assistance. She was on the phone bright and early the next morning telling Imani, Summer and Jasmine the good news. She had all of them on three-way. Summer was at Jasmine's when she called.

"Braxton proposed to me last night!" Mia exclaimed.

"Good," Imani said. "You two can stop living in sin now."

"That is good, girl!" Summer said.

"You can stop smiling now, wench!" added Jasmine.

"Ha! I know." Mia was beside herself as she shared the good news.

Summer asked, "How did he propose? Was it romantic?"

"Yeah, and what did he do? Anything spectacular?" Jasmine asked.

"Ain't they nosey?" responded Imani.

"Oh, Mani, you want to know too. Jasmine, she act like she don't want to know," Summer exclaimed.

"Yeah, she do, Summer. But if we hadn't asked, she'd be

fussing right now. So, you going to tell us how he proposed or do we have to go ask him?" Jasmine said.

The ladies all laughed.

"Okay. Let me tell you," Mia said as she told the women, blow by blow, about the preceding night's events.

"Go, Braxton," shouted Summer.

"That sounded nice," added Imani.

"It was. Jasmine, you jealous yet?" Mia laughed.

"Girl, go 'head. I'm glad for your bird head." Jasmine sucked her teeth.

The ladies talked on the phone for a few hours longer, discussing the wedding plans.

Mia decided to have a winter wedding. She got married at Imani's church, Lutheral Seminary Church. The church was covered with white roses all along the aisle seats and on top of the sanctuary. The ceiling was loaded with white and gold balloons. Candles were lit throughout the church. It was breathtaking and the mood was set with soft piano music.

Her bridesmaids came out, one by one. Jasmine and Summer were stunning. They wore silky light orange dresses. They were straight dresses that fell off the shoulders and dropped into a V in the front and in the back. The girls wore their hair up with soft white baby's breath in their hair. They wore jewels to complement their gowns. They were beautiful!

Mike escorted Imani, who wore a long, off-white gown that was very elegant. It had lace covered with beautiful teardrop diamonds. It was beautiful. Imani smiled and took her seat.

Braxton stood in a cream-colored tux and his groomsmen stood beside him with cream-colored tuxes as well with orange shirts and cummerbunds to match. When the doors opened, Tarel came out with the Bible. He was so handsome in his little tux. He walked slowly and he smiled. The wedding processional song started and Bridgett and Tashema came out wearing beautiful gowns. They were little short-sleeved dresses, fitted at the waist. They wore little baby's breath in their hair that was pulled back into curly ponytails on top of their heads. They dropped white, peach, and red rose petals as they came down the aisle.

The ushers opened the doors wide on both sides and there stood Mia. Her gown glittered and sparkled. It dropped slightly off her shoulders with a soft look. The arms did a V shape and diamonds hung throughout it. The back and front were al-most identical—it was a sheer look from top to bottom and was covered in diamonds. It covered her frame perfectly, and her train was also sheer and soft, covered with diamond sparkles. Braxton felt his knees go weak as Mia's father es-corted her down the aisle.

They said their vows that they had written themselves.

"Today, I take you, Mia, to be my wife, my friend, my lover, my confidant, my everything," Braxton said. "When God gave me you, He took a star out of the sky and I now feel like I'm a part of Heaven. I promise to love you with all my strength, and be the man in your life that fulfills your every dream and desire. I love you, baby, for now and al-ways."

Mia wiped the tears from her eyes and she spoke softly. "Braxton, I promise to love you, honor you and be all the woman you will ever need, till death do us part. I will be that friend, that lover, that confidant, that everything just for you. You are the reason I believe in love. I love you too."

The minister spoke. "The rings, please."

Mia and Braxton exchanged rings as the minister went over the significance of the rings.

"These circles are never-ending, therefore your love should be never-ending. Let no man put asunder what God has joined together. Love one another, cherish one another, and above all things, pray for one another and pray together.

"Braxton, this is your helpmate from God. Love her as you would love yourself."

Finally, Mia heard, "Braxton, you may kiss your new bride," and they became husband and wife.

The reception afterward was spectacular. Everyone sat at the outdoor reception with the wind blowing slightly across their heads. The sky was a beautiful blue-and-orange and the sun was just beginning to set. The long candle holders provided light above each table.

A fresh white, orange and red rose arrangement embraced the tables as centerpieces. All the

family sat around chatting and enjoying themselves. The buffet line seemed full of more people than the guests who were invited, and Jasmine sat at the head table, wondering out loud. "Cousins are here we ain't seen in five years and they still haven't spoken. People just come for the food."

"Normally I would tell you be quiet, but girl, that is the truth." Summer laughed.

"We got all our life to eat! Y'all ready to party?" Braxton grabbed his bride by the hand and went to dance. The old school music got everyone's juices flowing, and soon everyone was on the dance floor.

Imani laughed with Jamal.

"Dad, can I talk to you for a minute? Excuse us, Momma. This is man talk." Mike said.

Jamal got up and walked away with Mike.

"What's going on with you and Momma?" he asked his father.

"What do you mean what's going on?" Jamal replied.

"She seems to think there is another woman."

"Naw, just a lady she thinks I had something going on with."

"There's nothing going on?"

"Naw."

Mike looked away and then gave a stern look to Jamal.

TROUBLES WON'T LAST ALWAYS

"You supposed to be setting an example for a lot of people that are looking up to you, depending on you, to lead them down the path of righteousness. Be careful what you do."

"I know that, son."

"I don't have but one mom and I'm not going to let any man hurt her, and this is not coming from your son, but man to man." Mike walked off and left Jamal standing alone.

Chapter Seventeen

Mia, Jasmine, Summer and Imani stood in front of Mia's office. A host of invited guests and potential customers stood behind the ribbon, anticipating and celebrating the independence and confidence of this young doctor.

Mia dialed Braxton one last time because she had no luck reaching him that day. She hung up her cell phone and began to stare at the sign again with the ladies. The sign read: GYNECOLOGY AND PEDIATRIC CARE. The ladies toasted.

"To you, Mia," said Jasmine.

"Thanks, Jazz. It wasn't easy."

"But it was worth it," Imani added.

"I know, Mani."

"So all my patient care is free, right?" Summer joked.

"Mm-hmm, yeah, Summer." Mia twisted her lips up.

The ladies turned to the crowd and held up their champagne glasses. "Cheers." They turned and cut the ribbon. All the potential patients and guests flooded inside.

Braxton came in a little behind the women, looking at what they had accomplished. "I think my job here is done. I feel a little out of place."

"You can stay, honey. Mike, Evan and Jamal coming in
right behind you."

"Oh, all right then." The men greeted one another with
handshakes.

"Besides, it ain't any work going on in here today. This is
just a celebration."

The ladies walked around and toured the business and
grabbed pamphlets and enjoyed the refreshments.

Braxton walked over to his wife, looking proud.

"Thanks, baby," Mia spoke to Braxton as she watched the
ladies enjoy themselves and make their appointments with
the secretary behind the new desk.

After the celebration, Mia closed up the office and went
home. She showered and changed. Mia walked over in her
short silk housecoat and stood by the bed where Braxton
was waiting.

Mia looked at Braxton, remembering she had not been
able to reach him earlier that day for hours.

"Braxton, I called you from the office today several times.
Where were you?"

"I was here."

"Why didn't you answer the phone?"

"Maybe I was 'sleep."

"Braxton, it's been a year and things are kind of tight. Do
you have any prospects for work?"

"Don't see any. Maybe we need to leave this area."

"Braxton, I can't leave this area. My practice is my whole
life."

"What about my life?"

"Do I destroy my dreams to live your dreams?"

"I wouldn't expect you to."

"Then maybe you can do something else besides the construction thing. It seems to be pretty slow. Get something
normal, you know."

"What is normal? Nine to five? Then where does that leave me and my identity?"

"The bills are getting behind; that's all I'm saying."

"Okay. I'm the man, so I will take care of the bills."

"Nothing illegal."

"Of course not. Trust me."

"Thank you."

Within a few weeks, Braxton was working. Things seemed to be better, but Braxton was acting kind of distant. *Maybe it's my imagination,* Mia thought. *I think I will meet him at home for lunch today.*

Mia pulled up in her driveway. "His car is here. Great." Mia walked in. "Dang, it's quiet in here. Maybe he's in the back. Braxton, you here?" Mia continued to walk as she called his name. "Braxton?"

"Mia!" he exclaimed.

Mia dropped the lunch bags and her mouth fell open. Braxton was in bed with Tracie! Right in their house, in their bed! Mia ran to Braxton and started swinging. She was throwing punches all over the place. Tracie tried to gather her clothes and Mia turned to her and knocked her to the floor, still swinging. Braxton grabbed Mia, holding her while she was swinging all over the place.

"Oh, no! Let me go, you dirty lying cheat! Get your hands off me! I'm going to whip the black off of you and this wench's behind!"

"Mia, wait. Let me explain!" Braxton pleaded.

"Let you explain what? How your penis fell between her legs?" Mia tried to get past Braxton, where Tracie was trying to put on her clothes. Mia grabbed her hair and pulled.

Tracie got from beneath her pull and ran out screaming, "Help! Help me!"

"Get out, Braxton, before I catch a charge!"

"But Mia! Mia, it happened only this one time. I swear it was a mistake!"

"Get out, Braxton!"

Mia fell to the floor. "Lord! Why must love hurt so much? Why, Lord? I don't understand why!"

Mia slept on the floor until ten o'clock that evening. She had four messages on her answering machine. The first message was from her receptionist.

"Hey, Braxton and Mia. This is Devon. Mia, when you did not return to work, I took the liberty of rescheduling your appointments. Call me and let me know if you will be in to-morrow. Bye."

Second message: "Mia, please pick up. I'm sorry. I've been sitting outside in the car for hours. Please let me come back in."

Third message: "Mia, it's me again. She tricked me. She said she just wanted to ride out today, so I told her that I go home for lunch and that she was welcome to ride. Next thing I know, she is in our bed naked. I tried to walk away, but you know things haven't been the best between us in a while and I made a mistake."

Fourth message: "She means nothing to me. Please, Mia."

A knock startled Mia and then she heard, "Mia, baby, please let me come back in."

Mia cut off the lights and went to bed. Braxton knocked for what seemed like forever before he finally stopped. He slept in the car that night. The next morning, bright and early, he was knocking again. Mia finally opened the door. Braxton had been crying. His face was stained and his eyes were red.

"Our family is the most important thing in this world. She doesn't mean anything to me. I'm sorry. She had been trying for months, teasing me with her lustful remarks."

"And so you forget your vows?"

"No, I will never be unfaithful again. Please give me another chance."

"Why, Braxton? So you can hurt me again? I'm tired of being hurt. You're the last person I thought I would have to worry about hurting me."

"But the pain does not go away by ending our marriage. We have to deal with our problems."

"The problem now is that you're sleeping with another woman." Mia rolled her eyes at Braxton and shook her head in disgust.

"I was getting ready to get up. I hadn't even done anything to her. I couldn't do it. The guilt was too much. Girl, I love you. I couldn't hurt you like that. We've come through too much to turn back."

"When did you realize you couldn't hurt me? Between getting undressed and falling into bed, or getting on top of her and looking at a naked body beneath you?"

"I know it should not have gone that far, but I promise I didn't go all the way."

"What if I had not walked in? That is probably the only thing that stopped you. How do I trust you again? Do you know how it feels to see you in bed with another woman?"

"I understand how you feel; I am so sorry. I promise I never meant to hurt you and I don't know what got into me."

"So, is that the excuse next time?"

"There is no next time, Mia. Never again will I put myself close to a situation to hurt you. I promise. Please give me another chance."

"Why should I settle for a man who can't be faithful?"

"I slipped once in our three years of marriage. I will be faithful. Why should you let go of the best thing to come into your life? I love you, Mia, and I'm still in love with you; that is why I couldn't do this. You know I'm honest and my word is true, girl. I will never slip up again."

"Braxton, I need time to absorb this. Perhaps you should spend a few days at your brother's house. I will call you when I'm ready to talk."

"Mia, I never meant to hurt you. I'm not leaving, and we are going to work this out."

"Braxton, you are leaving and we will work this out my way or no way at all."

"Is that fair? Sounds like manipulation to me."

"Was sleeping with another woman fair? Should I be thinking about this? Or should I be taking you to court for all you're worth?" She looked him up and down. "Which ain't much these days."

"Fair enough." Braxton shook his head up and down and decided that rather than stand there and take his wife's insults, he'd rather grant her wish and go stay at his brother's. "Talk to you in a few days." Braxton left.

Chapter Eighteen

Mia was devastated. She understood what Imani had meant when she told her that things were going to happen sooner or later in a marriage, and if there is a love worthwhile, she'd have to figure out a way to work it out or move on. Mia loved Braxton and he loved Mia. That was all she ever asked for. For once in her life, Mia had to stand and give her husband another chance, but not because she deserved to be cheated on or disrespected or any of those things. It was because she knew what real love felt like, and Braxton was real love. She owed it to their marriage and their lives. She owed the maturity to the three women in her life.

It had been three days, and Mia finally called Braxton back home.

"You ready to talk?" Mia asked with spunk in her voice.

"Yeah, I guess. So tell me what we do from here or what it is that you have decided."

"I have decided that it will be a long time before I can completely trust you again. It won't be easy, and you can decide now if you want to go through it or not. It won't be my problem that I question you when you step out the door. It won't be my problem that I wonder what you're doing or who you are doing it with. You should not be expecting me to jump into bed with you anytime soon. I'm not ready. This is your problem, and I will deal with it the best way I can because you brought someone else into our life. I feel cheated, and I feel cheap and unloved, and I wonder what made you do it. I mean, aren't I good enough for you?"

"Oh, Mia, you're too good for me. It had nothing to do with you. Things just aren't meeting my expectations in life, and I turned the wrong way trying to handle it."

"But why? I thought I was your best friend," Mia exclaimed.

"You are, but I don't feel very manly coming to you crying about my problems."

"Then why did you marry me if you can't be who you are in front of me? Why can't you be both strong and weak in front of me? That is the meaning of our union; we hold each other up. At least that is what I expected."

"I know that now, Mia. I didn't get it before. As long as you can find the forgiveness in your heart to let me try again, I promise you I will never do that to you again."

"I will try."

"That is all I can ask for."

Things were hard over the next year. Mia couldn't deny that, and there was no use in her lying. She slept with Braxton a couple of months after. The pain of it all became overwhelming. She cried for a few months, at least every time she thought about it.

Braxton had been wonderful. His actions showed he was sorry and that he never meant to hurt her; so, she forgave him. That meant taking him off the time clock. It meant trusting him and giving him his freedom back by allowing him to let go of his guilt. Mia forgave Braxton, and he had a request upon her decision to let it go and never bring it up again.

"Mia, give me a baby," he requested of her.

"I don't think I want any more kids right now. Let me think about it, okay?"

"Don't think too long."

What is that supposed to mean? Mia shrugged her shoulders and let it go.

Chapter Nineteen

"Mia, someone is here to see you," her receptionist said to her.

"I have a patient. Can you take a message?" Mia replied.

"Will do."

Mia came from the patient's room about twenty minutes later. "Who is it?" she asked the receptionist.

"He's over there." Mia turned and looked. Her heart felt like it dropped in her stomach.

"Oh my God. Drake, what are you doing here?"

"Hey, Mia." Drake spoke nervously. "Just thought I would come by and see you. I heard about your practice and all. You finally did it, huh?"

"Yeah. I finally did it." The moment became quiet. Mia spoke. "It's been years. How have you been?"

"Good. Nothing much has changed with me. Still taking it day by day."

"Married yet?"

"No, but I hear you are."

"Yes, I am."

"You married what's his name, um, Bradley?"

"Braxton," Mia said coyly.

"That's right. Well, I would like to talk with you. Do you have time for lunch?"

"Yeah, I could eat."

"Where do you want to go?"

"Anywhere is fine with me. Your choice."

Mia and Drake went to a little Italian restaurant.

"So, what is it that you want to talk to me about, Drake?"

"I wanted to get that dead horse out of the middle of the room. I'm sorry about how things went down between us. I was scared and it was going to be my first child. I shouldn't have doubted you."

"Wow, to what do I owe the pleasure of getting an apology now? Do your mama think I'm good enough to have your baby now?"

"Was that necessary?" Drake said, obviously offended.

"You're right. I apologize. I had a lot to do with what happened. I'm over it now and trying not to live in the past. I wish I had handled things better, and if you want to make peace with me, then that's fine. I'm not angry with anyone—just myself."

"I never meant to hurt you."

"I know. I hear that a lot lately."

"Things not going good between you and Braxton?"

"Now, you know I'm not going to discuss my marriage with you, right?"

"I know. Let's order; I'm starving."

"I am too." Mia smiled.

Lunch somehow became a daily ritual for Mia and Drake. They began to get close again.

"So, Mia, have you told your husband that you're seeing me?"

"Yeah, right!"

"What you waiting for?"

"What reason do I have to inform him of my lunch schedule? We're not doing anything," Mia exclaimed.

"He cheated on you before?" Drake leaned over to touch Mia's hand.

"Why that question?"

"You're not the type to go out to lunch more than once for old times' sake, and look at us. Did he hurt you? I mean, otherwise you wouldn't be spending so much time talking to me."

"It happens." Mia dropped her head and shrugged her shoulders. "Doesn't it?"

Drake felt chills go down his spine. *This is my opportunity to win her back*, he thought to himself.

Drake responded, "And you stayed with him?"

"Yes."

"You must really love him."

"Yes, I guess I do."

"You know I never got over you."

"I'm married now, Drake."

"You're not happy. I can see that for myself."

"I am happy," Mia insisted.

"Don't you miss me at all?"

"You mean do I still have feelings for you?"

Drake nodded.

"Yes. But it's not what I feel for my husband. I love my husband."

"You sure that is all there is?" he asked.

"Yes, I'm sure. Where is this going, Drake?"

"Nowhere, but can't blame a man for trying."

"You're an idiot." Mia laughed.

"And you'll always be my girl."

"Okay, look, I have to get back to the office. Thanks for lunch. And this should be the last lunch we have unless it's with my husband as well. Spending time with you made me realize certain things about myself."

"That was my point earlier."

"I guess there is a lot to still get over, but I know two wrongs don't make a right. I needed to be reassured that I am better than being cheated on and someone else could love me too. Thanks for being a friend in my time of need."

"Anytime. Take care." Drake got up and walked away.

Mia sat and began to think.

I feel kind of bad now for not telling Braxton I had seen Drake and gone to lunch with him on several occasions. I kind of wish I hadn't seen Drake now. He could be a good friend, but he was up to his old tricks. Thank God I didn't betray Braxton, even though for a mere second I thought about what he did to me. But Drake isn't worth losing my marriage or my family over.

Mia felt her marriage was in a sensitive state. She and Braxton had been arguing lately about any and everything. Mia had stopped talking to him altogether. She was hurting because Braxton had started coming in all times of the night. If she said anything, he would blow it way out of proportion. She decided to just pretend everything was okay, but inside she was hurting. He didn't seem like a committed husband, so she felt she couldn't trust him, but she would try anyhow.

Mia began to gather her things to leave when she felt someone standing over her.

"Drake." She stood to face him. "Did you forget something?"

"Yeah, I did." Drake pulled Mia close to him and kissed her long and tender. Mia tried to pull away, but she didn't. She kissed him back. When their kiss ended, Drake looked deep into Mia's eyes.

"I wasn't sure if you understood what I meant when I said 'anytime'." Drake smiled and walked away.

Chapter Twenty

*H*ere *it is, two weeks since I seen or heard from Drake that day at lunch. But I know he's hunting me. I don't know how, but I can feel it. It seems no matter how good your intentions are, wrong always comes back to bite you in the behind.*

I feel nervous and Braxton has been short with me this week. I wonder if someone told him they saw me with another man at lunch. Naw, it could be a business meeting, so he wouldn't be upset about that, or at least he would have asked about it. Maybe he will cheer up after I tell him the news.

I just found out I'm pregnant. Four weeks today. I think I'll fix a romantic dinner and surprise him with the news. I would tell him I saw Drake, but like Mani says, some things are left better unsaid. I totally agree on this one.

Mia was wearing some jogging pants and a little tank top. She began fixing dinner. She fixed a nice salad, some deviled eggs and a shrimp plate with sauce. She then went to the main course and cooked up some crab legs, steak, collards and baked potatoes. "Whew, I'm exhausted." Mia pulled out the wine glasses and decided her work was done. She fixed the table with candlelight then went to shower and change. When Braxton entered, Mia was dressed in a long, red dress, smelling good and looking good.

"Mia, what is all of this?" Braxton said, looking around.

"This is dinner. Have a seat, big daddy."

"You never call me big daddy."

"Well, now I do, Daddy."

"What's up with the daddy?"

"That's what you're going to be." Mia waited for a big smile and then a bear hug. Nothing happened.

"You pregnant?" he asked.

"Yes." Mia smiled excitedly.

"Wow, Mia, that is good."

"I thought you would be a little more excited."

"Well, something is on my mind." Braxton was silent at first, but then Mia finally got it out of him.

"I was told you were seen with another man the other day having lunch."

Oh, man, Mia thought.

"Yes, he came by the office last week to see how I was doing and to congratulate me on my new business. It was Drake," Mia admitted. "I hadn't had lunch yet, so we went to lunch. Nothing big about it."

"Drake? Wow, why aren't I surprised? Then why didn't you tell me, since it was nothing big about it?"

"I didn't want you to make a big deal out of nothing."

"How long had it been since you last saw him?"

"It had been years. Why, Braxton? Do you honestly think anything more happened?"

"I don't know. You're pregnant, but you never got back to me on if you wanted to have a baby."

"And you're saying what?" Mia's spun her neck and put her hands on her hips.

"I'm saying could the baby be Drake's."

"I know you didn't say what I thought you just said."

"Why not? Maybe you were trying to get even with me."

"Do I look like a child who needs to play games with you? You go screw someone else and then try to put it on me?"

"For the last time, I didn't screw her."

"Might as well have; you were naked in our bed with her!"

"Okay, yeah, right."

"Okay, yeah, right. Is that what you said? I can solve this problem. I won't have it!"

"Like heck you won't have my baby!"

"Oh, now it's your baby? Whatever, jerk. You can put your wondering mind to sleep on the couch!"

Mia stormed out of the room and slammed her bedroom door and went to bed. Mia began fussing to herself. "The nerve of him! I got off my pills to have his baby and he thinks I'm putting up with this crap? I don't think so! I love Braxton and I'm happy I'm pregnant with his baby. Time will answer his questions. But by then, I wonder what will become of us? I couldn't imagine being in his shoes wondering if his baby is someone else's. But then again, where is his trust? He should trust me. This feels like déjà vu.

Mia swirled her head in anger. She sat on the edge of her bed and a dose of reality hit her. She suddenly turned sober and decided, *Yeah, I'm putting up with it because I'm having his baby. I'm having this baby.*

Chapter Twenty-One

Drake walked into Mia's office.

"Hey, Drake, I'm glad you came by," Mia said to him.

"What's the matter?"

"Word got to my husband that you and I have been having lunch together."

"He didn't take it so well, I gather."

"Not at all, because I had just told him that I'm pregnant."

"For real? Let me guess. I'm a suspected daddy again?"

"You got it."

"Maybe that's telling us something. Expected daddy twice, I should be your baby daddy."

"Drake, this is not the time for jokes."

"Okay, I apologize. What can I do? You want me to talk to him?"

"Are you serious? No way. I just needed to tell you."

"All right. I have to go. Call me if you need me."

"Okay, bye." Drake left the office.

Later on that evening, Braxton and Mia were at home when someone knocked on the door.

"Braxton, will you get the door?" Mia called out to him while she finished loading the dishwasher.

There was no answer from Braxton. The person knocked louder. By the time Mia reached the door, she realized Braxton had stepped out.

She peeped through the peephole. A beautiful, petite woman stood at the door. Her short brown hair and high yellow complexion almost threw Mia off guard for someone else, but it was indeed Tracie.

"Oh, no." Mia opened the door swiftly. "Tracie, what do you want?"

"I heard you were pregnant."

"Tell me something I don't know. It wasn't that long ago that it happened, so how did you hear that?"

This chick standing at my door. The nerve of her. If I wasn't pregnant, I would bash her in her head.

"Braxton told me," Tracie said gleefully.

"Um, and I'm sure he told you so your crazy self could leave us alone. So, Tracie, what do you want again?"

"Is it Braxton's?"

"Girl, if you don't get away from my door—could you be any dumber?"

"Word is, you were seeing someone else."

"And your point is?"

"Maybe you don't know your man like you think you do. Could be he was telling me because he wanted me to leave you all alone, or maybe he needed someone else again." Tracie turned her head, waiting for Mia to retaliate.

"Okay, whatever makes you sleep at night. I have no more time for this." Mia slammed the door hard.

"Wench. I tried to maintain my cool. I have a feeling that wasn't the last of her. Let me call Braxton."

"Yeah, Mia. What's up?" he answered.

"Tracie just came over here. Can't you keep her out of our lives?"

"Came over here for what?"

"To see if I'm pregnant with your baby."

"She got doubts too?" Braxton said sarcastically.

"Oh, so you got smart remarks? Since the two of you got so many doubts and you obviously still talking to her, why don't you let her have your baby?" Mia said angrily, then slammed the phone down in Braxton's ears.

Half an hour later, Braxton walked in the door.

"Mia." He was annoyed.

"Yes," Mia answered, irritated.

"I didn't mean it like that. And I haven't been talking to Tracie; we have mutual friends from when we were dating. She is toying with you. I'm sure someone we both know is running their mouth to her."

"Oh, but at first, you thought it was cute to have her in cahoots with you on who the daddy of this baby is! Joke now, Braxton. Go ahead, joke!"

"Look, calm your little self down. I said I didn't mean it."

"Start thinking before you talk."

Mia sped past Braxton and he caught her arm. "Let me go, Braxton." Mia tried to get Braxton to release his grip on her arm. She turned and faced him. "Why would she say that, Braxton? How she know what you have doubts about?"

"Because she is crazy and she thinks I want her."

"How do I know that? Tracie of all people telling me what you think. What's up with all of this?"

"Mia, she is crazy."

"Braxton, why are you tripping? I have enough class and respect if the baby wasn't yours to tell you. But I didn't sleep with Drake. Don't do this to us, Braxton. Just trust me."

"I'm going out."

"Where?"

"To the bar or something."

"Fine. You're going to regret all this in the end."

Braxton left.

"Dang, with all this grief, I might as well have slept with Drake."

Chapter Twenty-Two

Mia had forgotten the displeasure of morning sickness. It felt like someone was reaching into her stomach and pulling her guts out over and over again. She was ready to have this little person like yesterday.

Braxton was a real pain every day. This was his first child, so he shared the joy with everyone except Mia. He shouted joyfully at the ultrasound visits and hearing the heart beat. Then Mia had a scare. With all the stress that was going on, she started spotting. It scared Braxton and he finally realized Mia was carrying a life inside of her that required her to be happy. He started running her baths, talking to her and rubbing her belly and making sure Mia had enough to eat and drink; he rubbed her back and her feet. He was Mia's Braxton again. He was everything she needed and more.

Finally, their little gift arrived and it was a boy! Braxton named him Bilal. Mia thought that was a beautiful name. Along with Bilal came extremely sore and large breasts. Mia felt like she was carrying mountains on her chest. In short, Mia was not happy. Perhaps it was postpartum depression. But that wouldn't explain Braxton's behavior. He smiled at the baby, kissed him good night and called him his joy for living, all while he rolled his eyes at Mia. Then at long last, the bomb fell from the sky and it started to make sense.

"Mia, I need a blood test," Braxton spoke.

"Excuse me?"

"I can't have anything between me and my son. I need to know."

"Can't you look at that boy and see that he is yours? Your love should surpass a blood test. Even if you didn't think he was yours, what about the love we have? What about the fact you are the one who will raise him? So, since you need to be this way, then you leave me no choice. I can't get over this, so after you get a blood test, I want a divorce, and you're then going to pay with a child support check every month to make sure your son is provided for."

"What? That isn't fair!" Braxton protested.

"Fair? Your putting my character on the line. Much less, where is the trust? You have no concern for what you've put me through. This is your choice. You're the one bringing all this confusion back into our lives."

"What do you expect? Look at all the confusion and drama this whole ordeal has already caused. You started the confusion when you hid the fact that you were seeing Drake."

"Braxton, you're a hypocrite. The only drama here is coming from you! Think about how much of a mess you have caused in our lives. I couldn't come to you and talk to you in the beginning about seeing Drake because of your distrust. Second, you had the affair, not me, so stop putting your guilt on me. Third, you let me go through half my pregnancy hurting because you were too busy thinking someone hurt you. You are your own problem, and no one else has anything to do with this. Drake has gone on with his life and knows the baby is not his. Why can't we go on with ours?"

"Maybe you should have told me you saw him in the beginning and none of this would have happened."

"Maybe so, but then that means you would have to grow up and act like a man."

Mia was lost. She knew she was just as hypocritical as Braxton. But what she also knew was that it wasn't her righteousness or her prayers, or going to church that identified her relationship with God. She learned that the three women in her life—Imani, Jasmine, and Summer. These women understood that the love of Jesus was unconditional. Mia looked at the character of her mother and decided that like Imani, she wanted to establish a deeper relationship with God.

Mia's pride was hurt, but she knew that if no one else knew who the baby's father was, God knew, and she decided at that point God would see her through all of this.

Chapter Twenty-Three

Six weeks later, Braxton was coming in late every night. He was disrespectful and ignored Mia to the max. It was like a nightmare all over again. For Mia, it was the hardest thing to deal with. She already had issues with being validated and being needed. Every time Braxton pulled this stunt, it made Mia feel like a knife was being put in her back. She had had enough.

"Where have you been, Braxton?"

"Woman, when you start paying the bills up in here and taking care of this family, then question me."

"I contribute to the household. You wanted to be the man and you told me to spend my money as I pleased. Make up your mind how you want this marriage to work."

"Contributing isn't the same as taking care of this family. Looks like you contribute a lot to a lot of people. Holler at me after the blood test."

"Oh, all right. It's like that? You will regret it."

Mia looked at Braxton in disbelief and shook her head.

Strange, but at least Mitchell knew his own flesh and blood when he first laid eyes on each of them. I guess you get the good with the bad. Now I see why people divorce once, then stay miserable in the next marriage. How can you admit you messed up again? Even having people believe it's you is misery alone. Worse comes to worst, I could be one of those people who divorce three times plus until I get it right. I guess the grass isn't always greener on the other side.

Three weeks later, the blood test came back. The doctor called Mia and told her the results, and then Mia passed Braxton the phone. By the look on Braxton's face, you could have bought him for half a cent.

"Mia, I'm sorry for everything I put you through." Braxton spoke softly after hanging up the phone.

"Sorry? How do we get beyond this? You should love me enough to trust me. I would never lie or play with my baby's life. He would need to know who his real father is if anything ever happened to me. I would never do that." Mia became short of breath and sat down. "After all this, I'm having an anxiety attack. Thanks a lot, Braxton. I swear you're going to be the death of me." Mia turned red and held her chest.

"Mia, just calm down and sit still. Breathe. Breathe. Okay? Can I get you anything?" Braxton hugged Mia, but the pain didn't budge.

"Braxton, I don't think I can forgive you this time. And no, you can't get me anything. I think you have done quite enough. I think I need to go lay down."

Braxton felt like a nut, and an idiot. *What in the world made me trip like that?*

He began to wonder what he could do to get in good with Mia. Perhaps flowers, a vacation or a month-long apology. "Darn it, I should have known the baby was mine," he said out loud.

Mia knew Braxton was beating himself up pretty badly.

"Good enough for you. I will never forgive you as long as I live," she said out loud before closing her eyes to rest.

Chapter Twenty-Four

"Mrs. Hamilton, do you wish to keep your married name?" the judge asked.

"Yes, Your Honor," she replied.

Braxton stared with a cold, helpless look. He whispered, "Are you sure you want this?"

Mia looked away. The tears were warm against her face. Fear made her want to say no, to run into Braxton's familiar, strong arms. The pain was too deep. Mia didn't know from the pain if she could ever risk love again. She feared the next heartbreak could be fatal—people do die of broken hearts.

"Granted, this divorce is now final due to irreconcilable differences between—"

"Wait, Judge." Braxton looked desperately at Mia.

Mia felt her knees weaken underneath her.

"Excuse me, Mr. Hamilton. Is there something you need to say?" the judge questioned.

"Yes, I don't think we want this," Braxton replied.

"Are you speaking for the both of you?" The judge looked at Mia for a response.

"Am I, Mia?" Braxton asked.

Mia was speechless.

"Are there doubts about this divorce?" Mia's lawyer demanded an answer.

"Yes, Your Honor. I mean, but we're ready to go our separate ways," Mia spoke, embarrassed.

"I'm not, Mia. Please, for the sake of our family," Braxton pleaded.

The judge intervened. "If you leave out of this courtroom together, you won't be credible if you come back anytime soon for a divorce in my presence. I won't grant it."

"We understand," Braxton said.

Braxton walked over and pulled his wife in his arms. Mia sobbed uncontrollably. "Braxton, don't make me regret this."

A few hours later Mia was on the phone with Summer, who acted like she had just lost her breath. She sighed and then asked the question, "So, you didn't go through with the divorce?"

"Summer, I couldn't say anything. Before I knew it, I was walking out the courtroom still his wife."

"Hold on, girl. We need a threesome for this conversation." Summer dialed Imani. "Imani, hang up and dial Jasmine and connect her, and then I will call you back."

"For what?"

"Imani, just do it unless you want me to come through this phone," Summer joked.

Imani hung up and Summer clicked back over. "Hold up one second. I will call her back." The phone beeped. It was Imani.

"Hold on, Mia. You there, Mani?"

"Yes, I'm here."

"All right, hold on, y'all. Summer clicked back over to Mia.

"Okay, Jasmine and Imani, y'all there?"

"Yeah, what y'all want?" Imani asked.

"Tell them, Mia," Summer said.

"I didn't go through with the divorce," Mia said nervously.

"Why not, girl? Braxton is crazy." Jasmine scolded Mia.

"Jasmine, he is still my husband. I guess the divorce probably scared him pretty good, so maybe things will get better."

"Summer, you and Jasmine can't run Mia's life for her," Imani jumped in. "Let her make her own decisions. We all have made mistakes, but we didn't know they were mistakes until we went through them."

"All I'm saying, Mommy, is he don't treat her worth nothing," Jasmine stated.

"I agree with her there, Imani. He don't seem to be getting no better," Summer added.

"Mani, how are things at home?" questioned Mia, getting the attention off of her.

"Things are quiet, Mia. You know I give it to God and leave it alone. If I'm going to try and fix it, why pray?"

"So, you okay and all?" asked Mia.

"Yeah. I'm fine."

"What's going on with you, Jasmine? Is your man straight this week?" Summer antagonized.

"Summer, you better be glad Mani is on the phone," Jasmine replied.

"I was just joking. For real, how are things going?" Summer replied.

"Things are going fine. He went to rehab and he ain't even home. He got thirty days to pull, so hopefully drugs will be a thing of the past soon."

"That's good, Jasmine. As your mother, I would hate to see that break up your relationship, because maybe you two can get married soon."

"I agree, Mani; that is real good. I got enough marriage problems for us all with Braxton."

"Summer, you're mighty quiet all of a sudden. What's wrong with you?" Jasmine asked.

"Nothing. My life is just as boring as usual," Summer added.

"Ha! Girl, put on a sexy gown or something for that man. It seems he is never home or your life is just boring. Shoot, you can have some of my problems if you want. A few of my kids too, now that I think about it."

Jasmine interrupted. "It's not like you got your own kids anyway." Before Mia could respond, Summer continued.

"No, thank you, Mia. I'm fine," was Summer's reply. "I enjoy the quietness of a boring life, but I would like a little more excitement. My marriage has had its share of roller-coasters, so don't go wishing anything on me. I didn't say I wanted drama; I said I was bored."

"Well, look, girls. I need to go. My husband just walked in," Mia said.

"All right, bye," the ladies all said in unison.

Braxton walked into the room like he was thinking what he wanted to say before he got home. He approached Mia and grabbed her hands gently then called her name.

"Mia."

"Yes, Braxton."

"Look, I can't find any work here in New York City paying what I deserve to get paid. You know what I mean? The money I had in the beginning of our marriage was good. Now things are slow here and things are backwards. Now we are depending on your income to hold things together. I'm not good with that. I'm the man. I should be carrying the load of the bills, not contributing."

"Braxton, not that again. We are doing fine. Perhaps you should be careful what you say. Remember telling me that when I start paying the bills then I could question you? I don't roll like that, so we are good."

"Yeah, based on your income, but I'm the man."

"You are the man and my income doesn't change that."

Mia became playful. Braxton pushed her off.

"Seriously, Mia. I have a deal in the works closer to Central Los Angeles."

"But we have a future here. Construction is not a dependable field to just pick up and move the family."

"You may have a future here, but you can easily reopen your practice there."

"Braxton, it takes time to build clientele. Let me think about it. I swear, it seems like if it's not one thing, it's another; one ordeal after another with you."

"Everything is 'let me think about it.' Girl, what about do as I say? I'm the head, right?"

"Of course you're the head, but I do have a mind of my own. I'm not a monkey you can teach tricks to."

"I didn't mean it to sound that way. I'm just saying, you're supposed to follow me, for better or for worse."

"What is worse? You not being in control of the marriage the way you think a man should? We are a family, so let's just enjoy being a family. Please."

"You're not hearing me, Mia. I have to do me for there to be an us. Understand? Figure out what you want to do, then let's talk."

"I hear you, Braxton. Take it for what it is."

Braxton walked in the next room and Mia had to admit she already regretted her decision not to go through with the divorce. He had to have been thinking about this for some time to bring it up right after they got back together. Now all she could do was feel regretful.

Braxton was right back in Mia's face. "You coming to bed?" he asked.

"Yes, give me a minute."

"All right. Make it quick. We need to make up for lost time. I mean, we nearly divorced today."

"Sure, you right," Mia reluctantly agreed.

"You don't sound excited. I mean, what is it now?"

"What is it? We just got back together like hours ago and you talking about us moving, closing my practice and starting over. That is a lot to digest and think about at one time. Today was enough."

"I know it's a lot, but that is why you need to come to bed. I can relax your mind. We can remember one of the many reasons why we fell in love in the first place."

"Perhaps. I mean, we never had a problem in that area, now, did we?" Mia flirted with Braxton.

"Heck no. Come on, girl," Braxton said as he led the way to reconciliation.

Chapter Twenty-Five

Mia dialed her mother's number.

"Hey, Mani. What you doing?" she said into the phone receiver.

"Taking care of your kids, as usual."

"I know, Mani. I will come get them this weekend."

"Isn't it strange that I always have your kids and you get them on the weekends?"

"I get the point, Mani, but you don't know how much you have helped me over the years. Even when I come to get them you say that it is okay to leave them there at your house. I truly thank you."

"I know it's hard running a business with three small ones and a baby. How is my Bilal doing these days?"

"He is good, Mani. He's growing like a weed. And I promise you as soon as we get through this getting up at night, I will get the kids."

"I know you will. I got to go, child. Talk to you later."

"Okay, Mani."

Mia thought perhaps she would talk to Mani about Braxton's suggestion to move. But that chance passed her by.

She thought long and hard for a few weeks. She got headaches over it. She finally decided that it was time to move on with her husband. There was nothing left for her but bad memories and haunted faces. Her family could always come visit and she could come home to visit them. She felt good and complete about coming to a decision. Whether or not it was the right one was another story.

Later on that evening, Mia decided to call Imani back. She dialed the number.

"Hello," Imani answered.

"Hey, Mani, Braxton is going to take a contracting job out west near Central Los Angeles."

"What? What about your practice and the kids?" Imani asked her.

"I can open another practice and we won't be living in Central Los Angeles. We will be out of the city. The kids will go to a good school."

"Hold on, Mia." Imani said while she clicked over and called her other daughter.

"Jasmine, Mia is talking about closing her practice and moving to Los Angeles. Braxton is taking a job out there."

"Well, let him go. I know you're not closing your practice for any man. Especially Braxton. He is undependable," responded Jasmine.

"He is my husband," Mia reminded her sister.

"When he wants to be," Jasmine quickly replied.

"Jasmine, please," Imani said.

"Hold on, Mia," Jasmine said.

"Okay, let me guess, she is calling Summer," Mia said.

"Summer, hey, I have Mia and Mani on the phone," Jasmine said, clicking Summer in on the call.

"Oh Lord, what is going on now?" Summer sighed.

"Now, if your husband loves you, would he ask you to close your practice that you worked all your life to achieve and move for a contracting position to fulfill his temporary ego?" Jasmine asked Summer.

"Um, Mia, you need to think about that," Imani added.

"Mia, are you thinking about closing your practice? I know you're not," Summer contested.

"Summer, I have to do what is best for my marriage. He is not happy here," Mia stated.

"Well, I don't know. You know your marriage better than us," Summer concluded.

"Knowing him or not, I am your mother and I don't feel good about this in my spirit at all," Imani mentioned.

"Huh, I don't feel good in mine either, and mine ain't been around too often, so that should tell you something," Jasmine joked.

"Jasmine, you're crazy. But look, Mia, think about this. You know I don't speak too often against your choices concerning your marriage, but Mani is right. Something don't feel right about this," Summer said.

"I have thought about this. We may get completely back on track, having only each other to talk to, and we can leave the past behind," Mia reasoned.

Jasmine spoke. "You can leave the past here if it's true love."

"I know, Jasmine, but some people don't get over grudges as easily as others." Summer said.

"That's a problem right there," Imani protested.

"Yep, Imani, I agree," Summer spoke.

"A fresh start could be good," Mia said.

"Mia, a fresh start cannot be good when all the bills fall on him. It can only cause headaches. I'm telling you what I know as your mother," Imani told her daughter.

"Well, I haven't told Braxton yet, but I will have my manager run my practice on a trial basis before I decide to sell. My manager is a doctor also."

"Good idea, little sister," Jasmine said.

"Have you told your husband anything yet?" Imani questioned.

"Nope, Mani. I will, though. He is waiting on my decision. He needs to know by next week."

"If you're so sure, then why are you having the manager run the place on a trial basis?" Summer questioned.

"Summer, I wasn't born yesterday. I'm not putting all my trust in a man. What if things don't work out? I need to do this for my marriage in case it doesn't work out and for me. I've worked too hard to get this practice to just walk away now."

"Oh, okay. Whatever you say," Jasmine spoke.

"Well, I wish you guys the best of luck, but my babies need to stay with me until you guys get settled," Imani spoke.

Mia agreed. "I wouldn't have it any other way."

Mia hung up the phone from the girls and began to reflect. Why had she decided to try again with Braxton? Her insides didn't sit right with the entire situation. She was trying to trust her husband. She, however, never regained complete trust in him after catching him with another woman. She decided, in any event, she would move with her husband where she belonged.

Mani had taught Mia so many factors to make it in life; like how to just be strong. Mia felt at times Imani's character was cold and unfeeling. Mia didn't see her cry enough or laugh enough, or scream when she was angry at Jamal. When he hurt her, no one would know it. She was settled, but Mia saw her pain when it came to her. Mia heard her screams when she upset her. Mia heard her words of pain when she disappointed her.

It could be one of two things, Mia told herself. Mia either meant that little, or that much to Imani. It turned out she meant that much, and Mia was a little too valuable to let her just be. Mia loved Imani. Her strength before Mia's eyes was the only thing that helped her whisper to herself that she could go on with all the twists and turns in her life. Her character proved a man is only determined by your definition of a real woman. It takes a real man to love a real woman. Otherwise, she would move on without him. Mia stood on her decision not to allow her husband to move on without her.

Chapter Twenty-Six

The move was exhausting. Braxton, Bilal and Mia moved in and dragged all of the other kids' belongings into their rooms. They settled in over the course of a few months and Mia got employment quickly at a doctor's office not far from their home. They sent for the kids and it became home for them all.

Braxton's hours seemed longer and longer. He seemed happy, yet distant to Mia. One night, about a month later, Braxton never came home. He didn't even call. Mia filed a missing persons report only to be told he was alive and well. The next day when he sent word through a coworker that he had found another woman, Mia was devasted! He had promised to never hurt her again. He said he loved her.

Mia moved on daily with the kids as if nothing had happened. No matter how hard Mia tried to pretend that everything was okay when her mother and sisters called, it was growing weary on her being so far away from home with no one but her and the kids. Her pain was tender and intense, and she couldn't bear to talk about it.

Braxton eventually called a few weeks later, wanting to

explain why he had left her for another woman but didn't. The words had not yet come, and she couldn't bear to hear his voice.

Mia functioned as a single mother with a new baby as best as possible. She got up, got the kids ready and went to her nine to five. She came home, fed the kids, helped with homework, and put the kids to bed and plopped herself into bed right after. A Sunday to Sunday ritual, day in and day out, and Mia was tired. It seemed as though Mia was functioning until the days became longer and sleep would fall on her in the middle of her day with heaviness. The mornings were hard to get up out of bed. It was as if she woke up every day to a nightmare, but it was actually her tortured and lonely life—waking up to pain and laying down to pain. It seemed the pain would never stop.

Braxton had left her for a white woman. She was tall, blonde and skinny. Mia was crushed and overwhelmed at the same time. Her most defined emotion was anger.

Mia thought, *How dare he leave me and for a white woman at that? That no-good dog! I supported him, I moved my family away and tried to be there for him. Never have I deceived him or been unfaithful to him, and this is what I get for being the strong black woman? I can no longer walk this walk alone. I have to humble myself and call my family, in spite of the embarrassment. I need them right now.*

"Hey, Mani," Mia spoke into the phone, trying not to break down.

"Hey, baby. How you doing? You sound stressed."

Mia was crying before she could say another word. "Mani, could you get Jasmine and Summer on the phone, please?"

"What's wrong, Mia?"

"I will tell you all at the same time after you get them on the phone. I can only say this once."

"Hold on." Imani clicked over. A couple of moments later, all three women were on the line with Mia.

"Summer and Jasmine, you there?" Mani asked.

"Yeah, we're here. What's wrong with you? You sound like something's wrong," Summer asked.

"Summer, it's a long story," Mia replied. " I moved up here with Braxton and I tried to tell myself it was the right thing to do. But within months he began staying out later and later. Then one day, he never came home at all."

"What? I told you he was no good," Jasmine said.

"That is what she said, Mia."

"Summer and Jasmine, what does that change now? Mia, just come on home. You still have your practice and the place hasn't been bought yet," Imani told her.

"Mani, I am so embarrassed," Mia cried.

"Embarrassed for what? Things happen in life and you did your part, so don't worry about it, Mia. Just come on home. I have always been there for you and the kids, and that won't change now."

"Thanks, Mani."

"I know, and what you embarrassed about?" Jasmine asked Mia.

"Jasmine, he left me for some skinny, anorexic white woman." Mia sobbed. "I mean, she could have been at least a drop dead sexy white woman. I would have felt a little better."

"No, he didn't!" Summer exclaimed.

"Yes, he did. What was wrong with me?"

"How you find out, Mia?" Summer asked.

"Girl, he called himself coming over to get some of his things while I was not here, but when I was pulling up from work with the kids I seen them pass by. I had also seen her at one of the contractor sites but didn't know who she was at the time."

"Well, his loss. Right, Imani?" Summer said in a positive tone.

"You got that right, Summer. Plenty of men, white or

black, would love to have themselves an educated doctor that has her head correctly on her shoulders," Imani added.

"I wouldn't steer you wrong, as your sister. I say let him go, Mia, and good riddance to him. She will be getting rid of his no-good butt in a minute."

"Yep, as soon as she finds out he ain't worth a nickel. And I'm telling you that as your sister-in-law."

"Just make your plane reservations and come on home. Send for your stuff later," Imani demanded.

"I think I will."

"You okay, Mia?" Jasmine asked.

"Yeah, I will be fine, y'all. Thanks for everything. We will catch the next plane out tomorrow," Mia told them.

"Hang in there, girl. Everything will be okay," Summer added.

"I know. Bye." Mia hung up.

Mani, Jasmine, and Summer remained on the phone.

"I knew it was a mistake from the start. I told Mia I had a bad feeling in my spirit," Imani stated.

"Me too, remember, Mani? She should have listened," Jasmine exclaimed.

"Well, you all know she had to see for herself. I was hoping we were wrong. She don't deserve that," Summer protested.

"Well, I say we go up there and find Braxton and that woman, and beat some sense into both of them," Jasmine said.

"I'm down with that, Jasmine," Summer said.

"Summer, you and Jasmine know that is not the right thing to do. The Word lets us know vengeance belongs to the Lord."

Jasmine replied, "It can belong to the Lord. We just going to take care of it for Him. We will give Him all the credit."

"Like I said, I'm down with that," Summer said.

"Maybe you should hang up, Mani. Summer and I got this." Jasmine chuckled.

"I am going to hang up, and the two of you get off the phone talking stupid. Bye." Imani hung up.

"Like I was saying, Summer, let's handle this. What's the plan?"

"I say we tell Mike and Evan. And let him catch a beat-down for what he done to Mia."

"I agree. Let's do it."

Chapter Twenty-Seven

Mia and the kids sat quietly on the plane. Mia took a window seat and the tears began to flow from her eyes. She faced away from the kids, not wanting anyone to see her crying. Bilal looked up from her lap and cooed. Another era had come and gone in Mia's life. Her life seemed to always be dictated by love; what seemed like love anyway. None of her relationships seemed satisfying, lasting or even true. It finally occurred to Mia that maybe love was everything she thought it wasn't. Maybe love came in disguise—not perfect to the eye, not knocking her off her feet, but as a warm acquaintance followed by getting to know each other. Maybe love was running behind her and she was running away from it. Mia felt even though a major part of her life would be different, life must go on. Her pain was now tender and intense because it was still familiar from other heartbreaks. Hopefully, she thought, this too would pass.

She looked across the little specks that were obviously buildings, but she saw an orange-and-pink horizon with very thin cloud puffs and it seemed life was beautiful again. A sudden rush of hope and inspiration appeared out of no-where, and she thought as she looked down at Bilal that life wasn't so bad after all. Perhaps this was the start of beautiful beginnings.

Mia stepped off the airplane and went to baggage claim, pulling her kids behind her, with Bilal close to her heart. Mani, Jasmine and Summer were there. She could no longer hold the tears as they each grabbed her in a circle. She cried for at least three minutes as she heard soft whispers that spoke, "It will be okay. You're home now," and a cheerful "Stop crying, girl."

Mia managed to smile a little as she pulled away from the tightly fitted arms of Jasmine.

"Let's go home, daughter," Imani said.

"Okay, Mani," Mia replied.

They rode home in silence, which was different, and they all gathered at Mia's old place.

"You okay, Mia?" Imani asked her daughter.

"No, Mani, I'm not." Mia started to cry again and Imani pulled her close.

"You will be okay, baby. Time heals all wounds. I know it hurts now, but you will get through this."

Summer was fixing the kids some dinner.

"Where did this food come from? You all been here while I was gone?" Mia asked.

"Jasmine and I went shopping yesterday. All you have to do is relax and get settled," Summer assured her.

"Thanks, guys." Mia was so grateful for her family.

Although it was a cloudy day, Mia settled back in her old home after everyone left and she felt a sense of relief. She put the kids to bed and took a long, hot bath to ease her muscles and her mind. She knew she had to function as best as possible being alone and being a single parent.

Before Mia knew it, Monday rolled around and she had to

go get the kids registered back into their old school, to start her routine before she shipped them all to her mother—except Bilal, whom she couldn't stand to part with just yet. Imani insisted it was nothing and she could handle the kids during her time of strain and stress. She told Mia to get herself together first, and then come for the rest of the kids. Mia was relieved since she didn't know if she could handle all her kids alone at the rate she was going. It seemed when she did get the other kids back on the weekend, she was functioning, but by Monday morning, she was exhausted again. Bilal was still waking up at night, and it seemed she never slept or rested. The bills were taunting her when she did try to sleep. And even though she still owned her own practice, the cost of taking care of two households, so as not to inconvience Imani for helping take care of the kids, was a lot. She knew it would cost just as much if they were there with her.

Mia began to think about the changes Braxton had taken her through. She looked at all the pain she felt over the years, all the headaches and the sacrifices she had made. Now she sat alone and she realized she could no longer put the pieces together.

I'm going to call Braxton and tell him what I'm feeling. He is going to take Bilal until he gets a little older. I am going to call Mitchell and tell him to take his kids too. Why do I have to take the load alone? I have to be both Mommy and Daddy and I won't do it anymore! I can't breathe like this. I can't see my way. Where is my life going?

She stood with the phone in her hand. For a moment she couldn't move. Anger had literally taken hold of her and she began to feel pain her chest. Tears filled Mia's eyes. What was this? It was like a rushing well of water bursting inside of her except no tears fell. Mia trembled. She managed to pull herself together and her heart felt like it was in her throat. She dialed Braxton's cell phone number.

"Hello," he answered.

The anger rose up inside of Mia intensely, and suddenly she wanted nothing to do with Braxton, much less let him take their child.

"If you ever come near me again, I will kill you!" Mia screamed into the phone.

"Mia, don't be threatening me," Braxton said.

"Why not? Did you think about how you killed me when you left our children and me? Did you think about what you took from me when you left me for another woman—a white woman, at that?"

Click. Braxton hung up and Mia called back again.

"What, Mia?" he snapped.

"What! What!"

"Hello, Mia. This is Ann. I know you're hurting and all, but—"

Mia cut her off in mid statement. "Ann, are you talking to me?"

"Why, yes."

"Okay. Then perhaps you want to hear this. Braxton is still my husband, and even though I will never in this lifetime or the next want him back, I am going to sue you and him for everything down to the panties on your butt. So, since you were big enough to break up my home, let's see if your pockets are big enough to pay the cost."

"There is no need to go there. Things happen."

"There was no need, but since you want my husband, you took it there, and all my needs will be met. Good-bye, Ann."

Mia hung up. She had to laugh at herself when she realized how she put things into perspective so quickly. She decided she had the upper hand after all, and Braxton wasn't worth her time anyway. "Oh my God, what was I thinking by letting him get to me like that? Lord, help me. I need some time to pray, some time to gather my thoughts so I will never reach that point again."

Mia reflected on her feelings and emotions and it was scary; just the thought of letting another person have that much control over her emotions. It was time she distanced herself from the past and from Braxton emotionally.

Chapter Twenty-Eight

Once Mia had the kids back in their routine and at Imani's, she went back to her practice. She felt like she was finally where she belonged.

Mia saw her last patient and a sense of accomplishment came over her. She smiled as she reflected how far she had come in a short amount of time. In three months, she felt more like herself and she was happy. She was sure in a few weeks she would be able to get the kids back.

The independence she had gained over the course of time was part of her happiness. Proudly, she admitted that happiness didn't come in a new lover or a new husband, but from within her. The daily accomplishment of feeling like she had completed another day to the best of her ability was satisfying. It was overall just the rewards of feeling alive. It was living for the first time in many years. There were no heavy religious barriers in her life. Mia felt close to God and felt free and relieved that her tribulations were only exemplary of how much God loved her. Now with the knowledge of God's new grace and mercy, Mia knew she would continue to grow in God, and in faith.

Mia's happiness was finally realizing that if she was to ever experience Heaven, she would first have to accept that Heaven began on Earth; that God wanted her to live life to the fullest. With that thought, she began to practice the concept daily. Along her way, she asked God to clean her up and strengthen her. Ironically, God had already begun to clean Mia up before she asked.

Discouragement was the cause for her lifestyle, her attitude and her reason for becoming everything she was not. It occurred to Mia that she was weary, exhausted, beaten down and tired. She had taken little time to pray and hadn't stopped to look at her life. She thought she had prevailed. She was moving on, even in the mix of life, functioning and coping like normal single mothers, maybe even a little on top of her game she thought. But her mental and physical state said the contrary. She had lost weight, going from a size nine to six. She hadn't had a menstrual period in months, and she was physically and emotionally drained. All of this contributed to her discouragement and low self-esteem that she cared not to acknowledge.

Things from Mia's childhood haunted her that made her feel lower than other women. She had dreams as a young girl of being not only an author, but a model. She used to dance and feel the joy of it in her soul, until the day Imani told her she looked like the back of a monkey's butt. Those words stuck to Mia all the days of her life. She didn't know what beauty was, but she knew she was not it. Imani said if anyone was pretty, it was Jasmine. Mia was scarred for life. For a long while, Mia thought her color made her ugly; the smooth brown skin that covered her, or maybe her full lips or her nappy hair. Perhaps it was her narrow frame back then. Whatever it was, it had to be pretty bad to look like the back of a monkey's behind. Those words made it very difficult for Mia to love herself or accept anything about herself until she was old enough to know God made her just the way He intended. And God don't make no junk.

"Thank you, Lord, for your grace and mercy. I could have been, should have been dead and gone. I would not have known from the grave that You saved me. Thank You. I'm grateful."

Another day of work had come and gone. Mia walked with her head held down to her chest and her arms tight around her waist. It was windy and the air was brisk. She held her briefcase in her hand, moving quickly to her door. The night was quiet and the sky was clear. Her thoughts came to mind as quickly as she moved. It was hard being a single mother. She had the kids back now for about four weeks, and she didn't know if she was coming or going.

Mia helped the kids with their homework, fed them dinner and got the kids ready for bed. It was now 9:15 and she was just on her third trip to the car for the rest of the things she had left in there earlier. She came back in, plopped the bags on the floor and sat in front of the television. Immediately, Mia wanted to complain and name the countless errands, problems and unsolved financial beckonings in her life.

How Imani did it was a mystery to her. She had the help of Jamal, but a mother's work is never done among the many tasks a woman has to carry. Although it was just the three of them compared to her four, she watched Imani do it with ease. She raised her kids, worked her full-time job, and earned her retirement. Mia could see retirement nowhere in the near future.

Imani had seen the best and worst, not always knowing how the bills would be paid and perhaps not always knowing how she would make it. But one thing Mia learned from her mother was to take one day at a time. It's the only way she had made it this far. Truth be told, Mia did not see how she could be as strong as Imani. She had already seen worse days in her lifetime as an adult.

As a child, Mia had never seen the lights off at her home; she never went hungry or saw a day that Imani did not make a complete meal. The sheets always seemed new and the bathroom in order and tidy. Even though Imani worked, Mia never saw a messy house and didn't remember having too many toys to destroy the setting of the rooms as kids. She never knew they struggled because it was made comfortable for the kids.

Growing up, Jasmine, Mike and Mia thought they were living the good life. As Mia thought back, she now knew why they didn't get any money except for lunch; there was no extra money and their trips and desires to any store was limited. Mia understood why they got clothes and shoes only for school time and no in-betweens. It was called survival, and it didn't hurt her at all.

Now that Mia was grown with her own kids, she had already seen a few things in her household get cut off because of lack of money—the phone, the lights and the cable. But, God provided just the same. Mia thought they would be hungry, but Imani gave them food when they came to visit. Nothing ever falls through the cracks because of God. Mia strived to be where she was in life and Mani inspired her to be strong.

The phone rang.

"Hello," Mia answered.

"Hey, Mia. This is Celeste." It was Braxton's mother, to Mia's surprise.

"Hi. What can I do for you?"

"I know everything that has happened between you and Braxton has left a sour taste in your mouth. As his mother, I don't agree with his actions, and I need you to know that. But do you think I could see my grandchildren this weekend?"

"No." Mia spoke dryly.

"Is that it? Simply no?"

"Yep." Mia hung up the phone and didn't give the call a second thought, the same way she hadn't given Braxton one.

Chapter Twenty-Nine

Mia lounged on the couch across from Summer.
"Apparently love isn't love anymore, Summer," Mia said.

"I don't know, Mia. I still believe in real love. I mean, look at my marriage. We've overcome a lot of things many people wouldn't have been able to come through in a marriage."

"Yeah, but why does love have to hurt?"

"Mia, I don't think it should, but life is about hurts and joys. You can't really get to one level without touching the surface of the other. Emotions are so closely united. How do we know when we cry if we're crying in joy or pain? I mean, sometimes we are releasing something and we don't know that we even released it."

"How many days have I woken up lonely? You can't answer that, or anyone else. Neither can I. I'm just saying, I know there have been many and I'm going through it now. All because love is not genuine anymore. Everyone seems to want something for nothing. Give me, give me, is what love is all about these days. Someone is going to get screwed or be screwed in the end, so we hold back. In order for the relationship to work, we have to give completely of ourselves."

"Mia, I know it isn't easy. The worst feeling in the world is loneliness. But you're strong and you have gone through worse. I know how it feels to see a world of people and still be lonely."

"Yep, there is a world of people, and finding that special someone is hard."

"Mia, life is about connecting. Let that special someone find you. No matter what people say."

"Summer, did you ever think you would find love? I mean, how come it comes to some people so easy and others end up lonely all their life?"

"I don't think love is ever easy. There are ups and downs. I believe that love comes knocking at everyone's door, but I believe the hardness of people's hearts causes them to let love go. God doesn't intend for anyone to be alone who doesn't want to be alone."

"You believe that? I mean, sometimes that is just how your life turns out."

"I believe that. Don't you?"

Mia was obviously torn between her opinion. "I guess. I don't know. It's hard to say."

"Well, usually when you stop looking, there it is."

"Now, I believe that. I have heard that many times. People give up on love, and then there is Mr. Right, out of nowhere."

"Let me go. I will talk to you later, okay? I will see myself out."

"Okay," Mia replied as she heard Summer close the door behind her.

Mia walked along the shores of the rocky beach. The wind blew her hair and her sundress flew with the wind. She plopped down on one of the larger rocks. The waves of the ocean were fierce. She threw her sweater around her shoulders because the water blew chilling winds. It was bright outside, but the sun was not seen.

"Excuse me."

Mia looked up from the rock. *Oh my God, not again,* she thought as she looked at the stranger. "Yes, may I help you?"

"I just moved in a few houses down the beach and I just wanted to introduce myself. My name is Cashous."

"Hi, Cashous, my name is Mia." She stood to shake the stranger's hand, but a horrifying sight caught her eye. She looked down the beach and stood in shock. Then she began to trot, then run quickly.

"Oh my God! Oh my God! My babies!" Mia screamed.

Cashous realized what was going on too and began to run after her. A few other homeowners on the beach ran toward the scene. The house was engulfed in flames and burning furiously!

"My babies! My babies! Help! Help me!" Mia continued to scream. Mia scrambled down the beach and ran toward the flames. She ran with all her might toward the burning house on the sandy shores.

Cashous, right on her heels, caught her just before she ran in the burning house.

"Let me go! My babies are in there!"

Mia fought with the stranger, but he wouldn't let go. He yelled, "No! You will never make it out. Let me try!" He got as far as the entrance and the house blew. Cashous was thrown onto his back and knocked unconscious.

"No!" Mia ran inside and fought her way as far as possible through the mangled mess burning before her. Another stranger ran behind her and pulled her burning body from the flames. Mia's clothes were on fire, and the man tried desperately to put the fire out. One of the neighbors handed him a blanket they had been laying on on the beach. He threw the blanket around Mia and held her close. She lay helpless.

"No! No! Ahhh, my babies." Mia sobbed uncontrollably,

and people both known and unknown walked up and gathered to look at the burning house. A couple of minutes later, firemen arrived. They pushed the crowd away from the burning flames.

Mia, even in her state, softly spoke, "Please save my babies. They're still alive. I know. Can't you hear them? Please save my babies!"

The firemen continued to fight the blaze and spray the engulfed house. When the fire was over, it was a big pile of debris with no sign of life. Mia tried to get up, but the strange man who held her wouldn't let her. She was in a bad state, and he kept her covered until one of the paramedics was able to come get her. One by one, three mid-sized body bags were brought out, and one the size of a shoe box.

Mia rolled over in anguish and pain and wailed loudly. The paramedics took her into the ambulance, they asked her name, but she could not speak. She felt numb, and the paramedics realized she was in shock.

She began to fight the men. "Let me go! Let me go to my babies!" She began to scream and cry again. The paramedics restrained her and then gave her a sedative.

When Mia awoke, she began to cry again. She was in a hospital bed at Memorial General and noticed the stranger, Cashous, walk up to her. She was not sure how long she had been there. Her face was bandaged, and she felt very much still sedated. She was in a lot of pain and she couldn't see around the bandages that covered most of the right side of her face. She moaned. Cashous came forward.

"Hello, Mia. I thought someone should be here when you woke up. Is there anyone I can call for you?"

"Yes. Will you call my mother?" Mia replied.

"What is the number?"

Mia gave him the number. Cashous dialed.

"Hello," Imani answered.

"Hi, my name is Cashous. I am calling for your daughter,

Mia. She is here at Memorial General, and she needs someone here with her," Cashous said after Imani told him that
she was, in fact, Mia's mother.

"Why isn't Mia calling? What is wrong?"

"There was a fire."

"A fire? Is she okay? What's wrong with Mia?" Mani pan-
icked.

"Yes, Mia is alive, but she suffered second-degree burns
on one side of her body . . . but I believe she lost her children in the fire."

Imani felt like she couldn't breathe. She dropped the
phone. Jamal ran up to her side. "Imani, what is the matter?
Imani, what is the matter?"

"Mia's at the hospital. There has been a fire. All the kids
might have died in the fire."

Jamal leaned forward slightly as if he had been hit unexpectedly. "Let's go."

Jamal and Imani arrived at the hospital. Cashous just happened to be coming back from the bathroom when he heard
them asking a nurse what room Mia was in. Cashous quickly
walked over. "Are you the parents of Mia?" he asked.

"Yes, where is she?" Jamal answered.

"Right this way," Cashous said, and led the way.

Mia looked at her mother and father with empty eyes
once they entered the room. Imani ran over and grabbed her
daughter. Jamal sat on the opposite side. "Mia, honey, it's
Daddy. Are you okay?"

"No, Daddy. There was a fire. I laid the kids down for a
nap and I walked down the beach just to clear my head a little. When I looked back, the house was on fire. It happened
so quick, Daddy. I would have never walked away. I let my
children die, Daddy! I killed all of them." Mia sobbed in pain.

Jamal grabbed his daughter by her shoulders. "Look, you
would never kill anyone, especially those children. We know
you love your children, and they know it now more than

ever. Life is unpredictable, honey. You wouldn't have known this would happen." Jamal dropped tears from his eyes. "It's okay, baby. They're at peace. None of them are hurting."

Imani held Mia close to her heart and she cried softly as Mia spoke. She rubbed her head and shushed her quietly. "It's okay, honey. It's okay," she spoke over and over again. Mia dug her head in her mother's bosom and they cried.

A fireman walked up and Jamal got up. "What happened?"

The fireman went on to explain that a wire had initiated the fire. "A short caught immediately, and the smoke is what killed the children. They never woke up. There were gas heaters in the basement, and the fire caught quickly."

"Mani, how could I let this happen? How, Mani, how? It was me and all my problems and I wasn't concentrating on my children, who needed me the most."

"It's not your fault, baby. It's not anyone's fault." Imani cried on her daughter's head while Mia lay on her bosom. Jamal held them both.

Summer, Mike, Jasmine and Evan ran into the room. "I got an urgent call saying to meet you all here. What is going on?" Mike asked.

Cashous took the burden of filling them in because Mia, Jamal and Imani were too consumed with grief to even talk. They just held their daughter. Once Cashous finished talking, Summer screamed in horror, and Mike spoke softly, "No, no. Are they sure they're gone?" He grabbed his wife close and they held one another, walking over and sitting next to Imani.

Jasmine fainted, and Evan caught her in his arms and escorted her to Summer's side. They all cried and they all held onto one another. No one was left untouched, and the line was not broken as they tried to grasp what had just happened.

"Mike, can you call Mitchell and Braxton for me?" Mia stated. "Braxton is already in town, I believe. His mother called saying she wanted to see the kids. I told her no. I figured if she was calling out the blue, Braxton must have been home."

"Sure. I will call them now," Mike agreed.

"Thanks, Mike."

"Can I see my babies? Where are my babies?" Mia asked no one in particular.

Jamal motioned for a doctor. "Can we see the kids?"

The doctor came over and said, "She is a little sedated from the burns, but they are in the hospital morgue, and still nothing has been done."

"That is okay. Can we see them?" Jamal asked again.

"Okay," the doctor replied.

Jamal grabbed his daughter and the equipment that was hooked up to her while assisting her in a wheelchair, and pushed her down to the morgue slowly. Imani held her other arm and the others followed slowly behind.

There lay four small body bags. Jamal and Imani held their daughter tightly and Mike held Imani's arm. Mia struggled to stand over each bag. She opened the small body bags one by one.

There was Tashema, beautiful with her long braids, not burned at all. "My beautiful angel, my oldest. You take care of your little sisters and brother, okay? I will see you soon when I get there to Heaven, okay?"

Mia continued to drop tears upon her daughter's smoky face. Her body shook from desperation as she opened the second bag.

There was Tarel. Even though Tashema had Tarel by two years, he acted like the older one a lot of times.

"Tarel, now you behave up there in Heaven. No fighting with Tashema, because God is going to tell me all about it when I get there. My pride and joy, looking like your daddy. Oh, you were just like him too."

She tried to fight back the tears but they continually

rolled like rushing waters and she stood still in shock. "Bridgett, I haven't forgot you, doll. My little muffin." Bridgett was the youngest of the three by Mitchell. "Oh my goodness, so sweet with such a strong personality. Now, don't you go giving God much trouble. He know you were here for such a short time, but I will be there soon. I promise."

Mia looked over at the littlest bag of all. She unzipped it and held him close to her heart. She didn't say a word; just let her tears wash his smoke-filled body.

"Thank you, Bilal, for embracing us with your presence. I love you all so dearly." They all cried softly as Mia turned to say goodbye.

Imani wailed and Jamal held her close. She kissed each one of her grandchildren and told them they would have so much fun in Heaven. "No rules," she whispered.

Summer and Jasmine could not manage the sight at the time. They held tightly to their husbands with tear-stained faces and watery eyes. They held their heads down heavily in pain.

Mitchell and Braxton arrived at the hospital at the same time. The women all had Mia in their arms. She refused to ride back in the wheelchair. She looked up very wearily and the women lost their grip on her as Mitchell and Braxton walked over to her. They both searched her teary eyes, looking for answers.

Finally, Mitchell spoke. "Mia, what happened? Please tell me the kids are okay."

Mia hardly spoke. She shook her head slowly. She whispered, "My babies, they . . ." She screamed in pain.

Braxton's head fell on Mia's lap as he fell toward the floor and he wept. Mitchell never took his eyes off Mia. She looked at him and he at her. He grabbed her head close to his chest and he, too, cried. They stayed like that for a moment before Mike spoke.

"I can show you two where they are so you can see them."

The women immediately regained their places by Mia. Jasmine rocked Mia as she laid her head on her shoulder. Mia closed her eyes and continued to weep.

Mitchell broke down before he got to the morgue, and Braxton grabbed his shoulder and pulled him along as if to tell him he was not going alone. Braxton and Mitchell walked in and saw the little bags, still unzipped, and the tear stains from Mia on each of their little faces. Mitchell could go no further; neither could Braxton. They hugged one another and wept. It seemed all the hype about men not crying was just that . . . hype.

Chapter Thirty

Mia stood at the side of the caskets looking dazed. Imani, Summer and Jasmine stood in a circle, each holding one another around her. Mia wore a black veil over her face. Her white bandage still covered the majority of the right side of her face, which was still a little swollen. The skin was grafted from other parts of her body to replace the missing skin. Mia was no longer beautiful; her face was disfigured, her heart broken and her world shattered.

She didn't know if she stood or not. Her family held her on both sides. Four little caskets lay before her. The funeral proceedings were going on. Mia was a little sedated. She heard the words, stood in the church looking at each one of her blessings; yet she didn't remember walking in, getting dressed or how she got there. She felt like she was in a nightmare.

Her tears began to fall uncontrollably. Mia felt her knees buckle; her heart felt like it fell from her chest. She wanted to scream and she thought she was screaming but only soft *no*s fell from her lips. Her weak and feeble body began to shake.

"No, no, no." She sobbed and cried, leaning first back and then to each side of her supporting sisters. They too cried. They too held each other up for support. They all leaned upon one another. The men in their lives stood by with hands of encouragement on the shoulders of each woman. There were no hands holding Mia's shoulders, for both fathers, Mitchell and Braxton, kneeled over the little caskets and wept.

Braxton's body covered the small casket of Bilal. He talked to him softly. "You're always going to be my little man. I shouldn't have left you. Forgive me. I'm sorry, Bilal. I'm sorry. I shouldn't have left you. I didn't even get to say goodbye.

Mitchell stood up and looked at his three children. He, too, spoke softly to them. "I should have been there every day for you guys, but you know I love you. I love you babies, now and always. Forgive me for leaving your mommy to take care of you alone. I'm sorry."

They soon both turned to Mia, each with heavy hearts. Mitchell walked over and handed Mia a white rose to place on each of his children's caskets. He always told her he cared for them above any delicate rose. They were unique and they represented life. He said a white rose meant there is always life where there seems to be none—pure and beautiful.

Mia cried more as Mitchell pulled her from the grips of her sisterly support and pulled her close to his chest. Braxton, too, came over and embraced Mia from the back. Her two lovers, husbands, and friends; they cried in anguish and pain over the loss of her children and theirs.

Mia began to scream each child by name. She pulled away from the clutches of her ex-husbands. "Tashema, Bilal, Bridgett, Tarel. Get up, babies. Come on, babies. Get up for Mommy. Get up, babies, please," she cried. Mitchell grabbed her and held her close.

Imani ran up to her daughter. "No, honey. They can't get up. They're at peace now."

Jasmine walked over. "Come on, Mia. They're resting now."

"No, it's a bad dream. Get up, babies. Please, please, get up," Mia repeated.

The nurses Imani requested to be in attendance at the church followed closely as Imani and Jasmine escorted Mia out of the church. Summer followed closely behind. Before they made it to the door, Imani fell to the floor and her feeble body was lifted slowly. Jamal grabbed his wife and the family walked out without looking back at their deceased love ones.

The wind blew softly through Mia's bedroom window. The day was a cool, brisk sixty-five degrees. The sun shone, but with an overcast haze.

Mia lay in her bed. She didn't even know what day it was. The calendar days rolled on without her. It had been two months, and each woman did their shifts of coming by to see that Mia was okay. They had begun to grow weary. Mia hadn't spoken a word and had eaten very little and seldom ventured from her new furnished house on the beach, over-looking the still waters.

The three women gathered around Mia. They began to pray.

"Father in Heaven, most Holy God. It is Imani, and I am coming on behalf of my daughters and me. We have tried to understand what has happened in our lives, to be there for one another, but now, Lord, we need You to be there for us. We need strength where we don't have any. We need You to touch Mia and heal her broken heart. We know only You can fix what is broken and only You can put the pieces of our lives back together. We bless You, Lord, and we thank You for never leaving us or forsaking us, even when we can't see

the way. Help us, Lord, because we are unable to help ourselves. Amen."

Imani then spoke to Mia. "God has not forgotten you, Mia.
He loves you still and He loves those kids best. He knows
exactly what happened."

"I know, Mani. Thanks." Mia wept.

"Love you, Mia."

"Love you too."

Finally, after weeks, Mia looked at her three sisters in the
spirit of love and spoke. "Summer, Jasmine, Mani, I've thought
and I've looked at the beauty of God. I see Him in the waters. I see Him in the rising of the sun and the going down of
the same. I see His creations, and I have contemplated His
ways and tried to figure out His thoughts, but nothing comes
to mind. I am not even close to figuring out why my children
had to go.

"The fireman said it was faulty wiring and it spread
quickly. It was dry, and by the time it engulfed the condo, it
was too late. I was gone a few steps down the beach while
they slept. Overtaken by the smoke, they never woke up.
The one person who should have saved them was me. How
do I make sense of that? How do I make sense out of being
human, just walking along the beach, absorbing His beauty?
Where is the love in this story?" Mia looked out her bedroom
window and looked to the waters. No tears flowed, but she
went back into her empty stare.

"Look, little sister, I know it doesn't look like it now, but
God knows how much we can bear. Mia, you were tired, run
down and exhausted," Jasmine said.

"They were my life, Jasmine!"

"Of course. I'm not suggesting they were a burden so God
took them; I'm saying we don't know our strength or what
tomorrow will bring. Just know God knows all. It may not
have been about the children. Maybe it's about you. How
often did you stop to pray to God before all of this? Have

you considered stopping now and thanking Him for sparing your life? You could have been 'sleep as well."

"How many people don't acknowledge God and His presence and their children live on? Why spare my life when I have nothing left to live for?" was Mia's response.

"Mia, you don't mean that. Now, I raised my children to love God in spite of anything, because He could have taken you, so don't be ungrateful."

"Summer, do you understand what I'm saying?" Mia snapped.

"Mia, I understand what you're saying, but look at you; alive and beautiful. So trauma has hit your life. But your soul is still intact. Honey, we don't have the answers to what happened or why; we all hurt so deeply. None of us can explain the pain or even imagine your pain. However, we know only God has kept you in your right mind. Only God can bring you through this. Ask Him to help you get through this and show you direction and if He will give you some type of understanding. You may not be able to see it now, but He has not left you alone during all this. Ask him what He will have you do now."

Imani grabbed her daughter's hands. "I only know how it would feel to lose you after losing my other children. I don't understand, and my heart hurts because they were my children as well." Tears fell from Imani's eyes. "I cry and pray for you every day. Mani doesn't have the answers this time, but I know if we hold on a little while longer, everything will be all right. You just got to take one day at a time and one step at a time. Just pray, Mia. Talk to God because He is your friend and He hurts just as you do when you're hurting. Trust me; life is not easy, and it is unfair at times. Just remember, God loves us more than we love ourselves or could ever love those children.

"Now, we are going to each continue our regular lives. It

is time you try and get up from this spot. We love you, but we have to let go just a little bit now. Call us if you need us."

They each kissed Mia on the forehead and she heard the door close as they left. She was alone for the first time since her children's deaths. She sat, and she sat. The sun began to go down on her and still she sat in front of that window. She got up when she began to see blue dots in front of her eyes from staring in the dark. She walked down the hall to one of the bedrooms. She noticed her family had combined all her children's photos and memories in this one room. Mia looked at each of the photos.

Hours passed, and she fell to her knees. "Why, Lord? Why?" she sobbed.

She lay in a knot on the floor among her children's things and cried herself to sleep. When she awoke, she went to her room and grabbed a piece of paper. She began to write.

Dear Mani and Daddy, Jasmine, Mike and Summer:

I thought that I could make it through the trials of life. But I am finding out that life is too hard. Whatever God has against me, let's face it, He's God, and who am I to compete?

Mani, you said that nothing happens to us without God's permission, so I assume the permission was given for all these things to happen in my life. Some God, if you ask me. I mean, failed marriage after marriage, failed life, everything I put my hand to, I fail.

I didn't ask for much, just wanted love, someone to share my life with and a little peace. It wasn't like I was a bad person. I didn't do anything too bad in my life. Anyway, what I am trying to say is I'm sorry. I'm sorry that I have to leave you, and I am sorry things have to be this way.

I know you tried to be there for me as best as possible. I know you love me, but sometimes family love isn't enough. You know I needed more; I wanted a love of my own. I wanted something or someone to call my own, and my children were the best thing to love. Now what do I have left? I can't seem to imagine what I did so wrong in this lifetime; I mean why love seems to never work out for me. Whatever the reason, I can only say I'm not up to finding out. I'm tired and I just want to go home, wherever that is. It has to be a better place than this.

And Imani, if it is true that if I take my life then I will spend life in eternal damnation, then why did God take my life to begin with? This is eternal damnation, you know.

Jasmine, I tried to do like you and just take life as it comes and enjoy it, but some of us got it and some of us don't.

Summer, thanks for everything. You seem to always see both sides of the story but I can't see a bright side to this.

And Daddy, what can I say? We always found the humor in everything, but nothing is funny in this situation. I apologize for leaving you so soon. I love you all always and forever . . .

Mia sat down and reread the note and she began to cry again, then laughed. She balled the letter up and decided maybe she should try this another way.

Chapter Thirty-One

While Mia was trying to piece together the ending for her life, Jasmine's relationship with Evan was falling apart. At the time, she and Evan were having sexual problems.

"What is wrong, Evan? How long do we have to go through this? I think you should see a doctor."

"I don't need to see no doctor."

"Then why in the world are you having trouble performing? I mean, don't you love me still? Am I not attractive to you anymore?"

"Of course you're attractive to me. I don't know what it is."

Evan grabbed Jasmine's red robe off the bed and wrapped it around himself and tied the string tightly. He then rushed off to the bathroom with a little too much femininity for a man.

"I mean, Jazz, I'm not sure what it is. We can discuss it when you get back. You will be late for your flight." Jasmine was an event coordinator for her job at Holiday Inn.

"You're right. Let me get ready. Very seldom does the hotel send us anywhere. I better not miss that." Jasmine jumped up and grabbed a towel off the back of the bed and ran into the bathroom to get ready. She was out in a matter of minutes and grabbed her suitcase and was out the door. "So much for a quickie."

"Next time, I promise," Evan said.

Once Evan saw Jasmine was out of sight, he went back to the bedroom and went into his closet, and pulled out a box.

"Now, this is more like it." He pulled out a bunch of DVDs. He pulled out one in particular and put it in the DVD player. "Oh, I will be ready for you, Jasmine, when you, come back." Evan felt himself beneath the robe. When the first scene appeared on the television, it was two men kissing.

"This is more like it."

Evan left the house after his little movie and went to a gay bar. He looked at the men and he did a little flirting, but he couldn't bring himself to talk to any of them. He removed his jacket and revealed a little red top of Jasmine's he had chosen for the night and some tight black jeans. The gay men looked in admiration and whistled. Evan smiled and did a soft wave.

He sat at the bar. "Can I have a gin whiz, please?"

"Sure you can, doll," the waiter responded.

"Thanks."

"You new to the game, huh?"

"No. Well, yes. Well, not in the game, just curious."

"I can tell. You look a little too manly to have that top on. Trust me. Just be yourself."

"Okay. I just thought this was the way to go." Evan put on his jacket.

"Look, you never saw me here, okay?"

"Sure, lots of guys in here are on the down low. And they go home to their wives at night. This is what they do. No need to be ashamed."

"I'm not ashamed. Just feeling the waters," Evan reminded him.

Chapter Thirty-Two

Mia had fallen asleep again and woke up with a headache that felt more like a hangover. Her eyes felt like they would bulge from her head and her temples felt like they would explode from her brain. She got up and went to the bathroom. She splashed some cold water onto her face and gently wiped the drops of water and tears from her eyes. She grabbed her toothbrush and brushed slowly and carefully each tooth and then her tongue. She stood and looked at herself in the mirror.

"What is left for me to live for, Lord? Why have You forsaken me?" Mia unclothed herself and stepped into a hot shower. She let the water run over her hair and down her body. She let her head tilt down as she looked at the water swirl down the shower drain. She shook uncontrollably and she cried.

After an hour in the shower and the hot water running cold, she stepped out of the shower into the brisk, cool air of her bathroom. She thought she would feel rejuvenated, but instead, she still felt lost and alone. Everything she had set her hand to do in her life seemed worthless. The worthless feeling stemmed all the way to her marriages, her motherhood, her sisterhood and daughterhood and even her very own life.

Her business wasn't growing or declining, but just remained stagnant. She saw nothing worth living for, nothing worth running to, and she wondered what cruel joke life had in store for her next. She considered her options to see if she even wanted to stick around and find out. Life was too cruel for Mia, and she saw no purpose. Sure, being a doctor you would think offered its joys of helping preserve life, but who would preserve the preserver? She had nothing left to offer because life had nothing left to offer her.

Mia wondered, as she walked to the kitchen for a glass of orange juice, what kind of understanding or meaning was she to get from this last episode in her life? How was she to draw near to God when all life offered her were sour lemons? What was she to gain from losing yet someone else dear to her? Mia didn't feel like sticking around to figure out the answers. Enough was enough.

Why waste her time around here trying to figure out what to do next? *There is nothing to do now. God doesn't love me. God doesn't find me worthy of the ones who will be saved. They are already the chosen ones and I am coming to accept that I am not among them. I try to live my life to the best of my ability. I try to be a good person. I try to grow spiritually just as much as the next person, yet I see miracles happen in other people's lives. I see other people's happiness and changes. I see a God in other people's lives, but in my own life I see complete strife, disappointment and depression.*

All the negative feelings and hurtful emotions had Mia contemplating whether she wanted to live or die. This was her question even after helping others to live in this cruel and sad world.

Mia got dressed and returned to the office. She saw her

patients with little or no emotion. She prescribed medications and remedies. After a long day's hard work, she picked up Chinese food, went home and plopped down in front of the television. She rented *Deliver us from Eva* and curled up with a blanket.

Her phone rang. "Perfect timing," she spoke sarcastically. "Hello."

"Hi, boo. How you doing?"

"Hey, Mani. I'm doing okay. Just looking at a movie."

"Well, tonight is Wednesday. You want to go to Bible study with us?"

"No, not really."

"Okay. Well, I will call you when we get back."

"That's okay. I'll probably turn in early tonight. I will call you tomorrow."

"Okay. Well, good night."

"Good night."

Mia hung up. It was obvious to her, if no one else, she had a pretty large chip on her shoulder. Mia felt it and she decided she was all right with it. Who said while life dealt her a bad hand she had to smile about it and keep going on as if nothing had happened or pretend that her life would ever be the same? She decided she would keep going because she couldn't kill herself, but she didn't have to go along liking it.

Before Mia knew it, she was working twelve-hour shifts. Her life was consumed by useless energy that seemed to just pass the time. She saw little satisfaction in her job as a gynecologist/pediatrician. She began to feel like her life was dwindling away moment by moment with each passing day.

Immediately after hanging up, the phone rang again. Mia looked at the caller ID, picked up the phone and hung up. The bank was calling about her late mortgage payment. Suddenly, the blood began to boil in her skin. It seemed that she struggled to pay the mortgage on her house that she worked with sweat and tears to obtain, yet God had nothing in life for her but misery.

She looked at her life. She admitted she was not always the nicest person and not always honest, but definitely not the worst person in the world. She thought of people she knew throughout her younger years who sold drugs. These are drugs that moment by moment killed a thriving temple of God. Drugs that caused kids to kill one another at tender ages. Mia began to wonder if God was even there. At some point, people have to take justice into their own hands because it seemed God had left His people to fend for themselves.

To Mia, it seemed the people who had chosen the lifestyle of drug dealing were the only ones living happily, along with those multimillionaire preachers with the poorest people in their congregation. What separated them from the drug dealers? It was all about getting ahead no matter what the cost. She admitted that if she could get away with selling drugs and taking the easy way out of life, she would do the same. Mia's biggest regret was knowing right from wrong because God seemed to punish only those who knew better.

Why didn't God ever touch her family? What did she do that was so bad? Maybe she should have been praying for herself. Mia felt agitated and therefore decided she wouldn't worry about anyone else anymore. She was obligated to only one person, and that was herself.

Chapter Thirty-Three

Imani dialed Mia.

"Hello," Mia answered.

"Mia, what is going on with you?" her mother asked her.

"What?"

"You no longer have time for anyone. You're just sitting around the house and you act like somebody did something to you."

"I haven't done anything to anyone, and if I choose to just sit, I'm not hurting anyone."

"Well, why you acting like someone did something to you?"

"I'm not."

"Hold on." Imani called Jasmine and clicked her in. "Jasmine, you there?"

"Yeah, Ma," Jasmine replied.

Imani ordered Jasmine to call Summer. Jasmine obliged.

"Summer, you there?" Jasmine said.

"Yes," Summer replied.

"Now, both of you tell me; has Mia been acting like we did something to her or not?"

"Yes, she's acting like she has a nerve problem," Jasmine said.

"Jasmine, you shut up. You act like you've got a lying problem," Mia said in her defense.

"What's that supposed to mean?" Jasmine exclaimed.

"Nothing. Forget it," Mia responded.

"Well, Imani, I don't really know. She seemed fine to me. Just a little withdrawn, and that is to be expected. She's been through a lot lately," spoke Summer.

"Well, we all have problems, but we don't turn away from one another," Jasmine added.

"What problems you got? I mean, what type of problems do you all have? You have problems like maybe the occasional little boredom or a little frustration in the marriage, or maybe fussing about this or that. But seriously, what problems do you all have? Have your children been killed in a fire? Has your husband left you? Or do you work twelve hours a day or more to come home to an empty house and still can't afford the bills to live a comfortable life without crying at night from killing yourself to enjoy it? Does loneliness gnaw at you late at night and you think you're in a nightmare because you think you hear your children calling you, but they're not there? What problems do you have? Whatever they are, they are nothing compared to the problems I have just living! So, if you will excuse me, I want to be by my darn self and not with a bunch of fake people who pretend to have it all together and don't have nothing together!" Mia hung up on her family the same way she was hanging up on life.

Chapter Thirty-Four

The next morning was sunny and bright. It was a beautiful day, and Mia had just walked into her kitchen to make herself a cup of coffee. The doorbell rang.

"Who is it?" Mia called out.

"Mia, it's Summer," she said from the other side of the door.

"Hey, Summer. Come in. You know with the conversation on the phone last night I meant nothing toward you, right?"

"I know."

"But why the attitude with Mani?"

"Mani's always pretending like everything is about God. That is all I have always heard growing up. God this and God that. Well, where is God when I need Him most? I have prayed about losing everything I have, and no response. I prayed about the hungry, the hurt and the homeless. I prayed about my family. God won't answer my prayers."

"Mia, honey, you just had a hard time, that is all. You can't see the light right now, but things will get better. You'll see. I think you're angry and you need to figure out how to deal with that anger."

"I tried. I tried to give it to God. He doesn't seem to answer my prayers."

"He answers all our prayers. Just hang in there."

"I will. I have to run out to the store. Do you mind?"

"No, I will call you later."

"Bye."

Mia closed the door and went to take a hot bath. Truth was, she didn't need any more encouraging speeches. They had gotten her nowhere, and she didn't need it anymore.

In contrast to all the encouragement, Mia didn't go into work the next week. She moped around the house until she finally decided she had enough. She would sell her business and start over. This had to be the only reason for her sad life. She had made a wrong turn somewhere along the way. She needed to try again.

Mia sold her business and put the money in the bank. She paid her mortgage up for a year and put a little money aside. She figured it would be enough time to figure out what to do next.

Mia decided she would pursue her dream of being an author. She loved to write and had not done it in years. She decided that was what she would do.

Before she could grab a pen and paper, her faithful companion, the phone, rang.

"Mia, this is Mani."

"Hey, Mani."

"Girl, what in the world have you done?"

"What do you mean?"

"Sold the business."

"Yes."

"You worked hard all these years to get this practice and then you sell it?"

"It's not what I wanted to begin with. I wanted a career that made me indispensable, where I didn't have to go through the turns and battles of working for someone else and still never getting promoted or ever being treated fairly, so I started my own business."

"Then why give it up? It's done and accomplished now."

"It's not worth it. It's too hard. I barely made profit and people don't pay their bills and it's just too much on me to continue to do on my own. If I had a partner, it would be easier."

"Well, why didn't you seek some kind of help? There is help out there for minority-owned businesses, especially women."

"I'm just tired and I made a decision and now I'm going a new way in my life."

"So, now what are you going to do?"

"I'm going to try and write a book for a few months and see if I can't get a few chapters out."

"Mia, that is silly. How will you ever make it as an author? It takes years for the ones who make it to make a profit, and it's a lot of work. You still need to do something else."

"I know that, but for a moment, I can concentrate on just that."

"Look, it's your life. Do what you want. Bye."

Mia grabbed her pen and paper and began to write. She scribbled two chapters in no time and began to feel sleepy. "I shall resume my new career tomorrow."

Mia tried to rest her mind and ease her burdens and perhaps go to sleep. It wasn't going to work. She was worried and had her doubts. How many real people actually make it as authors? What would separate her from the millions of others who wanted to be authors? Then she began to say to herself that so many people could not want to be an author for the reasons that were deep in her soul. It wasn't about the fame or fortune, or her name being known. She just wanted to put her heart on the line for millions to see.

Mia had to laugh. So many thoughts came to her mind, so many books inside of her that had nothing to do with her,

but the deep desire in her heart to just take someone else
to a place they may not be able to go on their own; a different place without the expense or hassle. A mini-vacation
anywhere, anytime, with the benefits of home. That was
living.

Chapter Thirty-Five

"Surprise, Mia!"

Mia wiped the sleep from her eyes and looked up. She didn't even hear Jasmine come in, much less remember she had given her a key. Jasmine plopped down on the bed beside Mia.

"Hey, Jasmine, girl, where have you been all my life?" Mia yawned and stretched.

"So, you sold the place. Do tell, Mia, what is going on?"

"I had enough of working myself to death and nothing to show for it. I need a normal life like normal people."

"We don't know any normal people, Mia."

"Yeah, I know, girl. But I decided to try and write a book. Crazy, huh?"

"No. Not at all. I knew it would come out one day. That is all you used to talk about before you suddenly decided to change your journalism major to medicine."

"Should I just go back and pursue what is really in my heart? You know, I could be acting out of emotions."

"You should have done it anyway, Mia. People make decisions because it seems convenient and the best choice to survive. But don't you think life is about living? You should do what makes you happy and die trying. What do you have to lose? You would have died doing what makes you rich but not happy. Besides, girl, you know I believe whatever is in our hearts is our purpose."

"Girl, I should have called you when I had Mani on the phone. No one has put things in perspective for me like you just did. Thanks, girl. This is the first real joy I have felt since I lost the kids. Perhaps life may be worth living after all."

"Where did that come from? Life is always worth living."

Mia hugged her sister. "Thanks." Mia looked relieved. "I was worried for a while."

"Good, no regrets. Now, you want to go out today?"

"Sure."

"Let's go to the beach. You up for it?" Jasmine asked.

"Yeah. Let me shower and get ready." Mia rolled out of the bed and headed into the bathroom. Mia was out and dressed in a manner of minutes. "Let's go."

"What kind of darn shower was that? Wash in a minute?"

"I had already taken a shower earlier. I was just freshening up."

"Oh, well, a'ight. Let's go then. I didn't want you going to the beach smelling all fishy."

"Girl, come on with your crazy self."

The women walked the windy shores of the beach. They laughed and they walked. They stopped and laid their blankets out on the beach. "Life is full of surprises, right?" Jasmine said.

"Yeah, you told the truth with that statement. Here I am contemplating starting over at my age," Mia responded.

"Some of us get it right the first time. Some of us don't." Jasmine smiled.

"So, you got it right?"

"No, wishful thinking. Honestly, we never get it right. We die trying."

"I believe that about sums it up."

They looked over at one another with halfway smiles.

"How you really doing, girl?" Jasmine said to her sister.

"I'm making it. That is the truth; just making it." Mia looked sad.

"I wish I was doing better. Evan is so unpredictable. He has a funny attitude also. One day he's down, the next he's way down. He never seems to have much joy, or there seems to be a secret part to him I can't reach. But I love him."

"How can you love someone who seems to never have anything nice to say or never wants to be around you?"

"You've been through this. Tell me what to do."

"Leave him alone before he hurts you, or it's too late. I don't think he can be trusted."

"It's difficult."

"I'm here when you need me." Mia reached over and grabbed Jasmine's hand. "Just like you're here now when I need you."

"Thanks."

"Excuse me." Cashous spoke in a deep voice.

The women looked up. There stood Cashous.

"Hello," Mia said.

"I don't mean to intrude, but the last time I saw you . . ." Cashous paused. "Well, I was just coming over to say hello."

"No, it's fine. How are you?" Mia told him.

"I'm okay. How about you?"

"I'm surviving. This is my sister, Jasmine. Jasmine, this is Cashous."

"This is the stranger who was with you at the hospital," Jasmine recalled.

"Yes," Cashous replied.

"Well, it seems like a girl thing going on, so I will be going. Here is my card, so if you get the chance, call me and we can do dinner sometime, if you like."

"Okay. Thanks."

Cashous walked away and the ladies returned to their conversation.

"Will you be calling him?" Jasmine asked.

"Maybe."

"He's cute."

"Didn't notice."

"Me either. Ha!" Jasmine looked over at Mia with a big grin.

"No, really. I didn't notice."

"You will as soon as the blinders come off your eyes. You're entitled for a moment."

"Okay, so now can we lay out here like two white women and sleep in this hot sun?"

"Heck, no. Let's go for a swim."

"I'm with you. Then let's get some ice cream."

The ladies got up and ran into the ocean. For the rest of the day, Mia enjoyed life with her sister.

Chapter Thirty-Six

Mia rolled the paper with Cashous's number on it between her fingers. "Should I or shouldn't I?" She wondered for the last hour if she should indeed call Mr. Cashous or not. It finally became apparent to her more than ever that she really had nothing to lose. She dialed his number.

"Hey, Cashous, it's Mia," she said after he answered the phone.

"Hi, Mia. I really didn't expect to hear from you. What a pleasant surprise."

"If you didn't expect to hear from me, why did you even bother giving me the number?" Mia asked.

"A man can hope, can't he?" Cashous chuckled.

"Yes, I guess he can."

"So, this is a definite yes to my date?"

"I believe it is."

"All right, you name the day and time."

"How about tomorrow evening around sevenish? You know where I live."

"Okay. I will see you then."

"Okay. Good night."

"Good night." Mia hung up the phone and thought to herself, *That wasn't so hard after all.*

Cashous showed up a day later, dressed for a relaxing night out. He wore jean shorts, a T-shirt and sneakers. Mia had on a pair of shorts, a tank top and sandals. At least they both agreed on the attire. Cashous had planned a picnic in the park and a stroll through the mall, where he bought her an adorable necklace. At the end of the night, they settled in front of the television and both fell asleep.

Cashous and Mia's relationship grew quickly and it was very exciting. They took long walks, and they stayed up late talking. They did movies, dinners, and church every Sunday. Mia didn't even mind, because Imani made sure they were there anyway every Sunday, and Cashous loved going with Mia.

After a short courtship of eight months, when Mia least expected it, Cashous proposed and Mia accepted. It was simple and romantic. She came in from work and Cashous asked if she would like to go to the beach. He had rented a boat, and when she got on the boat, there were flowers on a table with candlelight and a spectacular dinner, which consisted of lobsters, clam chowder, salmon and a baked potato, with sweet tea and peach cobbler.

The sun was just setting and the waves were rolling softly with a small breeze. Cashous even had a little music playing—Luther Vandross. It was the most simple and romantic thing Mia had experienced. They sat and they ate, then they went to the front of the boat to lay in the lawn chairs with their blankets. Cashous got down on one knee in the moonlight and asked Mia to be his wife. Mia was speechless only for a second before she tackled Cashous and almost knocked the two of them overboard.

After a long kiss, Cashous spoke. "I guess that's a yes."

"It's a yes." Mia smiled. She hadn't done so bad for herself—from a construction worker to an attorney. Life was looking better.

Chapter Thirty-Seven

Frisno and Evan sat across the table looking at one another. Frisno, a very handsome man, gave a slight smile. He and Evan met twelve years ago at Samson Products, working on the production line. You wouldn't know he was gay until he opened his mouth and spoke.

"Okay, Evan. I can't read minds. You were quiet all day at work. What's the problem?" Frisno put his hands on his hips and demanded an answer.

"Frisno, I shouldn't get you involved."

Frisno threw his feminine gesture to wave Evan off. "I'm already involved, aren't I? Who has your back?"

"You do, Frisno."

"I didn't hear you, boy. Say it again, please."

"You do."

"All right, what's the deal?"

"I'm not feeling very manly lately. It seems Jasmine is not satisfied."

"Oooh, touchy. You sure you want me to speak frankly about this?" Frisno looked, with raised eyebrows.

"Will it change anything if I said no?"

"Heck no. Now, listen. I'm a woman. I may not have been born one, but you know I've always known that is what I was supposed to be. Now, I know about these things."

"So I know," Evan tried to intercede.

"Shut up, Evan. I'm as good as it gets. The problem with other women is they expect too much all the time. You're human. Women sometimes get so caught up in their desires— I being the exception, because I have been exposed to both sides of the track—that they don't know what a man wants. Evan, you just need to perform and be loved without the expectation of being made to feel like some type of mechanical sex machine. It will be the best sexual freedom you will ever know."

"How do I get there with Jasmine?"

"Talk to her."

"Not possible." Evan shook his head.

"And why not?"

"Same thing; expectations."

"Have another drink and another and another. You got problems. I will drive you home. Maybe after a good night's sleep, you will feel better in the morning." Frisno looked at Evan with a smirk on his face. "Exclusive of the hangover, of course."

When they arrived at Evan's place, Jasmine had not yet made it in.

"Where is your wife?" Frisno asked Evan.

"She's not in."

"Well, I guess it's up to me to tuck the big fellow in and make sure you're squared away before I go."

"Oh, Frisno. You're a good buddy. Thanks." Evan stumbled over to the bed.

"Child, you're worse than a pregnant woman on drugs. Let me help you." Frisno walked over and began to undress Evan. Evan kept pulling on Frisno.

"You know, you really do look like a girl. You sure you're not a girl?"

"Okay. Evan, you have had too many."

"Oh, you think? Maybe now I'm ready for my wife. I think I can perform now. What do you think?" Evan spoke with an inviting tone. He was flirting with Frisno.

"Not. You're a sloppy drunk."

"Okay, Frisno. Well, let me tell you a secret. I always wondered how you guys get into such a mess. What is that about?"

"Us guys? We're human just like you guys; just different strokes for different folks. Don't knock it until you try it." Frisno plopped Evan legs over in the bed. "You weigh a ton." Frisno sighed. "You feel like dead weight."

"Frisno, let me warm up on you." Evan looked like an innocent puppy.

"What?" Frisno looked over at Evan like he was crazy.

"You know."

"Evan, you been drinking. Let's talk about this tomorrow."

"Tomorrow I may not have the nerve. It has to be tonight."

"What about your wife, and our friendship?"

"I'm doing it for her, and our friendship won't change."

"You should talk to me when you're sober."

"Now or never, Frisno."

"Okay. But don't be looking at me all funny afterwards. This was your idea."

Frisno dropped his pants and revealed a red G-string with a cut-off red top to match. He shut off the lights.

"You on the down low, Evan?"

"Come and find out."

Chapter Thirty-Eight

Shortly after Mia and Cashous's marriage, Mia noticed that Cashous turned out to be very unaffectionate and non-conversational. The only thing he seemed to like to talk about was God. If it wasn't God he was talking about, he had very little to say. Even though Mia felt God blessed her with Cashous, she was not ready to give her trust completely back over to Him, so she desired not to talk about God at all. She still felt very betrayed and cheated in life by God.

"Cashous, want to go to a movie?" Mia plopped down beside Cashous and smiled.

"I can see a movie here on television," he answered.

"I know, but that isn't the point. It's about getting out and spending quality time together."

"I spend time with you every day."

"How? We both work, and when you get in, you eat and go to read the Bible or you're upstairs looking at some gospel show. I mean, I am here, you know."

"I don't feel like going anywhere." Cashous looked over at Mia and quickly back at the television.

"Okay, you went out to dinner with your church pals the

other night. You take the time to spend with them, but not with me?" Mia exclaimed.

"Look, I don't want to talk about this. I'm a grown man; I can do what I want to do."

"What does this have to do with being a grown man? What about just being a husband?"

"What else do you need me to do? I pay the bills, I'm not in the street, and I'm here, right?"

"And that is supposed to be enough to make a marriage work? You don't even talk to me. You laugh and praise God, but when it comes to me, you act like I'm just here for your pleasure. You expect things done in decency and in order to comply with your beliefs, but a marriage takes work, and you seem to put little effort toward ours." Mia folded her arms in frustration.

"Look, Mia, I'm going to bed. You act like you got a problem with who I am, but you married me." Cashous stood and walked toward the bedroom.

"I didn't know you would become Mr. Unaffectionate."

"I have to go read my Bible and go to bed. I have to go into work early in the morning." Cashous never stopped walking as he spoke.

"Does it say anything in that Bible like love your wife as you love yourself?" Mia screamed.

"I don't know why don't you pick it up and read it sometimes," Cashous said.

"You read it and it still don't help make your life any better. So what's the point? If I don't pick it up, God knows why I don't, so you think He will fix my problem if I don't pick up the Bible? No, I need to seek Him for Him to help me. Why He don't help those of us who can't help ourselves? But the Bible says He's present to help in the time of trouble. A little controversial, if you ask me."

"Whatever, Mia. Good night."

Mia was so angry. "Another trade-off, huh, God? What

looks good isn't always the case, I suppose. You send someone my way who turns out to be my knight in shining armor
for just that moment. But when I get him, he's a big, boring
toad. Is it too much to ask to have someone in my life who is
compatible with me? Someone who would actually be a husband? I love Cashous, but Cashous love Cashous, and only
cares about what other people think of him. Where does
that leave room for loving me? It doesn't, and once again, I
guess it means I'm just supposed to be alone and miserable
no matter how hard I try to find happiness. Thanks again,
Lord, for this wonderful life!"

Chapter Thirty-Nine

Mia walked along the sandy shores and wondered if her life could get any worse. Then it seemed the God who she felt no longer loved her, began to speak to her.

Life is not easy. I bless you then you need another blessing and another, and you will never find what you're looking for here in the world. You long for peace, sweet peace that is only given through Me, your God. The belonging you yearn for deep in your soul is just your longing for a closer walk with Jesus. Until you leave this foreign place and hate this world, you can never feed the spirit in its completion. But you can learn to be happy if you trust Me.

Mia began to cry. She wept for hours in that same spot on the beach. The wind was just about to make her return to her house when Cashous walked up.

"Are you okay, Mia?" her husband asked.

"No, but I will survive."

"What's wrong now?" Cashous sighed.

"What do you mean, now?" Mia looked up angrily.

"I mean you're never happy, so I know something is wrong again."

"And you're supposed to be helping by asking what's wrong now, implying that it's something you really don't care to hear? Wow, thanks."

"I never said that."

"Might as well have. You seemed disinterested before you ever let me say what was wrong."

"Okay, forget it. You going to tell me or not?"

"Not!" Mia rolled her eyes and continued looking over the sandy shores.

"Suit yourself. I'm not the one crying."

Cashous walked off and Mia jumped up and stormed past him. "Jerk!"

"Whatever."

In the meantime, Summer's life wasn't any better.

"Mike, want to hang out tonight?" Summer asked her husband.

"Nope, I made plans with the guys," he replied.

"Mike! You're always making plans with the guys. What about me?" Summer tossed her hands in the air and looked at Mike for an explanation. "Remember me?" she asked sarcastically.

"What about you, Summer? You go and do anything you want to do, so what about you?"

"But we don't spend hardly enough quality time together."

"Look, don't start that with me. You know I'm a man and I need to do my thing. I need my space."

"Why do things change when people get married? Your thang was me before we got married. You were with me all the time."

"Okay, and now I'm with you all the time. What do you want from me?"

"We live together, but we barely see each other."

"Look, stop following me like a puppy. You have your life and I have mine. Live your life and get out of mine."

"What? What is going on with you? You never spoke to me like that before. I mean, is someone else smiling in your face?"

"What is going on with me is I need you to get off my back."

"Okay, I'm off your back. I'll see you later." Summer turned to leave the room, grabbing her pajamas.

"Where you going, Summer?" Mike asked with concern.

"To live my life."

For the first time in their marriage, Summer contemplated having an affair. She thought about old friends and how good it would feel to be kissed, noticed and adored. It seemed her life with Mike had grown stale, like he'd rather do anything but hang out with her. It wasn't like that in the beginning. It was fun.

Summer began to ask herself if she had changed so much. Did she need to do something different, something new? She decided against the affair. She would just try a different approach, and if that didn't work, she would see if she still had it with someone else.

"Oh, shoot. I might as well stop thinking silly. God knows I ain't going nowhere." Summer picked up a book and went upstairs and began to read and eat ice cream.

Mike walked by the bedroom about an hour later. "You found your life yet?" Mike asked with a smirk.

"You found your brain yet?"

When Mike walked away, Summer pulled out her phone book. Her hairdresser, Cobey, had been itching to hang out for a while, even though she knew his intentions were far from innocent. "Let's see if he has time for me. Here he is." Summer dialed the number.

"Hello, Cobey?"

"Yeah, this is he."

Chapter Forty

Mia sat down to work on her newfound passion—the book she was writing, which still was untitled. She figured it would come in time. Mia never did anything that wasn't expected of her. She didn't know what to make out of it herself, much less anyone else around her. This move toward self-expression, desire and truth was not like her at all. She usually was an over-thinker, overachiever, indecisive, and predictable. Mia had decided that enough was enough. Nothing came easy in this world. Our dreams had to reflect our purpose, otherwise it wouldn't be deep in the pit of our stomachs and our hearts. Her desire to write and succeed was like a burning desire deep in her soul. Mia knew she had to birth her dream; otherwise, she would find herself continuing to wallow in the depression of life and its lack of satisfaction. Her rendezvous left her feeling lifeless.

Her old favorite pastime, which was talking on the phone, beckoned her at the worst time.

"Yeah," Mia answered, annoyed.

"Open up, Mia. I'm almost at your door."

"Okay, Mani."

Mia greeted Mani with a kiss after opening the door.
"What you doing here?"
"I came to talk to you."
"You could have done that over the phone."
"I was in the neighborhood."
"Okay, what is it?" Mia asked, annoyed.
"About the choices you been making lately. Mia, dreams
don't pay bills. It's okay to pursue your dreams, but can't
you do it while you work?"
"Mani, I'm tired. I've been in medical school half my life.
I've opened up my own medical practice and have been in
the field for over eleven years, never really accomplishing
what I anticipated for my business. I never really loved it,
but I chose a profession I felt would be tolerable and prof-
itable at the same time. Every day was a struggle. I was so
unhappy, and I continuously tried to convince myself differently. I can't convince myself any longer. I want what I
want."
Mia stared at her mother. "I just want to be me. I want to
be happy. I want to walk out my journey."
"Mia, people do things they don't want to do all the time.
Just change your career. Do something like go to school to
get into the writing business, but don't just give up everything
cold turkey. Work toward becoming an editor, an author or
whatever that field has to offer. I mean even journalism; you
like that."
"Mani, I know you mean well, but I have to do this my
way. I need to go cold turkey or nothing will change. That is
why so many people are depressed and on Prozac and many
other medicines, because we ignore the feelings deep inside
that are telling us our true purpose for being here. We need
to start listening to those feelings and even perhaps gain a
deeper understanding of who we really are."
"Mia." Mani called her name sternly.
"Mani, like you said, I'm the only one giving up every-

thing. I was the only one to make this sacrifice. I don't have any babies anymore to consider; just me and my husband."

"That's just it; you're not doing this alone. You're affecting Cashous as well. How are things with him? Have you considered the stress and strain one income will put on him in this lifestyle that you have become accustomed to?"

"It's okay, Mani. Cashous is in the legal profession. He is doing well in his practice, so we are managing fine."

"But it could be better; better if you were bringing in an income to help balance out any financial burden."

"Now, Mani, what is better? No offense, but you don't know what goes on here in my house unless I tell you." Mia shook her head. "Honestly, I think you take things too far."

"I know, 'cause I been there, girl. But a hard head makes a soft behind, so you do what you got to do."

"Okay, Mani." Mia's face turned into a snarl.

"And don't come asking me for a loan when things get tight." Imani picked up her purse and walked out without turning around. The door shut, leaving Imani on one side and her daughter, whom she thought was making the biggest mistake of her life, on the other.

Chapter Forty-One

Jasmine's long brown hair blew in the wind as she took a deep whiff of the fresh air. Work was a little draining today, so she headed off to the store before going home.

Jasmine walked in her house and put her bags down. She wondered if she should call Mia and show a little sisterly love or take a shower first. She decided she'd take her shower first. She decided since she was a day early from her flight, perhaps she'd surprise Evan with dinner.

Jasmine rushed to the bedroom but stopped suddenly in her tracks. She was speechless as Evan jumped up from underneath the covers. Frisno pulled the covers over his chest like he was hiding his breasts. He looked shocked and embarrassed.

No words came from Jasmine's throat as Evan spoke. "Jasmine, it's not what it looks like. I mean, I was . . . and we were—" There was silence.

Jasmine blinked hard and shook her head, still unable to move. Finally, she mustered up enough strength to say, "Evan, what is this? How and what?"

Jasmine could not form an entire sentence or much less

think when Frisno made his way by her ever so discreetly. Jasmine fell to the floor and then the confusion and shock passed by her for the moment. Evan ran over and grabbed her, but she pushed him off. "Get out of my sight," she spoke softly.

"Jasmine, wait! Let me explain." Evan tried to rationalize with his wife.

"Get out of my sight, you freak!" she yelled loud enough for the neighbors to hear.

Evan grabbed his things and ran past his gay lover, who followed quickly behind with a soft "whoo!"

Evan looked back sorrowfully. His tall stature looked smaller and different to Jasmine. He was a tall man and had the build of a football player. His low cut and his goatee around his chin made him look distinguished. That is what Jasmine liked the most. His skin reminded her of French vanilla cappuccino. She was crazy about her Evan, but now she looked at him in disgust and she had to wonder, what happened to the Evan she used to know? She knew things were tense. They had gotten a little offbeat and distant, but this? She couldn't begin to understand what she had just seen and what to do. She felt betrayed and lost. Most of all, she felt like a failure. What had she done wrong to make her man go astray?

Chapter Forty-Two

Mia woke up to a beautiful day. The sun was shining through her curtains and the chirp of a red bird made her gleam inside. She rolled over to see Cashous still asleep. He must have felt her eyes on him because he opened his eyes and smiled softly at her.

"Morning." Cashous spoke peacefully. He and Mia did their best to never hold grudges.

"Morning, Cashous." Mia spoke softly. She nudged herself close to him. Cashous responded by pulling her close. "Cash, what do you think about the decision I have made to become a full-time author?"

"I think that life is too short not to live your dreams. Go for it."

"You're not concerned about the bills and hassle of handling everything on your own?" Mia asked.

"I'm not handling it on my own. I will give you the cash and you can pay the bills. I know how to lay aside extra if I need it. We will make the most of what we have. Now, a man just woke up. Can we make the most of this time?"

Mia smiled. "You're so full of it."

"I know, but that is why you love me." A pause lingered for about a minute. Cashous looked down at Mia. "So, you sure this is what you want to do?"

"Yeah, as sure as I have ever been."

"Well, I support you then."

"Let's go out for breakfast. My treat."

"You sure you got money?"

"I always got money."

"All right, Ms. Lady. Your treat after I get my treat here first." Cashous pulled Mia under the covers.

Mia and Cashous dressed and drove out to Lepetite Café on the Boulevard. It was a wonderful morning and the high-rise dining area made it that much more beautiful. The mountains were seen in the distance, along with the water off the coast and the city strips along the way. Mia and Cashous chatted quietly.

"Hey, Mia." Jasmine said as she approached their table. Jasmine waved at Cashous. Cashous waved back.

"Hey, Jasmine. What you doing here?" Mia asked in the same tone.

"Look." Jasmine pointed to Mani and Summer at a nearby table.

"Oh." Mia's faced turned into a shocked look. "Why didn't you all call me?"

"We did, but we didn't get an answer. We tried your cell phone, and there was still no answer."

"I left it at home."

"You all can join us if you like," Mia said.

"No, I will go. I have a lot of work to do at the office," Cashous said.

"You sure, honey?" Mia asked Cashous.

"Yeah, I'm sure. Go on ahead with the girls," he said.

Cashous was really grateful for the relationship Mia had with the women, considering he had witnessed Mia lose her children.

"All right, I will see you at home tonight." Cashous gave Mia a kiss goodbye.

Mia watched Cashous walk off before getting up and going over to join Imani and Summer at their table with Jasmine. "Still the finest man I know," she said as she sat down.

Jasmine smirked. "Look who is joining us."

"Hey, girl," Summer said.

"Hey, Summer. Hey, Mani," Mia said.

"Hey, Mia," Imani said.

"What's going on?" Mia asked everyone.

"You should be telling us. I haven't heard from you in a while," Summer responded.

"Me either," Jasmine added.

"Jasmine, every time I call, you're in the street." Mia defended herself against the accusations.

"I have a cell phone number. Um, try using that," Jasmine blurted out.

"The phone runs two ways." Mia playfully rolled her eyes.

"All right, I didn't mean to start nothing. Chill out," Summer spoke. "I was just playing."

"But you did," Mia whined.

Imani scolded Jasmine, Mia and Summer. "Y'all cut out all that mess."

"Mani, it's just that everyone acts like I have to live according to their standards," Mia pouted. "I have my own life. People are so concerned with fitting into society that no one is different. Everyone got this same guideline to follow, and no one is concerned with just living. God created us different because of the beauty of it."

"God, Mia, that was deep!" Summer said. They all laughed.

"Are you serious? You all need to be in Hollywood with all this drama," Jasmine said.

"Jasmine, shut up," Mia replied playfully. They giggled again.

"So, how is the book coming?"

"It's coming good, Mani. I have a few chapters under my belt," Mia answered.

"What is it about?" Summer asked.

"Can't tell. You will see."

"Oh, come on, sis-in-law."

"No, you will see. Besides, I don't know myself. I take it as it comes."

"Duh, some kind of author you are."

"Mani, tell Jasmine to get a life."

"Summer, are you okay? You look a little weary," Imani asked.

"I'm all right, Imani. Just thinking about Mike. He's been acting weird lately. And I had the nerve to leave the house the other night like I was really going somewhere. I called an old friend and told him I would meet him. I didn't do anything like that, though. I went to Starbucks and had some coffee and came home."

"Give it to God," Imani said.

"Sound like she was ready to give it to someone else, while you talking about give it to God," Jasmine added.

"I know you not talking," Summer sharply said to Jasmine.

"Oh, you're getting an attitude for real? Why don't I just tell Mike what you were up to?"

"Mani, you better get here before I come 'cross this table," Summer said.

"Y'all shut up, please," Mia said.

"You shut up," said Jasmine.

"Okay. I'm gone." Summer got up and grabbed her purse and didn't say anything to anyone.

"Me too." Mia left behind Summer.

"Let them go, babies," Jasmine said.

Imani looked at Jasmine. "You need to stop playing so much."

"Oh, Mani, please." Jasmine got up and walked off as well, leaving Imani shaking her head while lifting her arms up to God.

Chapter Forty-Three

Mia had been out of work now for about six months. She had only 200 pages typed of her bestseller, and it was way out of the criteria for a credible publisher to pick up. She was at least 150 pages short of her goal. She began to get frustrated. She considered going back to work part-time in a doctor's office. She needed to talk to her husband.

"Cashous, things are getting pretty tight. Do you think I should go back to work?"

"I didn't want to push you, but our savings are dwindling and that is our cushion, so maybe a part-time job to catch up the bills isn't such a bad idea."

"I thought so."

"I mean, you don't have to, but it will make my life a little easier."

"I know. I will find something this week."

Mia looked at her life and began to cry. All she could see was a failed marriage, failed relationships, missing children and a desperate cry for help. *What am I to do now? Go back to work for someone when I've worked for myself? I don't like being given orders; I am a leader, a go-getter and I wasn't happy before, so how can I be happy working for someone else? I have no choice, though. And I guess that puts my book on hold, which means I will probably never finish it.*

Mia found a job in two days. She got a job from another colleague and worked as a doctor in his firm. She found herself pulling long hours again, and things fell right into place the way they used to be.

She dragged herself home, tired from talking, sticking patients, providing medical advice and standing on her feet. She looked over at the half-written manuscript and began to write. She awoke with the pencil and pad on the nearby dresser and Cashous sound asleep beside her. She didn't hear him come in or leave the next morning.

She got out of bed and fell to her knees. "Okay, Lord, it's been a long time since I got down on my knees. You win. What is it that You want from me? Why am I here? No matter how hard I try, You won't spare me any slack. I tried being a good mother and You took my children. I tried being a good wife and You let my husband despise me. I tried being all I could be in this prejudiced world and it seems You forsake me. What am I supposed to do if You don't love me? Who do I turn to if You don't help me? I have tried all that I can try, and it all comes to nothing. Tell me, Lord, what have I done to deserve this life of mine?"

Seek my desires and everything will fall into place.

"But, Lord, I am a doctor and I help people. How much more can I seek to do Your will and serve?"

Think about what I would have You do with your life.

"Did I hear that? If so, how much more can I do? I've sought, I've sought and I've sought. Why can't You just answer me?"

*Do good to all that you meet. Be a living example of Me
and you have done My Will.*

"I'm not You. I'm only human." Mia listened but heard nothing. "Lord, are you there?" Still she heard nothing. "Here I
go again. I'm still not sure of what to do with my life."

Chapter Forty-Four

Summer held the phone away from her ear, looked at the receiver, and placed the phone back to her ear before speaking, "Mia, are you serious?"

"Summer, I can't go back to work."

"Mia, you've only worked for about two months now!"

"I know, but it's not what I want to do."

"I understand that, but you have to do what your husband feels is best."

"I have done that. But I feel like I'm suppose to be doing more."

"I don't know what to tell you, Mia."

"What's wrong with you? You always have an answer."

"I'm going through some things myself."

"What's wrong?"

"My middle sister is leaving her husband for another woman."

"What?"

"You heard me right."

"What did your mother say?"

"Who? Girl, she asked my sister had she bumped her big head."

"I know she did!" Mia laughed.

"I know you're upset, but you got your other sisters to hold you up. Let me know if there's anything I can do. Call me later, okay?"

"I will. Bye."

Mia had forgotten her own problems as she dialed Jasmine. "You heard about Summer's sister, right?"

"That's a shame. I knew she was crazy, but dag," Jasmine gossiped.

"I didn't know she was that crazy, though," Mia responded.

"What's going on with you?"

"Packing my stuff."

"Where you going?"

"Leaving."

"Okay, leaving for what?"

"Evan is crazy. I put up with a lot, but I can't take any more. I had been keeping our problems to myself, trying to pray my way through them. I didn't want my problems to be the topic of our conversation.

"I put up with his drug problem, always been there for him, but now, his no-good butt wants to go get another man on the side. So he can have his no-good self. Shoot, after hearing about Summer's sister, I decided it was no need for me to bear these burdens alone. I'm not the only one with screwed up individuals in my life."

"Jasmine, you got to be kidding. How did you find out?"

"After my business trip, I came home to surprise Evan with dinner and found him in bed with another man."

"Not in your house, in your bed?"

"Sister girl, yes. That spirit of homosexuality attacks! As if the crack demon wasn't enough."

"Oh yeah, you got to go."

"I know."

"Well you know how them crackheads get."

"But where do the lies stop? We so much into lies that I don't know the truth anymore, Mia. When will he clean up? What about our children? What is his ignorance causing us all in the long run? Who is the father figure for our children?"

"Where do you plan on going?"

"I don't know. I had been staying at a hotel with the kids."

Jasmine thought for a minute then said, "Look, I gotta go. I'll talk to you later," Jasmine said hurriedly.

"Who—wait, hold up. What are you about to do?"

"Pack his stuff!"

Chapter Forty-Five

"You know what? You should be going, not the kids and I!" Jasmine screamed as she ran up the steps. She opened the bathroom door. "Do you hear me?"

Evan was bent over, sniffing coke.

"What the—I know you not in this house getting high! I will kill you!"

"Wait, baby! Wait! I was just finishing off what was left!"

"And I'm finished with you!" Jasmine slapped her husband across the face. He fell and hit the sink, busting his head.

"Woman, you crazy!"

"Mommy! Mommy! What you doing?" Jasmine's oldest daughter called out. When Jasmine ignored her, she went to call her grandmother Imani, who in return called Mia to drive her over. Mia happened to be on the phone with Summer, who said she would meet them over at Jasmine's house.

Evan stumbled woozily. He was losing lots of blood. Jasmine thought he was going to pass out, so she called an ambulance.

The cops and ambulance soon arrived.

"Can you tell us what happened here?" The police officer questioned Jasmine.

"We got into a fight," Jasmine replied.

"I don't see any bruises on you, and he is laid out," the officer said. They looked at Evan, whose head was all bandaged up from Jasmine wrapping a towel around his head.

Jasmine went to her purse and pulled out a cigarette and began smoking it. She had hid the terrible secret that at her worst times, she smoked, but tonight she didn't even care who knew.

Imani and Summer ran through the door, and Mia ran in seconds behind them.

"Officer, I'm her mother," Imani spoke.

"Okay. We have to take her into custody until her husband can tell his side of the story, otherwise it's attempted murder."

Jasmine puffed her cigarette and acted like she never heard the officer.

"Jasmine, are you okay? Say something!" Imani asked her daughter.

"Mommy, just call my lawyer and get me out please," Jasmine finally replied.

"I will, honey."

Summer and Mia stood close behind Jasmine. "Mommy, we can call him on the cell phone," Jasmine said. Jasmine reached in her purse and grabbed another cigarette and lit it.

"Let's follow the cop to the station," Summer decided.

The cop had handcuffed Jasmine and she began to cry softly with the cigarette hanging out of her mouth.

Summer ran up to Jasmine and snatched the cigarette out of her mouth. "Give me that cigarette, fool. You don't even smoke."

They laughed. Summer, who didn't smoke, put the cigarette in her mouth and took a good puff from it.

Mia walked up to her as they put Jasmine in the cop car and took the cigarette from her. "You don't smoke either."

Chapter Forty-Six

Jasmine was in the holding cell and Summer, Imani, and Mia sat in the waiting area and waited for her lawyer. When her lawyer finally showed up, they all rushed over to the lawyer.

"Hello, Mr. Denzel. I'm Imani, Jasmine's mother," Imani said, extending her hand.

"Nice to meet you, Imani," Mr. Denzel said as he shook Imani's hand. "I've already spoken to the state. Jasmine is free to go."

"Thank you so much."

"You're welcome, madam. They are releasing her now."

Before he finished his sentence, Jasmine walked into the waiting area. She threw her arms around Imani. She turned and looked at Mr. Denzel. "Now what?"

"We wait for your husband to recover. If he doesn't press charges, then nothing; unless the State tries to prosecute," Jasmine's attorney informed her.

"What do you mean unless the state tries to pursue it?"

"Well, the State, in a domestic violence case, has the right to prosecute for the alleged victim. But I don't think this is one of those cases, so it probably won't get to that point."

"Okay," Mia said.

"I'm going to the hospital," Jasmine said out the blue.

"Well, I will contact you ladies as soon as the prosecuting lawyer contacts me," Jasmine's attorney stated.

"Jasmine can they do that? Prosecute without his permission?' Summer asked. She continued, "Imani, she was mad. She wasn't trying to kill him. Right, Jasmine?"

"Well, all of you need to ask the attorney if she can do that," Imani replied. "I believe it's a good idea. If it turns out to be something more, she can plead temporary insanity for the reasons she hit her husband."

"Shoot, *temporary* is an understatement," Summer added jokingly.

"Summer, shut up. Like I said, I'm going to the hospital," Jasmine retorted.

"Call us," said Imani.

"I will."

The ladies left the police station with Mr. Denzel.

"Thank you, ladies. I will be in touch," he said.

"Okay. Thank you, Mr. Denzel. Thank you very much," Mia said as she watched Mr. Denzel walk off.

"He ain't bad on the eyes, is he, Mia?" Summer smiled.

"Got that right!" Mia replied.

"Bring y'all hot selves on. What difference is it if he ain't bad on the eyes? You all ain't nothing much to look at yourselves," Imani responded.

Summer's mouth flew open. "I know Imani ain't talking about me like that!"

"Girl, you know Mani don't care what she say to us, you included."

"I care, but the truth is the truth." Imani laughed hilariously.

Summer and Mia looked at one another.

"Mia, she must be riding in your car 'cause she ain't riding with me talking like that!"

Mia laughed. "I didn't drive." She shrugged her shoulders.

They reached the car. "Summer, open this car door and take me home," Imani said. They all laughed.

Mia went home and pulled out her manuscript again.

"Hey baby, everything okay?" Cashous asked after Mia entered the house.

"I guess it will be. Just waiting for Jasmine to call from the hospital," Mia replied.

"She really let him have it, huh?"

"Yeah, I didn't know she had it in her."

"Never underestimate a tired woman, my momma always told me."

"I guess you're right."

"No, I am right. You're tired, huh?"

"Cash, I guess I am. I mean, it seems life doesn't have more to offer than broken dreams and broken hearts."

"Yes, it does, Mia. Be thankful for what we got now, baby."

"What we got? We argue most of the time."

"A work in progress, Mia. We got us, we good."

"I can't seem to find what I'm looking for in this lifetime."

"Just give God praise. Watch and see; He will fulfill all your needs."

"All right, I can do that."

"Right on time," said Mia as the phone started ringing.

"Hello," Mia answered.

"Hey, Mia, It's Jazz."

"Hey, what's going on?" Mia asked Jasmine.

"Evan is awake," she answered.

"Oh, good. How is he?" Mia asked.

"He's okay. It was a slight concussion."

"So, what's up?" asked Mia.

Jasmine sighed before answering her sister. "He's not pressing charges."

Chapter Forty-Seven

"Jasmine, this is Mr. Denzel."

"Hey, Mr. Denzel, what can I do for you?" Jasmine said to her attorney through the phone receiver.

"I called to tell you the State is pursuing charges against you."

"What? What kind of charges?" Jasmine asked, stunned.

"They're going for attempted murder."

"What!" Jasmine kneeled over. "Are you serious?"

"Yes, I am. I am pushing for minor assault or at least temporary insanity."

"I'm pushing for all of you have lost your minds! How is the State going to press charges for something my husband didn't even pursue?" Jasmine snapped.

"Domestic violence is a serious issue. They can do it."

"So, this is why the jail is full of young mothers and young men. We're not putting one another away, the State is."

"Well, I can't say that."

"No, you can't being a man of the law, but you know it's the truth."

"I'm sorry, Jasmine. All we can do is try to beat the accusations as temporary insanity or minor assault charges."

"I'm not pleading temporary insanity either. I hit his tail and I meant to hit him. And I didn't lose my mind while I was hitting him. And if the courts didn't come stop him from killing himself with those drugs, then why are they so concerned now? A bunch of mess is all this is."

"Okay, you're right. Just the same, we have court Tuesday morning at eight."

"All right." Jasmine hung up on Mr. Denzel before seeing if he had anything more to say.

Coincidentally, Imani felt the Holy Spirit beckoning her to pray for Jasmine at that very moment. She got down on her knees and began to pray quietly. "I know that you, God, have purposed Jasmine's end, and I give You the glory. Amen."

"Mrs. Harris, how do you plead?"

"Not guilty."

"You may be seated."

The prosecuting attorney walked up. "Your Honor, may I call Mrs. Harris to the stand?"

"You may."

Jasmine walked up to the witness stand and lifted her right hand. She repeated after the bailiff and took her seat.

"Mrs. Harris, did you know what you were doing when you knocked your husband unconscious?" the prosecuting attorney asked.

"Yes," Jasmine answered.

"Did you know the ramifications for such an act?" the prosecutor asked.

"Didn't think of it at the moment," Jasmine replied.

"So, you didn't care?" the prosecutor asked.

"No, I think I heard myself say I didn't think of it at the moment," Jasmine snapped.

"So, have you thought of it now?" the prosecutor asked sarcastically.

"Are you an attorney?" Jasmine replied in the same sarcastic manner.

"Well, yes, I am. I recall going to law school and coming out with honors," he responded gleefully.

"Then you should know I had plenty of thoughts since then and since I walked up to this stand. I mean, did you go to school 'with honors' to come up with these ridiculous questions?" People snickered inside the courthouse.

"Mrs. Harris, do I need to hold you in contempt of court?" the judge asked.

"No, Your Honor," Jasmine answered sorrowfully.

Summer and Mia laughed. Imani gave them a look. "Well, she told the truth," said Mia.

"No more questions, Your Honor," the prosecutor stated.

"Your witness, Mr. Denzel," he said before taking his seat.

Mr. Denzel walked up to the stand and stood directly in front of Jasmine, folding his arms to indicate his comfort level as he began his questions. "Jasmine, you were tired and drained from Evan's drug usage, correct?"

"Yes, I was," Jasmine answered honestly.

"So, you could have been a little beside yourself or not completely yourself?" Mr. Denzel continued.

"A little, I suppose," she answered.

"How long has this been an issue?" Mr. Denzel turned and faced the jurors as he asked that question.

"A couple of years," Jasmine answered, also looking at the jurors.

"And not only had you found out that your husband had been unfaithful, but you caught him with drugs too?" Mr. Denzel questioned as he suddenly spun around to face Jasmine on the stand.

"Yes," Jasmine answered.

"That's all the questions I have, Your Honor." Mr. Denzel

walked confidently back to his seat before giving a wink to Jasmine.

"Will you be cross examining, counsel?" the judge asked the prosecutor.

"No, Your Honor. The part about the infidelity was not made known to me. We need a minute to confer."

Chapter Forty-Eight

Jamal and Imani sat across from one another in their lawn chairs. Both of them had newspapers in their hands with a small table with tea glasses in between them. They loved coming out in their backyard and enjoying quiet moments together. Imani bent the paper to the side in order to see what time her watched showed.

She looked over at Jamal. "Jamal, what you want for dinner?"

"My wife."

"What does that mean?"

"It means you're always being everything to everyone except me."

"Everyone, meaning who?"

"Meaning Jasmine, Mia and Summer. Aren't they grown yet? I mean, you're always on the phone with them or you're in the street with them."

"Okay, and you need me to do what?"

"Be home some more, woman."

"All right, I will."

* * *

Imani made herself comfortable the next couple of days. She walked around the house cleaning, cooking, and just being there whenever Jamal needed her. She read, she ate and finally she picked up the phone and did a three-way to Jasmine, Mia and Summer.

"Hey. What you girls doing?" Imani asked.

"Hey, Mani. This week has been quiet trying not to call you so much and all that stuff. I just been writing."

"What you being doing anyways, Imani?" Summer asked.

"Nothing, girls. Jamal is always riding to the store or going off to do this and that. I've been here all alone all week while calling myself being here for him."

"Typical," Jasmine said. "A man always wants you to be at their beck and call, but they never around when you need them. It's like they expect us to be tokens sitting around waiting to be used."

"Daddy never there," Mia added.

"Mia, you know men. Their elevator don't run all the way to the top," Summer said.

"Well, don't sit in that house and be miserable, Mama. He got his life and you got yours," Jasmine replied.

"I know, Jazz. I will see you all at court tomorrow."

"You nervous, Jasmine?" Summer questioned.

"Nope, it's in God's hands now," Jasmine answered nonchalantly.

"Summer, you believe she said that, and all serious?"

"She know who to call on in the time of trouble," said Imani.

"Bye, y'all." Imani hung up.

"Dag, with her funny attitude, how any of us put up with her so much is beyond me."

"You get it from your mama!" said Summer to Jasmine.

Mia began laughing really hard now.

"She sleepy, Summer. Let's get off the phone before she say something stupid."

"Bye then."

They all hung up.

Everyone flooded into the courthouse. Jasmine, Imani, Summer and Mia all walked in and took their respective seats. The ladies wore their best attire—all in suits—to reflect the classy family they were for the jurors. Jasmine took her seat beside Mr. Denzel, who was in the courtroom already waiting for her. He also looked like he wore his best suit for the occasion. The prosecutor looked over with a slight sneer since he only had on dress pants, a short-sleeve shirt and no tie.

The jury walked in.

"In the case of the State versus Mrs. Harris, do you have a verdict?" the judge asked the jury.

"We have, Your Honor," the chosen juror said.

"And how do you find the defendant?" the judge asked.

"We find the defendant guilty of minor assault," the juror answered.

Jasmine looked at the jurors, and then back to the judge. Mia smacked her lips and rolled her eyes at the jurors.

"Shush, Mia." Imani scolded.

"Very well. The State thanks you for your contribution to this case. Therefore, Mrs. Harris, you are to do five hundred hours of community service with two years' probation," the judge ordered.

Jasmine looked back at her family. She then looked over at Evan and rolled her eyes.

"Oh man, she really is going to kill him for real now," Mia said.

"Mia, it's not his fault," Imani said, defending Evan.

"Whose fault would it be, Imani? He should have left those drugs alone and no one would be here in this courtroom today," Summer exclaimed.

"People always looking to blame someone for their own actions," Imani snapped back.

"Oh Lord, Imani! We just saying!" Summer threw her hands in the air and shook her head.

"Darn, darn, darn, can't we all just get along?" Mia squealed.

Imani looked at Mia and gave her a stern look.

"Oh, sorry, Mani. I forgot you were who you was when I said what I said. I meant dag, dag, dag, can't we all just get along?" She snickered and hit Summer behind Imani's back.

The women left the courthouse and decided to go eat lunch.

"Jasmine, we are sorry." Summer said.

"For what? I married Evan. No one made me."

"I know, but if Mike take me through another thing in our marriage, I don't know where I might end up at." Summer sat back in her chair sternly and twisted her lips.

"Your time is coming," Imani said.

"Imani, don't put that on me," said Summer.

"She's right, Summer. You're either coming out of a storm, going in a storm or already in a storm in this lifetime," Mia spoke.

"You would know, Mia, but I am in a storm. Remember my sister?"

"How are things with that, Summer?" Imani asked.

"Imani, I don't know. I have never seen such a mess in my life. Turns out she is not a lesbian, even though I thought I caught her in bed with her lover."

"Don't that sound funny? Caught 'her' in bed with 'her' lover?"

"I know. It don't even sound right coming out my mouth, do it, Mia?"

"Well, girl, life is full of surprises. Look at me. I'm a bona fide jailbird."

"I knew you were crooked all along, Jazz." Mia laughed.

"Shut up, Mia."

The moment turned quiet.

Jasmine turned all red-faced and teary-eyed.

"What's going on?" Mia asked her sister.

"I can't pretend any longer. I can't do this anymore."

"Do what? You and Evan will come out of this all right," Summer said assuredly. "Girl, the infidelity was probably just doing cocaine with the lady."

"It's more than that. It's man trouble." Jasmine sighed.

"You mean you were involved with another man?" Summer asked with her eyebrows raised.

"No, Evan was," Jasmine said, disgusted.

"What? Come again?" Imani asked, confused.

"I left Evan because I caught him in bed with a man."

"Jasmine, you've got to be kidding me! You caught him what and with who? What in the world?"

"If this is all true, honey, he has the problem, not you." Imani comforted Jasmine by rubbing her hand gently.

"So, what did he say when you caught him?" Mia asked, pretending she didn't already know.

"He was like 'it just happened.' He said he always felt close to men and then he met Frisno and they connected," Jasmine answered.

"Fris-who? He sounds like a freak show instead of Fris-whatever!" said Mia.

"Frisno, girl, he some half-black-and-Spanish mixed man who is too cute for words." Jasmine soaked in her misery.

"Oh my God, Jasmine. So now what?" Summer waited patiently for an answer.

Finally, Jasmine spoke. "I kept it inside and he's calling every day saying he wants to come home."

"He wants to come home? Yeah, right," Mia said.

"Yes, he said it only happened once and he will never do it again. I asked him how can I believe that or trust him, and he said after he did it he realized it was just a thing, like curiosity. He said he was sick to his stomach for two weeks every time he thought about it," Jasmine replied.

"But, Jasmine, he experimented with a man. He went to

another grown man. I can't get over that," responded Summer.

"Okay, but who knows how you, or anyone else for that matter, would have reacted catching their husband in bed with another man!" Imani added.

"I'm considering letting him come back home," Jasmine said under her breath.

"Jasmine, are you crazy?" Mia asked softly but sternly under her breath as if someone was listening to their conversation. "He went to another man, you caught them, he nearly pushed you over the edge and you want him back?"

"I love him," Jasmine stated.

"There isn't that much love in the world. Honey, you're insecure and not sure of who you are. You can get a man that is sure of who he is, at least sure of his sexual preference. It's too much of a risk. What if he does it again?" Imani asked her daughter.

"I don't think he will," Jasmine answered.

"But how can you be sure?" asked Imani.

"I can't be sure, but how many things can we be sure about when it comes to matters of the heart?" Jasmine looked for an answer in the women's eyes.

"Just think about it, Jasmine, before you take him back. The fact that he went there is too much for me to even bear, but you're not me and you love him, so just pray about it," Imani asked of her.

"I will," said Jasmine.

"I mean, were there any clues or ideas to make you think he was interested in men?" Summer asked.

"No, none. We were like rabbits in heat a lot of the time. Sometimes, when he came in from playing basketball with the fellows, he would attack me while he was all sweaty and girl, that was the best."

"Okay. Too much information. I feel sick," Mia joked.

"He says his reason was he needed someone to hold him,

and it seemed only another man knew that a man can have vulnerable moments," Jasmine said in a disgusted tone.

"He should have came to you, then, not gone to another man," Imani mocked.

"That's what I told him. He said he didn't have to tell this man what he needed; he just knew." Jasmine saw the bewildered looks on all of their faces and her head titled slightly to the side.

"And that makes it all better?" Summer sighed.

"No, I didn't say that," Jasmine answered.

"Girl, you on drugs or what?" Mia began to get annoyed with the conversation.

"All right, whatever. You finished?" Jasmine asked her sister.

"Yeah, I'm finished, before I say something I will regret. Look, I love you and we're sisters and I'm here for you. Call me when you need me. I will check on you later on today. All right?" Mia gathered her things and said bye to the other women.

"All right. Bye. I love you too," Jasmine replied as Mia walked away.

"I love you too." Summer reached over and kissed her sister-in-law on the forehead and walked out.

Imani reached over and rubbed her daughter's back. "It will work out somehow. Nothing is too big for God; this is just another way Satan is trying to destroy the family. But remember, greater is He that is in you, than he that is in the world. Tell that homosexual spirit to leave in the name of Jesus and then bind it up in Jesus' name. Whatever you bind on Earth, will be bound in Heaven."

Chapter Forty-Nine

Mia found herself feeling isolated. It seemed each one of her sisters and Imani had gone in their own direction and problems seemed to separate them for the first time in their lives. No one was calling anyone. No one was visiting, and there hadn't been any brunches, lunches or dinners between them in about two months. Life was hard.

Mia sat looking over her terrace and held the phone in her hand. She placed it down on a nearby table. She began to weep. She hadn't been able to get anyone all day, and she was not sure what was happening, but it didn't feel good. It seemed she was alone. And for the first time in a long time, she knew Jesus was beckoning her to talk to him.

"Here goes. Father, Lord Jesus, I am not sure what I'm supposed to say right now, but I want to give You thanks for my sisters and my mother and my families. I realize that You have been our strong tower and have kept each of us along the way. Protect us please, and if You separated us for a moment so that You could get your time in, then here it is. Now if You will only let me hear from one of them and know everything's all right. Amen."

Almost instantly, the phone rang. Mia looked up. "God, you are awesome!" She then answered the phone, still shouting in the process.

"Girl, what you shouting about?"

"Hey, Mani! I was wondering where you all were at. I couldn't get anyone and the calling has dropped short."

"Yes, I know, and that is why I'm calling. I have Jasmine and Summer on the phone. We need to get together soon. Okay? I feel something in my spirit and I don't like it."

"What is it?"

"I don't know. I been praying, though, so God will reveal it soon."

"All right."

"What's good for you all?" Summer jumped in the conversation.

"How about Thursday. Let's do brunch," Mia suggested.

"Okay, call me with the details. I have to go," Summer blurted out.

"Summer, you ain't been on the phone two seconds," said Mia.

"I know, Mia, but I have to go."

"All right, bye," Mia said to her sister-in-law.

"All right, I need to cook," Imani said.

"Me too, Mama," said Jasmine. "Bye, Mia."

"All right. Bye, y'all."

The women all hung up.

Well, You did exactly what I asked, Lord, so no need to complain for them being fast about getting off the phone.

Chapter Fifty

"Jamal, don't you know that if the head isn't right, the family can't be in balance?"

"Imani, what you talking about?"

"You know good and well what I'm talking about. How you going to be a shepherd and lead the sheep if you're fooling around with the women in the congregation? You have to answer to God, not just me."

"I'm not fooling around with anyone. Just because you see someone smiling in my face, I have to be fooling around with them?"

"It's more to it than that and you know it. How come you don't preach where God brought you from? You preach what feels good to your carnal man. But what about your testimony? Does anyone know your story?"

"God didn't say anyone had to know my story to preach. I preach the Word and that is what is required of me."

"So, who did He deliver when He brought you into the marvelous light? Did He deliver all those people you preaching to or did He deliver you? If no one can see how the preacher got delivered, can you deliver them? You fooling around with those women and I'm not going to be a part of it. You're going to look up and I won't be sitting in that front pew, and then you're going to explain to the church why I left you. But I'm not going along with your lies and your scheming because my soul is too valuable for me to mess around and lose on account of your foolishness."

"Imani, trust me; there is nothing going on in that congregation. You're letting those women get to you, and perhaps you have too much stress on you, but I ain't doing nothing!"

"All right then, if that's what you say. But my tears carry weight, and like I said, you have the Father to answer to, just like I do."

Jamal just looked over at Imani and shook his head.

Chapter Fifty-One

"What do you mean you don't know how long you have to live?" Jasmine asked Evan.

"Jasmine, like I said, I went to the doctor and I'm HIV positive. I know this is a shock, but don't keep asking me what I mean!"

Jasmine sat down on the edge of the bed, almost dropping the phone. "It's a mistake, I'm sure. I mean, you can't, and I don't—I won't accept that," she exclaimed.

"I took three tests. And Frisno confirmed he had it as well."

"Oh my God, Evan! Oh my God!" Jasmine screamed.

"Jasmine, calm down . . . you may not have it. It was a terrible mistake, and now it's cost me my life and our marriage."

"What about my life? Look what you did to us!"

"Jasmine, don't." Evan pleaded. "Just go get tested. I'm sorry . . ." Evan sat on the bed in his brother's room and cried into his hands.

* * *

Mia knocked on Jasmine's door. Jasmine opened it swiftly and plopped down on the living room recliner. "What's up, sis?"

"Nothing."

"Okay. Then why you look like you just found out you only have twenty-four hours to live?"

Jasmine burst out crying.

"What's up, for God's sake?" Mia demanded to know.

"I may have AIDS," Jasmine confessed.

"What? What are you talking about, Jasmine?"

"Evan is HIV positive."

Mia sat down on the end of the couch, speechless.

"He found out a few days ago."

"Oh, honey. I'm sorry. There's a big chance you don't have anything. Let's make an appointment today. I will go with you."

"No, I'm not ready."

"But, Jasmine, the longer you wait, the worse it could be if you did get it. I mean, we hope you don't, but we don't have time to waste."

"Who wants to know that there is a chance your life could be cut in half or you will be sick the remainder of your days? Or what about knowing if I will be here to see my children grow up? I've lost one of my loved ones already, and he's not even dead. I can't stand to see him deteriorate or just watch him die. I want to be there for him, but I don't know what I will do if I have it."

Mia stood and looked at Jasmine. She didn't have words, so she just embraced her. They cried.

"I can't see life without you. You're not going anywhere, okay? And when you're ready, we will go together. I can't believe I'm saying this, but Evan doesn't need to be alone now. No one wants to die alone. Let him come home, okay?"

"Okay," Jasmine whispered softly.

Jasmine called Evan at his brother's and welcomed him back home. It had only been a couple days and as Evan lay on the couch, he looked sick to her all of a sudden. She figured it was her imagination, but already the mental toll had taken hold of him and caused the physical attributes of HIV to surface.

Evan looked over his shoulder and didn't speak to Jasmine. She walked over and sat on the coffee table in front of her husband. She cried all the while.

"I never meant to hurt you or for things to turn out this way. Jasmine, what happened? I mean how?" Evan sat up slowly.

"We both know how. Why, perhaps, is the better question. It shouldn't have happened."

"Why did you let me come back?"

"Do you want to be alone?"

"No."

"All right then, you're not going to be."

"Look at me, Jasmine. I look like I haven't eaten in years. I don't have any energy and I don't feel so good."

"Have you even considered that you may beat this thing? Perhaps you can live as long as anyone else."

"No, I haven't. It's probably a fight I'm going to lose anyway."

"*Probably* is not a fact. You have to think differently. Who is going to help me if it turns out I have it?"

"Don't say that. I couldn't live another day if I infected you. Have you gone to get tested?"

"No, but I will. I just need a few days to get myself together. You know, gather my strength up."

"Pray."

"Yes, pray."

After her meeting with Jasmine, Mia called Summer and told her everything. Mia decided that they all needed to get together to tell Imani. Next, they were all getting together for lunch. They decided to meet at Mia's condo.

"Lunch wasn't supposed to be until tomorrow. Why we here now?"

"Mia asked us to come over here."

"Mia, what's wrong?"

"Jasmine, you want to tell them?"

"I don't have the strength," Jasmine answered. She started to cry.

Mia paused before saying, "Jasmine may be HIV positive. Evan found out he had HIV a couple of days ago. He has no idea how long he's had it."

"Oh, Jasmine." Imani broke down at just the thought of her daughter's fate.

"Just pray for us. I mean, I feel like a ton of bricks are on my back, and I don't know what to do."

"Well, that is why we are here. In times like these, we need a savior. God will do what's best for Evan at this point, and all we can do is pray for you that God will grant His mercy upon you."

"Well, have you taken the test yet, Jasmine?" asked Imani

"No, not yet," Jasmine answered.

"Scared, I bet," Summer said emotionally.

"Yep, how you know, Summer?" Mia asked her.

"I could only imagine," replied Summer.

The women joined hands and prayed. As they prayed, it seemed God looked down upon His daughters and the rain fell from the sky. The wind blew and the wind turned chilly. The women stayed on their knees a long time in front of the fireplace, and not one of them said a word. They all gathered around Jasmine and held her as she cried softly.

"His eyes are on the sparrow, and I know He watches me . . ." Imani sang the song slowly, as Jasmine laid her head and chest in Imani's lap. Mia and Summer lay next to her.

Chapter Fifty-Two

Evan and Jasmine spent the last couple of days praying. It seemed to have lifted his spirits. The doorbell rang unexpectedly.

"Evan, can you get the door?"

"Yea, hon. I got it."

A police officer stood with Jasmine and Evan's oldest son, Alex, in front of him.

"Officer, what is the problem?"

Jasmine came behind Evan to the door and pulled Evan aside to let the officer step in with Alex. She gave Alex a sneer.

"I remembered you and your wife from court. So, instead of hauling your child off to jail, I brought him here. He was pulled over in a car with a juvenile, and they had possession of some illegal substances in the car."

"What type of illegal substance in the car?" asked Evan

"There were a few pills of Vicodin in the car and some marijuana."

"Okay. Thank you, officer. His father and I will take it from here," Jasmine said.

"You all know that this is the start of something harder unless you really tell him the consequences. Next time he's going in."

"Thank you, officer." Jasmine closed the door.

"Alex, what in the world are you thinking?"

"I wasn't doing anything, Mom. That stuff wasn't mine," he said in his defense.

"Okay, then why would you be with guys like this? You're only thirteen. Don't mess up your life," Jasmine told her son.

"Dad, will you talk to her? I'm a big boy." Alex looked over at his father with his hands raised in question.

"What do you want me to say, Alex? It's okay?" Evan asked sternly.

"You did it," Alex said sharply.

Evan grabbed Alex by the shirt. "Let me tell you something, boy. What I did I did as a man. I wasn't thirteen; I wasn't under my mama and daddy's roof, and I wasn't some pissy smart-mouth who thought he knew it all. Matter of fact, as a man, I almost lost my family and ruined all of your lives in the midst of it. So, until you're a man and can make man decisions, if I catch you smoking up anything in this house, I'm going to beat you like you were a man."

Alex stood shocked, and so did Jasmine. It had been a long time since she had seen her husband in true character. She was proud, and he hadn't touched a thing since he came out of the hospital.

"Understand, Alex?" Jasmine said with her shoulders held high.

"Yes, Mom," Alex answered, not so manly.

"Go to your room and don't expect to go out for another month," said Evan.

"But, Dad!" Alex shouted.

"Dad what? Get moving now!" Evan shouted back.

Alex scrambled up the steps.

Jasmine smiled at Evan. He stood a little taller and said, "Now, get in that kitchen and cook me some dinner, girl."

"Don't get carried away." Jasmine smiled.

"Oh, yeah. I mean, can you cook me some dinner?" Evan restated the demand jokingly.

"Much better! I think I can," said Jasmine.

Chapter Fifty-Three

Jamal walked around his church sanctuary and quietly gave thanks to God for all He had done. He went into his office and sat behind his desk chair. He opened his Bible to Psalms and began to prepare for his next sermon.

Ann entered the room. Jamal stood to greet her. "Have a seat, Ann."

"Thanks, Pastor Reese. I wouldn't have bothered you, but I need someone to talk to."

"That is why I am here."

Ann flipped her long legs over one another and pulled her dress up slightly to show a bit of her thigh. She leaned forward to get her Bible and gracefully exposed her cleavage. She leaned back and caught Jamal admiring her beauty. He became embarrassed and quickly went back to business.

"Um, Ann, what is it I can help you with?"

"I'm having marital problems. My husband, he treats me more like a slave than a wife. He expects me to be the perfect wife, to be the perfect mother, sex partner, and fill his every need, but he doesn't want to tell me where he's going or when he will be back when he goes. He doesn't want to go to counseling or make any compromises. It's his way or no way."

"Have you asked him to come here with you?"

"Yes, I have, and he has declined."

"Well, it's hard to counsel your marriage when your husband isn't willing to participate."

"I know, but what else can I do?"

"Okay, let's work on you. We will make sure you're being the virtuous woman and you're not missing something that perhaps is making him act out like this toward you."

"Okay. Great. When do we start?"

"I have to check my wife's schedule and get back with you."

"Why your wife?"

"I prefer the women be counseled by my wife. Of course, I will be present."

"If you don't mind, I haven't quite gotten there yet with the first lady. I would feel embarrassed, and I would rather it be between us."

"Well, okay, but what problem do you have with the first lady?"

"I don't have a problem with her, I just don't feel comfortable with her. You know it takes us women a while to trust one another."

"All right then, let's begin. What can you tell me that makes you the woman you're husband needs or that God has ordained a woman to be? What do you classify as a good wife and a Godly wife?"

"Let's see. I cook, I clean, and I'm a good mother. And oh, I'm not too bad in the bedroom either. Once, when he came home from work, I had placed rose petals from the door to the bathtub. I had a bowl of strawberries with melted chocolate on the tub with a fresh bottle of wine. I had bubbles and soft music playing. I wore provocative lingerie that was see-through. I washed him down—"

"Um, excuse me, Ann. That is more detail than I need to know." Jamal felt the bulge in his pants. Ann noticed him twitching and she began to cry.

"I'm sorry; it's just that I have tried so hard," she said.

Jamal handed her a tissue over the desk and she embraced his hand. "What am I supposed to do, Pastor?"

"Read these scriptures and study these scriptures on marriage." Pastor Reese gave her scriptures from the book of Corinthians. "Read chapter seven, The Principles of Marriage. Come back to me in a few days and let me know if any light was shed on the situation from studying what God says about marriage."

"Okay, Pastor. Thank you."

Ann walked out and Pastor got up and closed the door. "Whew! Talk about yield not unto temptation." The door opened and he turned quickly.

"I forgot my purse," Ann said. She picked up her purse while looking at Pastor Reese. "Do you have something in your pocket, Pastor?" She smiled and walked out.

Jamal started home. He couldn't get Ann's breasts and legs out of his head. He knew women were his weakness. "Lord, give me strength," he mumbled. He pulled up to his house and got out and walked in.

"Imani, you here?" Imani was not home. "Probably out with the girls again," he said. His cell phone rang.

"Pastor speaking."

"Pastor, hi, this is Ann. I came home today and my husband was gone—no note, no anything. I just don't know how much longer I can do this. If I'm not wondering where he is because of his attitude, I'm wondering who he is doing."

"Ann, don't let the devil play with your mind. Until he gives you reason to suspect anything, just continue to pray on it and do what you have to do to stay in the will of God."

"Okay, Pastor." Ann paused for a moment. "Pastor, I sense

my conversation on how good of a lover I am got to you today."

"Why do you say that?"

"Was something in your pocket?"

"Yeah, something was in my pocket."

"The wife not taking care of home?"

"I guess she doing okay, but I'm only human."

Jamal heard Imani's keys in the door. "Okay, Mrs. Ann, I will talk to you and your husband when he's ready to talk. Okay. Thank you."

Imani walked in. "Hey, still working?"

"Yeah. Marital problems in the church," Jamal responded.

"Did I hear you say Ann?" Imani asked.

"Yeah. She is having problems with her husband."

"Maybe if she got her eyes off you she could take care of her husband."

"Look, Imani, I don't know where all this craziness is coming from lately, but let it go. I ain't messing with no one in the church, including Ann."

"Then why aren't I in these counseling sessions? This is not the first time she has had a problem and I wasn't told she needed counseling."

"She isn't comfortable with you yet."

"Then she's not comfortable with you. Don't you see? I'm your wife, and you should not be counseling any woman in the church without my presence."

"Look, I don't have time for all this. I'm going out."

"Going out where?"

"Anywhere I want to. I'm a grown man, right?"

Jamal walked out and slammed the door. Imani went and sat on her bed and began to pray.

"Dear Lord, You said You give us authority to trample over servants' heads. You give me authority over the earth, and greater is He that is in me than he that is in the world. I know the seducer sits and waits to steal my husband, my peace and my family. But, Lord, I pray that no weapon formed will prosper because that is Your Word. I bind up every lustful spirit, whore spirit and everything that comes against this marriage, and I call her by name. I demand that Ann move in the name of Jesus Christ. Amen."

Chapter Fifty-Four

Jasmine lay across her bed. It was still early morning, and she hadn't even gotten up for her morning coffee.

After a lot of sleepless nights and crying herself to sleep, Jasmine finally felt like she needed to go to the doctor. She couldn't hide her pain any longer; she couldn't pretend she wasn't losing her mind. She watched what was happening to Evan, and all she knew was that she needed help.

"If there is a God out there, please do this for me. Let me live to see my children grow up. Have mercy on me." She didn't know if anyone heard her, and she didn't feel any different, but she decided she would go to the doctor. She couldn't bear not knowing another day. She reached over to her nightstand and picked up her phone and dialed Mia.

"Hello," Mia answered.

"Mia, can you go with me to the doctor?"

"Jasmine, you okay?"

"Yeah, Mia, I'm okay. Just wondering if I'll get to see my kids off to college or not."

"I will be there in a few minutes."

Jasmine hadn't got her clothes on good before Mia came walking in the door.

"What happened to knocking?" Jasmine asked her sister.

"No time to waste on small details. Ready?"

The ladies drove the doctor's office in silence. As they arrived, Jasmine signed in and they took a seat.

Mia grabbed her sister by the hand. "You're going to live and be just fine."

"That is what you say."

"That is what God says. He died on the cross that we may be healed. You're going to live. And if you continue to confess that, you allow Him to do good work in you and you will have no HIV, no nothing."

"How is that, Mia? I have a husband who has it for God knows how long, and I slept with him for the last year and a half."

The nurse called out, "Mrs. Harris, you can go back now."

"Mia, will you go back with me?"

"You don't have to ask."

"Excuse me, ladies," the doctor said.

Mia reached over and grabbed Jasmine's hands. Both ladies looked on nervously.

"Your test was negative."

"What?" Jasmine asked.

"Your test was negative," the doctor repeated.

Mia looked at Jasmine, who stood still in shock, and pulled her close. She sobbed loudly and Jasmine sobbed softly and the tears fell.

The doctor walked out. "Take care, Jasmine. You can see the nurse when you're ready on your way out."

"Did you hear that, baby? You're negative."

"I heard. Wow, how did this happen?"

"Girl, God's favor. It's all about who you hooked up to.

Mani has been praying, and I believe that she had everything
to do with it."

"Didn't you pray?"

"Yeah, but I be slipping. I ain't going to lie. I wasn't sure
He would hear my prayer; good thing Mani stood in the gap.
But she didn't do it, God did."

Jasmine rushed straight home and into the house. "Evan!
Evan! Are you here?" Jasmine's voice was unpredictable, so
Evan proceeded with caution.

Evan walked slowly out of the bedroom. "Here I am.
What's wrong?"

"Evan, my HIV test was negative!"

"Are you serious, Jasmine?"

"Yes, Evan, I'm negative."

"Oh, baby, that is good. That is the best news I have heard
in my entire life!"

"Evan, I want to try something."

"Anything, tell me."

"Let's try and see if God or Jesus is worth trying, for you.
Let's pray that He will heal your body and see what happens.
We don't have anything to lose."

"I don't know how to pray."

"You speak English, don't you? Let's just tell Him we accept Him into our hearts and believe Jesus is the Son of
God; and that we will serve Him as our Lord and Savior.
Then we'll tell Him we want Him to heal you because people
say He can do anything."

"Okay then, let's do that."

Jasmine and Evan both said those exact words together
and asked Jesus to heal Evan.

Chapter Fifty-Five

Jamal dialed Ann's number. "Hello, Ann. I was just checking on you, praise God."

"Oh, Pastor, thank you. I'm okay. A little down today, though."

"You need to talk?"

"Yes. Can you come by?"

"I'm not sure I should be there if your husband is not home."

"He's out of town for a few days."

"How about you meet me at the church?"

"All right then; half an hour?"

"Yes, I will be there."

Jamal went to his office. He fixed himself up and ignored that little voice that told him he had crossed the line. Temptation had overtaken him, and he enjoyed every minute of it. Ann walked in. She wore a flimsy little sundress that was just a little over her thighs and showed too much cleavage to be in the church. Jamal swallowed hard.

"Hi, Ann, have a seat."

"Pastor, how long are we going to play this game? I can see that you want me. I have needs and so do you."

"But we are both married."

"Then why are we here? I know you saw the signs. I needed to talk to you without your wife. How about the flirting? Did you think I was doing it for my health?"

"Well, I thought we were just having fun. I'm not sure I want anything but a little fling on the side. You know, to spice up the old life a little bit."

"I have a fling on the side; he's my husband. I need a godly man." She talked seductively. "I need a man that I can depend on and who I know won't run out just to be running out."

"How can you trust me to be that man? I'm considering running out on my wife now."

"I know your weakness is women and you have come a long way. The only reason you're fighting with me is because I'm irresistible."

"Yes, you are."

Ann walked over and played with Jamal's shirt. She moved a little closer. His phone vibrated.

"Excuse me," Pastor said, then answered his phone.

"This is Pastor Reese."

Imani looked at the phone bewildered and then put the phone back to her ear. "What's wrong with you? You didn't see it was me?"

Jamal moved uncomfortably past Ann, who looked annoyed.

"Hey, Imani," he said.

"Where are you and what are you doing?"

"I just had to run by the church for a little while."

"Oh, well I'm around the corner. I will be there in a bit."

"All right." He hung up and pushed Ann out the door. "My wife is around the corner."

"Okay. You can say you were counseling me."

"No, I can't. It's in the middle of the day and no one is here at church but us. I don't think so."

He pushed Ann out the door like a rag doll.

Imani arrived five minutes later. "What you doing here?" she asked.

"Just meditating on some stuff. I'm finished, though; let's go to lunch."

"Oh, good. I can eat, but before I do, let's mess around for a minute."

"Here?"

"Yes, here."

"All right." Jamal smiled and thought, *I got what I needed after all.*

Imani dropped her long dress to the floor and underneath was a little nightie that put a big smile on her husband's face.

Chapter Fifty-Six

Evan had suddenly become sick from a touch of pneumonia. He was miserable, thinking that the disease was already taking its toll on him.

Jasmine stood over Evan's bedside at the hospital. He looked halfway dead and the doctor didn't seem to know what made him take a turn for the worse.

"Here, honey, let me put some Chapstick on you." She rubbed the Chapstick on his dry lips.

"Thanks."

"So, are you feeling better today?"

"I still feel awful. It seems since we prayed that prayer things got worse for me."

"I know, but if God is who people say He is, you probably would be dead and gone by now. Maybe worse isn't the worst."

"I guess you're right. What have the doctors told you?"

"Same things they told you; that they don't know what is going on with you. They increased your dosage and you got worse, so they dropped off adding any more medicines until they can run the blood tests again."

"They ran blood tests."

"Yes, but the doctor said something was weird, so they needed to run them again."

"When did they say the test results will be back so they can tell me what's wrong with me, besides the obvious?"

"They said in a few days."

"If I make it a few days."

"You will, honey. Just rest."

Chapter Fifty-Seven

Mia, Jasmine and Summer walked in church looking sharp as tacks. They took their seats and Ann leaned forward from her row on the other end of the pew and smiled at the girls. They all looked back at her and rolled their eyes.

"Why is this heifer on our pew?" Mia said.

"I don't know, Mia, but she act like she think she's somebody," Summer said.

"Well, Mani been acting kind of funny lately to Daddy. And I believe that snake got something to do with it," Jasmine added.

"How you know, Jasmine?"

"Summer, I hear things."

"I know you do," said Mia.

Summer turned serious. "No, but for real, Jasmine, how you know?"

"Well, if you must know, one of the girls in the back, you know Tara, she said Ann been telling people in a matter of time she's going to be the first lady."

"Oh, no she didn't! Then looking at us and sitting on our

pew like she special. I can solve this now." Mia got up and started walking toward Ann.

Summer pulled Mia's arm and sat her back down. "We in church, girl. Wait until we get in the parking lot and then we can talk to her."

All throughout service, Mia seemed anxious. She was furious and she couldn't believe her daddy would betray Imani that way. After church, the three ladies waited until Ann finished sucking up to Mani and then watched as she hugged Pastor, switching off like she was ready to star in a porn movie. The girls followed her outside.

"Excuse me, Ann. I am Mia, if you don't already know me. I was wondering, why are you a homewrecker?"

"Oh! Excuse me?" Ann asked in a confused tone.

"You heard me," Mia responded.

"Look, dear girl, I don't know what you've heard or perhaps think you know, but you shouldn't be angry with me if Daddy wants a new model and not a wagon," Ann stated matter-of-factly.

"Hee-hee, Jasmine, you see she got jokes about Mani," Mia replied.

"I see she do," said Jasmine.

Summer walked in front of the woman and she stared Ann in the eyes like she wanted to slap her.

Mia stepped close to Summer. "Since you're the new model, I guess you know you ain't made out of nothing and it won't take much for me to whip your behind out here."

Ann stepped back and looked shocked.

"Oh, threats? And you're supposed to be a preacher's daughter?"

"Supposed to be? I am the preacher's daughter and still will be after I kick your behind. So if you think you're brave enough, then try me." Mia took off her earrings and motioned for Ann to come on and fight.

Ann walked off in a hurry. Jamal walked up to the ladies.

"What is going on?" he asked, looking from one woman to the next.

"You should know," said Jasmine.

Imani walked up.

"Mani, we have to go. We will call you," Mia said while putting her earrings back on, and then the women walked off.

Imani looked at Jamal. "What's wrong with them girls now?"

"Who knows?" he answered.

Later that day, Ann called Jamal on his cell phone. Jamal excused himself from the dinner table. "Excuse me, Imani. I will take care of this."

Jamal went down the hall a little ways. He answered his cell phone.

"What can I help you with?" Jamal said softly.

"I'm having a hard time tonight. I mean, I'm only human and I need to see you."

"I told you when you called earlier at the office I couldn't get out."

"Just for a few minutes?"

"Okay. Meet me at the church in fifteen minutes."

Jamal walked back into the dining room. "Imani, I need to go let one of the ministers retrieve his papers from the church."

"Can't that wait?" she asked her husband.

"No. He needs them now," Jamal answered.

"All right, but hurry back," said Imani.

"Look, I'm not a child. I know when to come back," Jamal said rudely.

"Okay, but why be so rude? I was just saying," protested Imani.

"You're always just saying. Have you noticed that?" Jamal walked out and slammed the door.

Imani spoke out loud. "God, you would think I did something to him just because he had to go out. Wonder why he didn't give that minister that's calling him away from his dinner a piece of his mind."

Jamal pulled up, and Ann was already at the church. "Come on and be quick so no one sees us."

They went inside Jamal's office and cut on the lamp light. "I needed to see you desperately, Pastor. How long can we play this game?"

"But what is it that you want from me?"

Ann reached over and kissed Pastor affectionately and passionately. A bulge grew in his pants and he pulled back. "Ann, I can't."

"Yes, you can."

"Wait. Perhaps I gave mixed signals. I can't do this to Imani."

"E who?" Ann asked as if she didn't know who the first lady was.

"Imani, that is First Lady's name. Remember her?"

"Oh, that's right. I never really bothered to ask anyone her first name. I'm used to hearing First Lady Reese."

"Look, things are getting out of hand. I have to go. Let's just act like this kiss never happened."

"It happened, and I will act like it happened. You want me, and the something in your pocket tells me exactly that. So why are you fighting it?"

Chapter Fifty-Eight

"Evan, what is it?"

"You're right on time."

"I guess I am. You look like you just seen a ghost. So what am I on time for?"

"The nurse just informed me that the doctor was coming in with my test results. She told me to brace myself. She said she had to say something and that was it."

"Oh my God, Evan. What could it be? Let's just prepare ourselves and thank God for every moment he has given us together."

The doctor walked in. He looked perplexed and puzzled. Jasmine had a nervous stomach.

"Mr. and Mrs. Harris," the doctor said, "I have a bit of alarming news."

"Oh, how long, doctor? We are ready," Evan said.

"Oh, the contrary. We have decided to eliminate the medicine altogether that we have been giving you for HIV. We found the reason you were getting sick is because the HIV medicine was making you sick, due to the fact that it was not finding anything to fight against anymore. Your system has been trying for the last seven weeks to reject it."

Jasmine looked at Evan and then at the doctor. Evan said, "So, doctor, you're telling us what? There is nothing there for the medicine to fight against? Have my insides all been dried up and I'm going anytime now?"

"No, Evan." The doctor chuckled. "What I'm saying is, there is no sign of HIV any longer in your system."

Jasmine nearly fainted. The doctor gave her a chair. Evan looked on and began to laugh uncontrollably. "I mean, doctor, are you sure?"

"Yes, we did two days' worth of extra testing and every test known to man. I don't know. You have a clean bill of health, and my question is, what did you do?"

Jasmine looked at her husband; he then grabbed Jasmine's hand close to his heart.

"We prayed."

"No, seriously, what kind of things did you do? I mean, it's a medical miracle."

"No, seriously," Jasmine said, "we prayed and our Lord and Savior answered our prayers."

"All right, well, prayer works then. As soon as the nurse brings in your papers, you're free to go, but I would like you to come back in a few weeks and let us check you to see how you're doing."

"I may come back, Doc, but I feel like I can live forever."

Chapter Fifty-Nine

The next Sunday in church, Jasmine, Summer, Imani and Mia talked about Evan's miracle. They were all on fire for the Lord.

"Evan, you're living testimony, and we want people to know what God did for you and your family," Jamal said, signaling Evan with his hands to come down to the altar. The crowd began applauding as he walked forward. Jamal extended his hand toward Evan. "Bless you, my child."

"Um, Daddy didn't waste no time, did he?" said Mia.

"Mia, if he was as interested in God like he says he is, this church wouldn't have all this confusion in it all the time," Summer said.

"Oh, shut up, y'all. What's wrong now?" Jasmine snapped, sounding like Imani. She was caught up in the moment of excitement for her and Evan.

"Jasmine, I didn't open my mouth. I don't know what's wrong with that girl." Summer laughed while looking at Mia like she was talking to herself.

Jasmine and Mia laughed. As they took their seats, Ann walked by with a full-brim pink hat on with a pink suit and bad pink shoes to match. She walked in like someone off the front page of a magazine. She strolled past and sat right in the seat where Imani was usually seated as first lady. Imani usually came in right before Jamal preached so she made an entrance.

"Oh, um, can someone tell me why she just sat in Imani's seat?" asked Summer.

"Let's go ask her," Mia said.

"No, Mia. I know your temper. I will just ask her to move. I mean, I don't understand. She's been coming here a year now. She knows that is Mommy's seat."

Mia and Summer followed Jasmine. Evan made his way back to his seat as Jamal was taking his place in the pulpit. He looked on nervously.

"Excuse me, Ann. How are you this morning?" Jasmine asked.

She looked up from the program like it had some kind of intriguing detail. Imani walked directly up behind the women, and looked at Ann.

"Hi, First Lady. You don't mind, do you? I feel more in place here."

The girls looked on and stood behind Imani like bodyguards.

"Well, yes, I do mind. This is the first lady's seat."

"Oh, I know whose seat it is." Ann looked back down at her bulletin.

Mia removed her earrings once again. "Stand aside one moment, Mani," Mia said.

"Mia!" Imani squealed, annoyed.

"No, it's okay, Mani," Mia replied. "I got this." Mia stepped in front of Imani. She gently took the big hat off Ann's head and set it down on the seat next to Ann. Ann looked up and grabbed her head.

"I beg your pardon!" she screamed.

"I took your hat off very nicely because Mani asked you to

get up nicely. But the rest of you may not land as gently as your hat did."

Jamal ran out of the pulpit. "What is going on here?" he asked.

"I don't know," said Jasmine. "Would *you* care to explain what is going on? I mean, Mrs. Ann feels for some reason she needs to be in the first lady's seat today."

"Ann, what is the point of all this?" Jamal asked her.

"I mean, Pastor, I felt that after you reach a certain point in a relationship, you're entitled to bigger and better things."

"All right, enough talking." Mia pulled off her earrings and stepped out of her shoes.

Ann jumped up and began to run, but with her three-inch heels on, Mia caught her before she got very far and grabbed her by her hair and pulled her backward. She stumbled to the floor.

"Help me, please! Get this crazy woman off of me!" Ann yelled.

Imani and Summer, along with Jasmine, pulled Mia off of Ann. Mia stood to her feet and adjusted her clothes. She then sat in the pew in the second seat, waiting for the choir to sing. The choir noticed her looking at them, and the director pounced to his feet and began to direct the choir.

They sang "Jesus is a Balm in Gilead." They sang softly, still looking at Ann gathering herself. Jamal went scrambling back to the pulpit, and Imani took her seat as Jasmine and Summer took theirs. Ann scrambled her way out the door. Imani threw the pink hat behind her. Summer caught it and put it on her head. It just happed to match her outfit. They never cracked a smile or missed a beat, but sang along with the choir. The director looked at the choir and snapped his fingers and instructed the people to sing loudly.

"Sing, people! Sing! Show is over!" he shouted, excited. "Jesus said he came to make war, not peace! Jesus is still Lord!"

"Amen!" Mia, Summer and Jasmine and Imani spoke in unison.

They all smiled because they knew if Imani wasn't so lady-like, she would have kicked Ann's butt herself. But as far as Jamal was concerned she couldn't wait to get to him after church. Usually, she would holler "You better preach," and "Amen" during his sermons, but this time, Imani didn't even move, not even for the offering. The girls took her cue, and they didn't move either.

Jamal began to speak as if he had something that was going to bring everyone around. "Today we have a special visitor, or should I say visitors, that have an amazing testimony for the Lord Jesus Christ. God said greater works shall we do, and by faith they have been made whole. Well, why don't I just let them tell the story." Jasmine and Evan stood up.

"Well, I was pretty sick," he began. "I was diagnosed with HIV, and it was awful. You know, I knew I was dead. I didn't want to live. My wife didn't have it, but she stayed with me and told me that all we could do was pray. Right, honey?" Jasmine nodded yes. "So, we prayed, and seven weeks later, I think I'm dying, right? But I'm not dying at all. What is happening is I have to stop taking the HIV medicine because it's killing me. I have been healed, and there is no reason for me to be taking the stuff."

Jasmine shouted. "Praise our Lord and Savior! Tell them!"

Evan continued talking. "It was like poison to my bones! I had to stop taking that stuff. The doctor said I don't have nothing; I have a clean bill of health." Jamal jumped up and start to shout "Hallelujah!" and the rest of the church followed in with clapping.

At that moment, Summer fell out in the Holy Ghost, and as soon as Mike picked her up, he fell out in the Holy Ghost. Around this time, the choir director was screaming and jumping in the Holy Ghost and fanning himself like there was no tomorrow. "Praise God! Praise God!" A few minutes later, he laid out with the Holy Ghost for a brief second and suddenly jumped back up, instructing the choir to shout. The choir shouted "Praise God!" The choir director fell out again and immediately stood back up with the same instructions to the choir, "Shout 'Praise God!'" As soon as the choir shouted "God," he fell back down in the Holy Spirit.

"Oh my God, girl. Why Daddy let this fool direct the choir?" Jasmine said.

"Girl, why you playing, Jasmine? He the best singer in town," said Summer.

Jasmine responded. "I know, but look at this nut, will you?"

"Maybe his redemption draws near," said Mia.

"Yea, um, I guess you're right." The three ladies laughed so hard, they didn't even notice Jamal had given the benediction and church was over until Imani walked over.

Imani looked at the girls curiously. Before she could ask what they were up to, Summer stared at Imani, then said, "Imani, you think he had HIV for real?"

Imani shrugged her shoulders. "I don't know. He was pretty sick, but then again, God can do all things, right?"

"That he can!"

Chapter Sixty

"Did you think you could get away with an affair right under my nose?" Imani spat.

"There was no affair," Jamal replied nonchalantly.

"Okay. Then why did Ann feel the need to sit in my seat, as if to make some type of statement that she had just cause to be there?"

"I don't know what Ann felt or why she did it!"

"Oh, yes you do, and you're going to tell me, unless you want me to get the girls involved. They have been upset with you for some time, and I thought they were just being unbearable, but now I see it's more."

"It's not what you think. Ann—well, Mrs. Ann—needed counseling, but she started to get a little personal, so I told her I wanted to include you, but she wasn't comfortable telling such things to you."

"Such things like what?"

"Well, she was explaining how she was a good wife and how she takes care of her husband but he neglects her."

"Okay, and why wouldn't she be comfortable with me hearing that?"

"It was about what she does in bed with her husband."

"And you couldn't see the trap in that? You couldn't see what she was up to? Of course you did, you idiot! When will you change? Preacher or not, you wanted her to pursue you or things to go over the line or whatever!"

"Nothing happened, I swear. She kissed me is all."

"Kissed you?" Imani rolled her neck with a bewildered look.

"I didn't kiss her back."

"Kissed you when?"

"That night I needed to take the papers to one of the ministers."

"There was no minister there."

"Um."

"Um! Um! You lied to get out the house and meet her! You were considering having an affair. What stopped you, the fact that she exposed herself today?"

"I wasn't going to have an affair!"

"You will never learn. I mean, the more I talk to you about the schemes of women, the more you fall. It's not because you can't see; you refuse to see. You don't have any strength but the strength God gives you. How can you play with fire and not eventually get burned?"

"I didn't do anything."

"You never do anything, let you tell it. But that's okay. You stay right there."

Imani went in the bathroom and fetched the anointing oil.

"What are you going to do with that?"

"Pray over you."

"So why you feel like you have to anoint me?"

"I'm going to get that devil out of you; that lust and adultery devil."

"Imani, go 'head now! You can't be playing around like that. I'm a preacher. I don't have no lust and adultery devil in me, woman!"

"Oh, yes you do!" Imani slapped oil on her hand and slapped Jamal so hard against his forehead, he stumbled back.

"Woman, have you lost your mind? Get off me!" All the while Imani was still holding with a fierce grip on Jamal's forehead and quoting scriptures and praying to God.

"Yea, though I walk through the valley of the shadow of death, I will fear no evil, for you are with me."

"Imani, I'm not playing. Get off of me!" Jamal slapped Imani's hand away and she got louder and regained her grip even harder this time.

"I demand that those lustful spirits and adultery spirits come out of him and go back to the pits of hell from which they came, in Jesus' name! Come out, in Jesus' name!"

Jamal pushed Imani's hand away and walked out the door.

"Jesus, please let him get sick to his stomach and get a headache as evidence that you have done this thing, and let him know it was by Your power and Your Will. Amen."

Chapter Sixty-One

"Just a minute," yelled Jasmine.

"Jasmine, get the door!" Evan called out.

"I'm getting the door, Evan!"

Jasmine opened the door and almost fell over, but then she composed herself quickly and realized she wasn't having an illusion. "Frisno, what are you doing here?"

"Evan called me and I needed to see him, according to his message," he responded dryly.

"What? Evan, come in here."

Evan entered the room. "Frisno, good. I'm glad you came."

"You are? Would you care sharing with me what this is about?" Jasmine replied.

"I'm sorry, honey," Evan said to his wife. He then turned back to Frisno. "Frisno, come in and have a seat."

Frisno looked over his shoulder as he slipped past Jasmine. He was in a linen baby blue outfit and Jasmine had to admit to herself that he even looked good in that.

"Jasmine, after what God did for us, I couldn't help but want to tell Frisno that he too can be healed. I didn't tell you I invited him over because I didn't want you to say no."

"You're right. I would have said no," Jasmine gritted.

"I can go," Frisno said as he watched the expression on Jasmine's face turn to a sneer."

"No, Frisno, we can pray for you, if you want." said Evan.

"I heard your story and I don't buy it. Only cats have nine lives. Evan, do you have nine lives?"

Evan looked confused.

"Didn't think so! So, if this is all you wanted, I have to go," Frisno said, getting ready to leave.

He looked frail beneath his clothes, and Jasmine began to feel sorry for him. She realized how he felt because they were just there.

"Frisno, it's true. Evan is no longer affected. I mean, what do you have to lose?" Jasmine told him.

"I have time to lose, Missy! I don't have time to be day-dreaming." Frisno's tone began to quiver. "I have to enjoy what God will let me have left."

"That is what we are trying to tell you, Frisno. Your time can be as long as anyone else going through this," Evan said to his friend.

Jasmine began to feel sick as she watched Evan touch Frisno's shoulders and talk to him like he would talk to a woman in need. Seeing him touch Frisno so tenderly made her wonder if he was completely healed of his one-time fling. Frisno stepped up and loosened himself from Evan's grip like a woman would.

Jasmine stepped in between Evan and Frisno. She touched Frisno's shoulders as Evan had done. "You have nothing to lose."

"Again, my time." Frisno looked at Jasmine and Evan with sadness in his eyes.

"Thanks for thinking of me; however, goodbye." Frisno left just as quickly as he had come.

Jasmine looked at Evan, annoyed. "Do you think you could have discussed this with me first?"

"I knew you would be against the idea."

"If you knew me so well, we wouldn't be in none of this mess in the first place."

"You were the one who asked me to pray. Shouldn't we show that same love to another one of God's children? No matter what the circumstance?"

Chapter Sixty-Two

After Jamal got back home from his argument with Imani, he lay in bed a few hours later with the covers over his head and his arm over his stomach.

"What's wrong with you?" Imani asked

"Wifeitis," he joked.

Imani laughed. She then turned and walked out of the bedroom. "Thank you, Lord."

It turned out that not only did Jamal have a bad day, but Mia finally broke down and went to the doctor.

"Why do I feel so full and sick, doctor?" Mia had asked the doctor.

"Mia, you're pregnant with twins," the doctor replied.

"With who whats!" Mia exclaimed.

"That's right, twins. I can't believe it myself."

Mia cried tears of joy. "Oh, thank you, doctor."

Mia rushed over to the beach where everyone waited for her for their mid-week get-together. She settled herself on a chair.

"Well, I finally found love," she said to the ladies.

"What you mean, Mia?" Jasmine asked her sister.

"Jazz, I wondered why God allowed so many things to happen to me. I always said why me? But I heard him say 'why not you?'"

"I don't get why you telling us this," said Summer.

"I get it," Imani broke in.

"Mani, I know you do. It took this much to happen to me before I realized that God is love. That family, children, men, nothing should be more important than Him."

"He's a jealous God," Imani added.

"Not only jealous, but He's a just God. He takes away and He gives. Even though

I've never been on track and times I wanted to curse God and die, He still blesses me."

"Yeah, I guess you're right," said Summer.

"Well, let's see. I have a house better than before. My husband and I are happy and I'm pregnant with twins." Mia smiled an enormous smile.

Jasmine spit what she was drinking from her mouth and she looked bewildered at Mia. Summer screamed, "What the hezzie did you say?"

Imani looked like she was about to pass out. "Girl, what did you just say?"

"Yep, He restored me and gave me one of the sevenfold blessings the Bible speaks of. It's like He said the storm is over now, and your faith has made you whole!"

"Oh my God! Hallelujah!" shouted Imani.

"God, Imani, I think that popped God's ear drums," said Jasmine.

"Mia, that's wonderful!" Summer exclaimed.

"Thanks, Summer."

"How Cashous feel about all these babies?" Jasmine asked.

"I haven't told him, but a first-time father, girl, he's going to be tore up from the floor up. I will tell him tonight."

"Ooh, can we come?" Summer asked.

"Naw. Let me tell my husband alone, please. I just had to share it with you all first because you been with me through it all."

"Yep, through it all," said Jasmine.

Imani then added, "Double for your trouble, baby; double for your trouble."

Chapter Sixty-Three

Summer and Mike were at home watching a late TV movie. "Mike, who was that?" Summer asked her husband as Mike hung up the phone.

"Summer, I already told you it was Kendra. Why you ask me the same question again?"

"It's almost twelve midnight. Why is Kendra calling this time of night?"

"She wanted to know if I could come over first thing in the morning to work on the report due Monday."

"But tomorrow is Saturday."

"I know it's Saturday, but the proposal is due Monday."

"Oh, all right. I see."

"Good night." Mike stood up and removed the blanket off of them they had been cozy in.

"What, you going to sleep? I mean, it's been a while. I was hoping, you know, we could fool around a bit."

"I'm tired, and you just heard me say I have to get up early and go over to Kendra's to work first thing in the morning."

"Why doesn't she come over here?"

"We can't get anything done over here."

"Why not?"

"Most of what we need is at her apartment."

"Maybe most of what *you* need is at her apartment."

"Don't start talking that mess to me. You always tripping, I swear."

"Why wouldn't I trip? It's been almost three months and we haven't had sex. I mean, are you gay, fooling around, or what? Perhaps you need to see a doctor."

"I don't need to see a doctor. I'm just fine."

"Then what is the problem?"

"Your mouth is the problem!"

"I mean, what is the deal? You touch me once a month, if that much. We are young and you act like you have no interest in sex."

"Who says I'm not having sex?"

"What?"

"I mean, you keep bringing up stupid accusations; maybe that is what you want to hear."

"Oh, it's what I want to hear, huh? Good night, Mike, and you can sleep on the couch."

"I think this is my house. Do you have a house where you can put someone on the chair? Otherwise, I sleep in the bed I paid for."

"You're stupid."

The phone rang, interrupting the argument. "Hello," Summer answered the phone. It was her sister-in-law.

"What's up, Jasmine?"

"Evan is acting like he's depressed since Frisno is doing his own thing, not trying to get better." Jasmine told Summer about the incident at their house when Evan invited Frisno over to pray.

"Jasmine, what you want me to do about it?" Summer asked with an irritated tone.

"Dag, what's your problem?"

"Nothing, I just don't feel like hearing about Evan considering all he has put you through. What can I tell you?" Summer never looked back at Mike as she grabbed the blanket and headed to the guest bedroom.

"Nothing, obviously. Looks like I need to be telling you something. What is bothering you?"

"Nothing, I'm just tired."

"All right. Well, call me later."

"Okay."

Mike peeped in the guest bedroom. "Who was that calling this late?"

Summer hesitated, then answered with a lie. "It was Kendra. She said she will have to finish up by herself on the proposal because she had something come up."

"Then why she couldn't tell me that herself?"

"I told her you were 'sleep."

"Well, I can call her in the morning."

"Call her for what? I just told you what she said."

"To see if there's anything she needs me to do. Unless that is a problem too."

"Whatever." Summer turned over and went to sleep.

Mike didn't know how to approach the lie Summer had just told since he told the initial lie about going over to Kendra's to work in the morning. He figured Summer knew he told a lie, but Summer just told the lie out of spite. In any event, Mike didn't have an excuse to leave the house in the morning; Summer had just shot that to hell, and all he was going to do was go fishing alone. But since he went so often and knew he neglected Summer, he made up a lie.

"Darn, a lie never pays off, and on top of it, two lies beat all; I still don't get none tonight."

Chapter Sixty-Four

Mia struggled to carry the twins. Never did she believe someone could feel so miserable all the time. Cashous sometimes seemed excited and other times very withdrawn. Mia sat and she thought; she was five months pregnant and was on bed rest for the remainder of her pregnancy. The time off was with pay, but she could not bring in overtime money, which she had grown quite accustomed to. Mia was sure she wouldn't carry the babies to term, and she wanted to be prepared. This setback had taken her off schedule to have the babies' room ready and get all the shopping done. Now it was up to Summer, Imani and Jasmine to fill in the gap, since she could not do excessive walking or moving. Mia knew God was faithful, but she wondered what had she manifested with her thoughts. The months seemed to pass by so slowly.

"Geez, I am going to drive myself crazy looking at the walls," Mia said.

"Mia, it's not that bad," Cashous told her.

With a flustered look, Mia responded, "How you know, Cash? You ever been on bed rest with twins?"

"That is all you have to worry about? How about double everything with twins? The least you can do is try and bring them here healthy."

"You got all the answers, don't you?"

"That is not what I'm saying."

"Then say what you mean."

"Nothing, forget it."

"No, let's not forget it. You obviously have something to say."

"All right, the way I see it is we already live paycheck to paycheck now. So, how are we supposed to make it with two babies at one time and maintain our lifestyle?"

"Is that what you're worried about? Our lifestyle? We have more than enough; we are highly blessed, and of all people, you should know that. You sit with your head in that Bible so many days, but you don't really know who God is, do you?"

"Yeah, I know who He is."

"No, you don't. You haven't been through anything, so how you supposed to know him? You stay close to the line so you won't be the sinner. Yet, you don't step over the line to be sold out for God. You go to Bible study and you go to church to maintain the image of the holy and righteous. Yet, you don't even know Him."

"And I guess you do."

"I do. The same God who helped me live when I lost all my children and my life all at once is the same God who will help us make it now. He is Jehovah Jireh and you need to learn His ways."

"I can understand all that, but God gives us common sense, and I may have to pick up a second job, then where does that leave me time to see our new babies?"

"So, if God gives us common sense, He doesn't give us spiritual sight? Did he make a mistake with these babies, so now we have to see ourselves out of His mistake? Or do you think He knows the ending before the beginning and whatever He allows to come to us He is just and able to help us through it?"

"When did you become Juanita Bynum? You talk to me like I don't know the Word."

"Then act like you know the Word. Faith without works is dead. Don't put your stuff on me because you don't have faith to believe He will make a way. You're worried about our lifestyle. We are blessed. We have more than enough and it just means we have to cut out eating out all the time, and unnecessary spending, but that is the sacrifice you make for love."

"Look, I have to go out. It's not like you pay the bills anyway. What would you know?"

"I pay enough, and I bet you couldn't make it without what I do pay, so what's your point?"

"Nothing."

"Oh, you burn me to the core. It is amazing how you put your issues on everybody else for everybody else to deal with."

I understand, Lord, the fear he must feel as a man. I mean, I worry about bringing them here and caring for them, but he has them and me on top of his worries as a man. However, Your Word says You're just and able to perform that which we ask of You and believe it and that settles it. Thank You, Lord.

"Mia, I'm running out," Cashous told her, tired of arguing.

Mia wobbled her way up. "Going out where?" She followed Cashous.

"Anywhere but here."

"I mean, for what? Going somewhere else is supposed to make your life better? It sounds like we are the problem. You resent the babies and me because you have to help care for us. It's not like you will be doing it alone. I have income coming in too."

"And what is that you're bringing in, milk money? We have to still live and eat, right? I swear you don't get it!"

"No, I get it. I swear you can't know Jesus, because a little bit of trust would at least put you talking somewhere in proportion to having a little bit of faith. I don't hear it."

"See if you can hear this." Cashous slammed the door as he walked out.

Chapter Sixty-Five

Summer rolled over and looked at the bright sun shining through the guest bedroom window. She lazily eased out of bed and went into her and Mike's bedroom. She went to her closet and pulled out a sky blue suit and the shoes to match. She looked over at Mike, who was pretending to be 'sleep. She went and stood over his bedside. He moved slightly then opened his eyes to see Summer standing over him.

"Mike, you going to church with me today?"

"Naw, I think I'm going to skip church today," he responded sluggishly.

"You haven't been in a while," Summer protested.

"I don't need to go. Why you going?" asked Mike.

Summer threw her hands up slightly and gestured. "No big deal. I just feel better when I go."

"I feel better when I drink a beer," Mike joked.

"All right, but you need some kind of outlet to deal with life."

Mike sat up in the bed and looked at Summer. "If that is

true, I don't think it will be Christianity. It's the white man's religion."

"Mike, what in the devil are you talking about?" Summer exclaimed.

"I mean, Malcolm told me about the trick to get us over in their country to serve their white God," Mike said confidently about his source.

"Malcolm don't know Jack! He is trying to be like Malcolm X just because his name is Malcolm." Summer rolled her eyes in the top of head and shook her head at Mike.

"No, baby, I think he right. We got to stop eating that pork, and no happenings with them white devils, and we going to start going to the temple." Mike shook his head in complete agreement with his statement.

"Mike, what you going to the temple for? You still in their country. Carry your black ass to Africa and do your thing. Me, I'm going to church." Summer turned and grabbed her undergarments out of her dresser drawer, walking toward the bathroom.

"Cursing and all, still going to church, huh? You always got to be over-dramatic, but you know what I mean," Mike shouted as Summer walked out of sight.

Summer yelled from the bathroom, "Yep, that is the good thing about my God—I'm saved by righteousness and not by grace. I just have to keep on doing my best; He will do the rest. And by the way, I know what you said, but I'm going to eat what I want. And Muhammad never made a way for me when times were hard, but I know Jesus has."

"Ahhh! No, girl, that was gas." Mike shouted and rolled back down into the comforter.

"Then if I got gas, what you got?" Summer shouted back at her husband.

"I got the truth on my side!"

Summer peeped only her head out of the bathroom. "Okay, I tell you what; you go with your truth, and I will go with mine. Like my daddy always told us, I would hate to mess around talking about there ain't no heaven and find out there is a hell," she said softly.

"Girl, your daddy only saying what the white man told him."

"Mike, were you doing some type of drugs when Muhammad set you free?"

"How you know who set me free? He may have," he responded.

"Did you ask him?" Summer questioned.

"Why would I ask him to set me free when I didn't want to be free?"

"So the answer is no, you didn't ask him." Summer went back into the bathroom.

"What's your point?" Mike leaned over, trying to see Summer in the bathroom.

"Well, I asked Jesus and He answered me. If you have a God who doesn't answer your prayers, he isn't much of a God," Summer said proudly.

"You need to read the Koran then you will understand," replied Mike.

"I don't need to read no Koran! You need to go back through detox and clean the rest of that crack out your system."

"That was low. Oh, baby, that was real low," Mike whined.

"Whatever. I have to take a shower." Summer started her shower, got in and left Mike to his thoughts about salvation.

Chapter Sixty-Six

Evan came up with the idea for everyone to come over for a picnic at his attempt to preach Jesus to Frisno. Frisno could never turn down free food, and Imani agreed that because of the love of Jesus Christ and the miracle he performed on Evan, they should all do their part.

Imani said, "We were all feeling Frisno's pain only a couple of weeks ago. We shouldn't wish that on our worst enemy." The ladies all agreed. Jasmine was not thrilled, but she knew God would want her to be a disciple for Him in Frisno's time of need.

Frisno walked in and sat at the picnic table and looked around sluggishly. His weight was down to skin and bones and he walked with a cane.

"Frisno, you hungry?" Jasmine asked him.

"No, Jasmine. Thanks anyway, but I can't keep anything down, so why eat?"

"You taking your medicines?" asked Jasmine.

"Yeah, but they make me feel sick because I always have an empty stomach because I can't keep anything down," Frisno replied.

"Can't win for losing, huh?" Jasmine stated.

"Something like that," Frisno responded.

"I'm sorry to hear that. I can make you some tea and perhaps that will be okay?" Jasmine walked off to get the tea. Summer looked at her as she came toward the picnic table where she, Imani and Mia sat.

"Jasmine, don't tell me that is who I think it is," Mia asked.

"Mia, give it a break. He's dying from AIDS. Do you think now is the time to pick?"

"I'm not picking, but how do you even stand and look at him or be around him after what he did and what Evan did to you? I didn't think he would show up for real."

"Are you ever going to let that go? I know God spared my life and Evan's and it wasn't to be selfish. It's not about us; it's about God and His mercy that we need to share with the world."

"I hear you, but you're a bigger woman than I could ever be, 'cause my foot would be up his behind," Mia bragged.

"That's what makes you, you and me, me."

"All right," Mia said, while throwing her shoulders in the air.

"Mia, why you so hard on her?" Summer asked.

"Summer, I just don't understand it."

"Then just leave it alone. You don't have to understand everything; just go with it," Summer replied.

"I mean, can't we all get along?" said Imani. She laughed hilariously at herself.

Mia looked at her mom and shook her head, but continued on with her conversation with Summer. "Well, that is my sister; it might as well had been me."

Imani butted in. "But it wasn't you, and your sister is surviving and doing a darn good job at it too."

Mia shrugged her shoulders. "I guess you're right, Mani."

"I am right. When have I ever been wrong?" said Imani.

The women looked at one another, knowing none of them would have the nerve to answer that question.

They all nodded their head in agreement while murmuring, "Mm-hmm, yeah."

Frisno looked up from the table. "Look, ladies, you ain't whispering, so you might as well say it to my face."

Mia swung around like a robot and Imani, Summer and Jasmine turned slowly with delayed reactions. Jasmine was by Evan's side in an instant. "Evan, what the ham sandwich did he say?" She looked sternly at Evan like he better answer quickly. Evan just looked back at Jasmine blankly.

"I understand you're frustrated with your illness and all, but watch out with the attitude, Frisno," Mia stated. "And have some respect for my mother."

"I wasn't including your mother; just you three wannabe Charlie's Angels," he said, referring to Jasmine, Mia and Summer.

"Oh, no he didn't," said Summer.

"Frisno, that is enough," said Imani.

"It doesn't have to be enough. I can end his sorrow right now," said Summer.

"No one did this to you but you, Frisno," Jasmine finally said.

"But why you got to talk behind my back? At least talk to the hand!" Frisno held both his hands up as if to stop traffic and swirled his neck around in the opposite direction.

He dropped his hands wearily and slumped back over. The girls fell limp on one another, laughing.

"That is enough, I said!" Imani looked at all the parties involved. "You never know what will happen to you in your lives. Stop that foolish laughing, and Frisno, you never know who you may need from here on out. Let your words be few in the sight of a just God."

"A just God," Frisno said, looking away. "I guess my life is just."

Chapter Sixty-Seven

Mia managed to take the twins to seven and a half months of her pregnancy. They were born early; first the girl and then the boy.

"A girl and a boy!" hollered Cashous. "Hot dang, I got my girl and boy in one shot!"

Dr. Wynn began to speak. "Both your babies are five pounds each, and they look wonderful."

"They so tiny," said Mia.

"Honey, they are good, though. You hear Dr. Wynn?"

The nurse came up. "Do you have names yet?"

"Not quite. We need a little time to decide on the last few names we picked. We didn't expect them yet." Mia spoke wearily.

"Okay. They will be baby A and B with your last names." The nurse set the babies in each of Mia's arms. Mia looked down at her twins and she began to weep.

A tear came to Cashous's eye. "I know." He looked down at his twins. "You have given me so much. Thank you, Mia. I love you."

"God has given us so much."

It wasn't a second longer before Jasmine and Evan, Mike and Summer, Jamal and Imani ran through the door. Imani squealed, "Oh, my babies here!"

"They look like their Aunt Jasmine. They so beautiful!" Jasmine exclaimed.

"Now, Jasmine, why you want to say those babies look like raccoons?" Mike joked.

"Shut up, Mike."

"Oh, my baby so funny and cute!"

Jasmine put her finger to her mouth as if she had to throw up. "Please, I just ate."

"Both of you are wrong. They look like their precious Aunt Summer. Yes, they are so cute."

"Summer, how did your blood get in this?" Imani asked.

Summer looked stunned. "Oh, no you didn't go there, Imani. I have told you about being grown. Mike, she going to make me take it outside," Summer stated.

"Summer, sit down somewhere, girl," Mike said.

"Y'all always got to play. Shut that noise up in here. Cashous, bring them babies over here to Grandma and let me hold them," Imani demanded.

"Be careful, Ma. They so tiny," said Cashous.

"Mm-hmm, I got them. I had three tiny ones of my own," Imani replied.

One of the babies began to cough excessively; she began to turn blue. Mia had crawled to her feet, and Imani was holding the baby in the palm of her hand and patting her back.

"Call the nurse, Cashous!" Mia yelled.

Cashous ran for help.

"Help, my baby is choking," he said nervously to the nurse.

The nurse ran in and grabbed the little baby. She patted the baby very hard and her color came back. Mia held the bed with a look of terror. The tears streamed down her face. "Is she okay?" Mia asked between sobs.

Cashous grabbed her closely.

"Yes, she just got strangled like little ones can do in their first hour of birth. She has to learn how to swallow as well. She's just fine," said the nurse.

"Thank God!" said Mia.

"I figured she had just choked," said Imani.

She gave Mia the little baby girl, and she began to weep and could not get herself together.

"Mia, stop crying. She's okay," Imani said as she stroked her daughter's head.

Jamal went over and rubbed Mia on the head. "She just takes after her papa. If one of them didn't choke before I left this room, I would have sent both of them packing." Jamal laughed. "Yeah, that's right, I said it."

"Mmph," spoke Mike.

"Was that supposed to be funny?" Jasmine asked.

"Jasmine, you will have my talents one day. Don't hate," said her father.

"Oh my God! Jasmine, Jamal told you don't hate!" Summer laughed out loud.

"Summer, it wasn't that funny. Keep your day job, Daddy," Mike responded.

"Wooh! Its getting hot in here!" Imani blurted out of nowhere.

"Ma, it's thirty-five degrees outside and even colder in here," said Mia.

"Shoot, Mia, you stay cold and you don't know what I feel anyways." Imani started taking off her sweater and undoing her blouse.

"Dag, Mama, you getting ready to give Daddy a strip tease?" said Mike.

"I can. He would like that." Imani strutted across the

room in model form. Jamal looked and shook his head with a smirk.

"Whoof!" Mike startled the babies and they jumped. "Oops."

Summer and Mia laughed hilariously.

"I don't know what you're talking about. Like my sister said, who ever seen a model with big legs?"

While Imani talked, she started to dress again.

"Imani, what the devil is wrong with you?" Summer asked intently.

Imani looked up in the sky with frustration. "Why don't you all mind your business, please?"

"Whatever it is, I hope she take it with her when she go," said Summer.

Imani rolled her eyes at the girls. Mia, Summer and Jasmine exchanged looks with Mike.

"Well, Mia and Cashous, have you given the babies names yet?" said Imani

"We haven't decided yet," Mia answered.

"Cashous, you all had almost eight months to decide," Summer stated.

"We just haven't picked out of the ones we chose. We wanted to see them first."

"So, what you going with, Mia?" Jasmine asked.

"Don't know, Jasmine," she replied to her sister.

"Poor babies," Mike said out loud.

"Shut up, Mike. You got a name and nobody still know who you are," Mia said jokingly.

"Girl, you are crazy. I'm more famous than Stevie Wonder. You didn't see that crowd of girls following me down the hall?" Mike ran to the door and looked both ways down the hall as if to see if women were there.

"Like heck there is," said Summer

"She ain't got used to it yet, being a groupie and all. I told her I married her, so she's safe," Mike teased Summer.

"A crowd of flies, more like it." Jasmine rolled her eyes at her brother in a friendly manner.

"Jasmine, kiss my foot."

"Oh, it's your foot now since Mommy and Daddy here."

"It's always my foot. Anyway, Summer and I got to go. Let's go, groupie."

"Mike, I can't stand you."

"Yeah, we going too, before I pass out. Come on, Jamal."

"Well, I know I'm going before she pass out."

They all kissed Mia goodbye.

Cashous laid the babies in the hospital beds and Mia drifted off to sleep. Cashous lay across the bed and held his wife. "You're right," he said to his sleeping wife. "God will take care of us."

Chapter Sixty-Eight

Frisno had called several times since the cookout and made peace with Jasmine and the other women. They decided that they would do what was right in their hearts and in God's heart and be the family he didn't have. Frisno decided to pop up at Jasmine and Evan's house.

"Frisno, hey, honey!" Jasmine said.

"Hey, Jasmine," Frisno replied.

Jasmine stepped aside to let Frisno in while speaking. "You look good."

"You don't look so bad yourself." Frisno spoke as he walked in.

Frisno is looking well and fine, Jasmine thought.

Frisno noticed her staring at him and practically read her mind. "My features are very defined, aren't they?"

"They are," Jasmine said in amazement.

"So, what are you doing?" Frisno asked Jasmine as he took a seat on the couch.

"Just waiting for Roselyn to come over," Jasmine answered.

"Who's she?" Frisno asked in curiosity.

"A coworker of mine."

The doorbell rang.

"Speak of the devil herself, there she is."

Roselyn walked in, and all of a sudden, Frisno manned up and stood tall.

"Hello," he said in a deep and unfamiliar voice. Jasmine almost stumbled over as she looked at Frisno over her shoulder in shock.

"Hello," Roselyn said softly and seductively.

Still in shock, Jasmine introduced them. "Roselyn, this is Frisno."

"Nice to meet you, Frisno," Roselyn said. She extended her hand toward Frisno.

Frisno kissed the back of her hand, and replied, "I'm pleased to make your acquaintance."

"Well, Frisno, I'm on my way out. You coming?" Jasmine asked her friend.

"Yeah, I will hang with you girls for a moment," he answered.

The three went out the door and went to an outside café by the beach. Roselyn was captivated by Frisno.

"So, Frisno, what do you do for a living?" Roselyn asked him.

"I paint a little here and there. I have begun to really try and captivate the beauty of life. Life is not promised, you know," Frisno responded proudly.

"Wow, that is so beautiful," Roselyn exclaimed.

"Thanks. If you don't mind me saying, you're beautiful too." Frisno looked at Roselyn up and down.

Roselyn blushed. "Thank you, Frisno."

"Frisno, you mind if I see you alone for a moment?" Jasmine stood up.

"Sure, I have to go to the men's room anyway."

"I have to go to the restroom myself. If you can hold it, Frisno, may I?" Roselyn said.

"Sure." Frisno watched as Roselyn walked toward the restrooms.

"Frisno, what in the devil has gotten into you?" Jasmine spat.

"What?" Frisno squealed in his girlish way.

"What?" Jasmine imitated Frisno's behavior. "You know exactly what I mean. You turn from drag queen to Billy Dee."

"I'm just enjoying her company."

"Oh, so is that what you were doing when you went for my husband?"

Frisno put his finger in the air and began to swirl his neck aggressively. "Oh, no you didn't go there! Wait a darn minute, Jasmine. Now, that isn't fair!"

"No, you're right. I apologize, but I'm not understanding. You play with people like this?"

"I do not play with people like this or like that. Truth is, I have been missing the company of a woman lately and the feeling of being a man. I've been thinking I can't change who I am, but as sick as I have gotten and may become again, one day I want to have family—children, you know?"

"Where is this coming from, Frisno? Is this just the fear of dying or what is it?"

"It may be, but if I am going to die, I want to at least have a child that can carry on my legacy—the beautiful experience of living through a child forever."

"With technology, there is a way I'm sure, but what does Roselyn have to do with this? I mean, you're not thinking of trying to get her to carry your child, are you?"

"No, of course not; just practicing up on my man skills."

"Well."

Roselyn broke the conversation as she walked up. "Is everything okay?"

Frisno stood up and went back to his man voice. "Everything's good." He pulled out her seat for her and smiled a devilish smile.

Chapter Sixty-Nine

Cashous felt a little agitated as he ran through the grocery store to get milk and Pampers again. The babies were the joy of his life. They named them Ailjon and Angelina; however, they were more expensive than he had anticipated. They were growing like weeds, and the price of milk and Pampers seemed to go up every other day. It seemed all his money went to the bills and to feeding the family. Cashous felt overwhelmed, and it seemed as if the walls were closing in around him. He couldn't tell Mia he was beyond his limitation and stressed beyond belief because being a man meant withstanding the pressures of life and finding a way to provide for his family.

"Man, life is hard. I can't win for losing. I always wanted kids and I got two in one strike. Lord, please help me see my way. I know I don't talk to You that much lately, but if You help me just a little bit, I won't forget to give You your glory," Cashous prayed.

"Cashous, what's up, man?" Cashous heard a male voice say from behind him.

"Evan, what you know good?" Cashous replied, giving Evan a hand slap.

"I can't call it. What's going on with you besides the obvious?" He pointed to the items Cashous had to pick up.

"That's it, man. Baby Pampers, baby milk, babies, babies, babies."

"You killed two birds with one stone, stud muffin!"

"Make it do what it do, baby."

"Hey, I'm having a few guys over for the game tonight. Won't you come by?"

"I'm not sure I should leave Mia at home with the babies. She still gets quite tired, and they are only two months. She hasn't got used to having twins yet."

"How about I ask Jasmine to come over for a few hours with Mia while you hang with us for a few?"

"Deal. I'll see you around eight."

"Okay. Later."

"Later."

Cashous went home hoping Mia wouldn't flip when he decided he wanted to spend a night with the guys.

Chapter Seventy

"What is it, Doc?"

"You're in stage four of prostate cancer."

"What?" Jamal's heart felt as if it stopped. His heartbeat went irregular.

"Your family history indicates it's not common, so let us do a few more tests. Of course, we will have to operate, but the rest is up to faith."

"But I didn't have any signs or pains; nothing."

"I'm sorry, Jamal."

"I know, Doc, but I confess Satan is a liar. I will be all right."

"That is fine, but in the meantime, you will have to be admitted."

"Admitted?"

"Immediately. Perhaps you should call your wife. I will give you a few minutes alone."

Jamal sat for a few moments. He pulled out his cell phone and called Imani. His voice trembled as he spoke.

"Imani, can you come down to the hospital?" Jamal said, almost in a whisper.

"Sure, what's up?" Imani exclaimed.

Nervously, Jamal answered, "The doctor says I have to be admitted to the hospital immediately."

"For what?" Imani asked anxiously.

"The doctor says I have prostate cancer and it's in the last stages."

"Prostate cancer? Jamal, we know Satan is a liar," his wife protested.

"I know." His response was dry and unconvincing. "You coming?" he asked his wife with urgency.

"Of course. I'm on my way."

Imani hung up the phone and tried to regain her composure. What would she do without Jamal? "Later stages?" she moaned out loud. "It has to be a mistake. God is too good to let this happen."

While Imani was on her way to the hospital, Mia was over the stool again for the third time this week. She didn't know what it could be since she was getting sick all times of the day for the last few weeks. She stayed so stressed all the time she figured she must really get her some rest, take it easy and stop stressing. She decided rest was what she needed; however, she was scared it was something more serious, since she was also losing weight. How much could one girl take in one lifetime?

Imani ran into the surgical unit of the hospital and Jamal was dressed in surgical wear and in an assigned bed already.

"They were just waiting for you," Jamal said as he reached for Imani's hand.

"Why? I mean, why you in surgical clothes already?" Imani asked fearfully.

"They need you to sign some papers and the doctor said it's best to do this right now. They're not sure at this stage if my body is strong enough to withstand the surgery," Jamal stated.

"Of course it is. You are healthy as a horse," Imani said with an upbeat tone.

"That is what I told them. They said there's always a risk with surgery."

"We know that, but we got the doctor on our side that has never lost one patient." Imani pointed her finger up.

"It's normal procedure for them to tell everyone that. I will be fine," Jamal assured Imani because of the look of fear in her eyes. "Remember who our God is. His name is Jesus, a name above all names."

"I know. I love you," Imani answered with a little more assurance.

The nurse walked in while Imani and Jamal were still talking.

"Love you too. See you when I come out."

The nurse took the papers from Imani's hands. She then gave Imani a nod and they turned and wheeled Jamal away. Imani sat in the chair, trying to absorb what had happened in a matter of an hour's time.

Could something possibly go wrong? she thought. *What do they mean 'strong enough'? Should I call the girls? No, I will wait until he comes out of surgery. No need to worry them; he is coming out fine.*

Chapter Seventy-One

Cashous rang Evan's doorbell. Evan opened the door to smoke, beer and cards with three other fellows.

"What it be like, baby!" Evan yelled out to Cashous.

"I made it, man," said Cashous.

"Good. Come on in," Evan said as he moved to the side and extended his arm out toward the card table.

"You know I ain't into all of this," Cashous spoke while walking toward the table and looking back at Evan, who was closing the door.

"I know. Just let your hair down and chill a few," Evan responded. Evan was swinging his hand around Cashous' head like he was styling it.

"All right, I got you," exclaimed Cashous.

"A'ight. Damon, Brock, and Chuck, this is my man, Cash," Evan introduced.

"What's up, man?" Chuck asked Cashous.

"Nothing much. What we playing?" asked Cashous in return.

"Nothing for real; just don't want to look like chicks while we express ourselves. The only thing we really know how to play is Go Fish," Brock responded with an embarrassed look on his face.

"Dag, that is sad," Cashous responded.

Evan added, "You know how we do. We businessmen."

"Yeah, you know, so we just holding the cards," Brock said. "Right, Chuck?"

"Yeah, but we drinking the beers, right?" Chuck confirmed.

"Oh, heck yeah!" Evan shouted.

"So lay it down. What's on your mind, Cash?" Evan said.

"Man, life. We can't even live at my house because of the price of milk, electricity, food, Pampers, car payments. Should I go on?" Cashous intensely answered.

Chuck followed quickly, adding, "I believe if they can't get us where it hurts by our color, since we have educated ourselves and are well-rounded and developed men, they hit us with our children and our livelihoods. We can't even have kids to carry on the generations because it's hard to raise and feed them in this day and time. How can we reproduce when we can't afford them? That is the reason why so many women get abortions. It cost too much to keep them."

"Yeah, black women genocide, and no-good daddies. I mean, let's be real. These young dudes ain't hitting on nothing these days," Evan responded.

"Okay, but it goes deeper than that. This whole 'man' thing gets heavy," Brock added.

"I feel you. I work, I work and I work, and sometimes my white coworkers with five kids live in a bigger house, got more cars and can still take two-week vacations in Disney World and we work at the same company, in the same position. Does it take a genius to know the white man gets paid more? He can't budget that well," Cashous stated.

"It's like Brock said; it's deeper than that. It's almost like we are not supposed to have a family, much less the privileges associated with having a family."

"The pressure is rough," Damon finally added.

"Make me want to rob a bank sometimes," Evan exclaimed.

"I know, Evan. I'm tired of robbing Peter to pay Paul."

"What's a black man to do?" asked Damon.

"My man, far as I can see, we doing it. Keep it moving," said Chuck.

"Cheers to that."

The men leaned back and sipped their beers again.

Chapter Seventy-Two

Summer and Mike were loading the last of their things in the trunk of their car in front of their house when Kendra, Mike's coworker pulled into the driveway. As she pulled up, Summer took her seat in the front of the car. Mike took Kendra's bags to the truck.

"Summer, do you mind if I sit in the front? I have some numbers I need to go over with Mike," she asked.

"Sure, go ahead." Summer mumbled "heifer" under her breath to Kendra.

"Excuse me?" Kendra asked.

"Oh, I didn't say anything." She mumbled "heifer" again.

"Did you call me heifer?" Kendra asked, astonished.

"Is that what you heard?" Summer looked questionably at Kendra.

"Well, I thought. . . ."

"Get in the car, ladies. We are running behind," Mike said, interrupting the little spat.

Summer noticed Kendra's strikingly beautiful body. She had short hair and looked like a black Imani. *This heifer is with my husband all day*, she thought.

Kendra turned and looked at Summer. "Why did you say you were going with us on this business trip?"

"Because I want to. Did I need another reason?" Summer answered cunningly.

"Oh, no, I'm just saying we have so much work to do. We will be busy most of the day," Kendra responded.

"Mike told me two days, and the rest of the days were his and mine," exclaimed Summer.

"Mike, are you sure we can finish in two days?" Kendra questioned.

"Yeah, Kendra. We're almost finished now. We only have two presentations. I wasn't sure why you planned three extra days in the first place, but since it's on the company, I figure we might as well make the most of it," Mike said.

"I thought we may run over or need more time." Kendra stared at Mike for a response.

"Bull," Summer said.

Mike laughed and Kendra pulled out her numbers and started talking business.

Chapter Seventy-Three

While Mia's parents were going through a crisis, Frisno had worked his magic on Roselyn and got her to accept his invitation on a date.

Roselyn and he were at the club dancing, and Frisno held Roselyn close on the dance floor.

"This is nice, being close to you like this," Roselyn said shyly.

"It sure is," Frisno agreed.

"So, Frisno, where you been all my life?"

"I been most of the places you've been, I'm sure. Just wasn't your time to see me," he said seriously.

"How do you know it's time now?" asked Roselyn.

"Oh, believe me, I know. Life is not promised to anyone; we have to take what we want when the opportunity knocks," Frisno stated.

"I believe you're knocking." Roselyn flirted with Frisno.

"I am." Frisno grinned. He leaned over and kissed Roselyn.

"Um, that was nice. It seems like you know what a woman wants," Rosleyn said, staring in Frisno's eyes.

"I know. It seems we are so connected, right?" responded Frisno.

"I wish this feeling could last forever," Roselyn said while laying her head on Frisno's chest.

"A lasting feeling is what I'm after. You know, something to last forever or someone to carry on my name," blurted out Frisno.

"My goodness, you think like that? Most men run from such topics," Roselyn exclaimed.

"I'm not most men." Frisno smiled.

"Amen to that. My cell phone is buzzing. Let me get that." Roselyn looked down at her cell phone. "It's Jasmine," Roselyn said.

"Jasmine doesn't want anything. Call her back later. You're all mine now."

"But we haven't talked much at all. I've been seeing you. Not that I'm complaining—let me see what she wants." Roselyn answered the phone. "Hey, Jasmine, what's up, girl?"

"Hey, Roselyn, how you doing?" Jasmine asked.

"Good. Me and Frisno are at the club," Roselyn said, excited.

"That is why I called. Can you call me back as soon as he drops you off tonight? I have something to tell you," Jasmine demanded.

"All right. I will call you back," Roselyn agreed.

"Promise, Roselyn. You been saying that a lot lately. We have to talk," said Jasmine.

"I promise."

"Okay. Bye." Jasmine hung up.

"Is everything okay?" Frisno asked Roselyn after she ended her call with Jasmine.

"Yeah, she wants to talk girl talk, I'm sure. I will call her back tomorrow."

"Cool."

Jasmine paced the floor of her home. It was a quiet night

around their house and the TV was on softly in the background. Jasmine sat behind the kitchen counter and just held the phone in her hand. She looked up at Evan with a concerned look.

"Did you get her?" Evan asked.

"I got her, but she said she will call me back tonight when Frisno drops her off."

"Are you sure you want to tell her, Jasmine? I mean, maybe he told her already and they just hanging out. Then you would have betrayed his trust."

"Well, if he told her, then it's no problem. I have nothing to worry about. I just would feel better if I knew he told her," Jasmine responded.

"All right, it's your call," Evan said.

Back at the hospital, Imani was sitting nervously, and it seemed like all night and day had passed. The nurse came out. "Madam, is there anyone who can come up here with you?" she asked Imani.

"Why? What's going on with Jamal? Is the surgery over?" Imani replied.

"I'm sorry."

Imani felt shaken and the nurse helped her to her seat.

"He slipped into a coma during the surgery."

Imani stared off. After a few minutes, she spoke. "What does that mean? I mean, didn't you get the cancer?"

"We did, but somehow he wouldn't wake up from the anesthesia."

"So, how long will he be in this coma?"

"It could be a few hours to a few months, or years. We never know with a coma."

"Can I see him?"

"Yes. Can I get you anything?"

"Yes. Call this number, please. Tell my oldest daughter to call the others. Her name is Jasmine."

Imani walked in the room and stood over Jamal. It was weird seeing him so still. She laid her head over his bed and began to cry and sing, "Nothing But the Blood of Jesus." She recalled in her mind the moments she and Jamal and their family had shared.

About half an hour later, Jasmine, Evan, Mike, Summer, Mia and Cashous walked in and broke her thoughts.

"Is he going to be all right?" Mia asked sadly.

"Yes, Mia. The nurse said he will come around," Imani replied.

"What if he doesn't? Why didn't you call us before he went into surgery?" said Jasmine.

"For what? What could you have done?" Imani looked at her daughter and questioned her.

"Maybe see him before he went into a coma!" Mia yelled at Imani.

"Mia, you will see him again, and not in a coma," Imani said sternly.

"But Mani, you don't know that. You should have called us," Mike added.

"Okay, Mike, it's done now. Let's not get on each other's nerves. We have to pray he will come out this coma like yesterday," said Summer. "How is he doing?" she asked Imani.

"He's stable, but they're not sure why he slipped into a coma," said Imani.

"Well did they say about how long he could be in this coma?" Mia asked.

"They are not sure."

Evan walked over and put his hand on Imani's shoulder. "Be strong, Mrs. Imani. He will come around."

"I know he will, Evan. Thank you."

Chapter Seventy-Four

Evan walked in the house, yelling at the top of his lungs. "Yo, Jasmine!"

No answer.

"Yo, Jasmine!"

He ran upstairs, and there was Jasmine on her knees. She hadn't responded because she was in the midst of her prayer.

"God, You said a family that prays together, stays together. I've seen Mani and Daddy praying. We've served together and worshipped together. I may not be sold out for You, Jesus, like I should be, but You're real and I know You are, and I need You to touch Daddy and wake him up for even a sinner like me. You said ask and it shall be done; I'm asking in Jesus' name."

Evan turned and walked out. The phone rang. Jasmine got up off of her knees and answered it.

"Hey, Jasmine, it's Mommy. Come to the hospital and call your sister and brother."

"Okay. What's wrong?"

"Just come. You will see when you get here."

"Okay."

Jasmine couldn't read Imani's emotions. She did a three-way and did what Imani had asked her. She then went and found her husband.

"Evan, come take me to the hospital."

"What's up?" Evan asked.

"Just come on."

"I'm on my way, baby."

Jasmine had called Mia and Summer. Summer called Mike. "Mike, where are you?"

"At work. Where am I supposed to be?"

"I called your work phone and you didn't answer."

"I said at work. Can I get every call?" Mike exclaimed.

"Your mom said to come to the hospital."

"What's wrong?"

"I don't know. Jasmine only said your mom said we would see when we got there."

"I'll meet you there."

"Why can't you come get me?" Summer whined.

"Kendra is at the doctor's office and she's ready to be picked up."

"What the . . . What you mean Kendra need you to pick her up at the doctor's office?"

"She forget she had an appointment while we were out, so I dropped her off before I came back to the office."

"Then she needs to find a way from there."

"Look, Summer, I will meet you there. You tripping about nothing." Mike hung up.

Summer grabbed her keys and headed to the hospital. She pulled up at the hospital and waited for Mike. Mike pulled up and he and Kendra got out.

"Why is she here?" Summer asked Mike.

"Oh, I told him not to bother to drop me off. He can do it after we leave here," Kendra answered before Mike could speak.

"Oh, you did, huh?" Summer looked sternly at Kendra and then back at Mike. "Mike, you can't think for yourself, so I'm going to help you out. Kendra, we don't need you here for this type of occasion. It is a very private matter." Summer looked back at Kendra and said, "So you can go."

"Mike didn't say that," Kendra protested.

"Mike didn't say this either. You're fired!" Summer yelled.

"You can't fire me!" Kendra yelled back at Summer.

Summer turned to look back at Mike. "Mike, tell her she is fired."

"What?" Mike asked, dumbfounded.

"Let me say it again. You want my husband, you come to the hospital with my family, and you impose upon our privacy. Tell her, Mike. She is fired."

"Look, Kendra, take this money for a taxi." Mike pulled out some money and handed it to Kendra. "I will talk to you later. Just go," Mike said impatiently.

"Just go? Negro, what?" Kendra placed her hands on her hips and looked at Mike, waiting for a response.

"Hold up, Negro who?" Summer pulled off her shoes.

Mike looked over at Summer and held his hand up as to get her attention. "Wait, Summer, I got this." He turned to look at Kendra. "You're fired, and give me back my money." Mike snatched the money out of Kendra's hand.

"Yeah, catch a cab with those strings hanging from your dress you call legs!"

Mike looked at Summer. "No. That wasn't funny."

"That wasn't good?"

"Nooo!" Mike exclaimed.

"Hey, guys." Jasmine and Evan walked up. "Wasn't that your coworker, Mike?"

"Was," He told Evan.

"What?" Evan asked.

"Later. Let's go in," Mike said while walking toward the hospital.

"Wait for us!" Mia and Cashous walked behind them.

"Anybody know what's wrong?" Mia asked.

"Nope," Summer responded.

They all walked in. When they walked in his hospital room, Jamal greeted them from his bed. "What's up, kiddos?"

"Daddy!" Mia screamed. They all rushed up to Jamal.

Imani stood with tears in her eyes.

"Our God is still alive, and He still answers prayers," Imani said.

Evan stood back and looked. "What's wrong, Evan?" Imani asked.

"I just saw my wife praying a few hours ago for her God to wake Daddy. And now Jamal is up."

Jasmine looked over from where she stood at Jamal's bed. "I believe Jesus is the way," she said.

Jamal spoke. "Come here, Evan. I know He's the way. I could feel His presence the entire time I was 'sleep. Do you believe that?"

"I do. I believe," Evan responded.

"Would you like to receive Jesus as your Savior now?" Jamal asked Evan.

"I would," Evan responded.

"Just repeat after me. If you confess with your mouth the Lord Jesus and believe in your heart that God has raised Him from the dead, you will be saved. For with the heart, one believes unto righteousness, and with the mouth, confession is made unto salvation."

"I believe and I confess Jesus Christ is Lord, and God raised Him from the dead," Jamal said. "That's it."

Evan smiled and said, "Glad to have you back, Dad."

"Good to be back."

Chapter Seventy-Five

Roselyn laid in Frisno's arms in her apartment. She felt like a new woman after being intimate with Frisno. Frisno laid with his arms behind his head, looking at the ceiling. Roselyn broke the silence between them.

"That was nice," she said.

"Roselyn, yes, it was. I didn't remember what I was missing."

"Frisno, it couldn't have been that long," she exclaimed.

"Yeah, it was that long, and it was worth the wait." Frisno looked down at Roselyn.

"I believe you, and that is why I couldn't resist going bare with you," snickered Roselyn.

"I know, but I didn't pull back, so a little Frisno may be running around soon." Frisno laughed.

"That is okay. When it's right, it's right," Roselyn commented.

"Yeah, how could something that feels so good be wrong?" said Frisno.

"It can't," Roselyn stated.

"Roselyn, you don't know what you have done for me."

Frisno turned over on his side so he could look into Roselyn's eyes.

"Perhaps you don't know what you did for me?" Roselyn said as she rubbed her fingers up and down Frisno's chest.

"I have some idea. It makes me both happy and sad," Frisno said in a somber tone.

"Why sad?" Roselyn questioned.

"Because it can't last forever," Frisno answered.

"What are you talking about? Don't tell me after all this time you got what you wanted and now you're prepared to walk out of my life." Roselyn sat slightly up on her side and looked intently at Frisno.

"Never will I walk out of your life. This is a marriage now. Believe me, I'm with you until death do us part," Frisno said pulling her close to him.

"Are you serious?" Roselyn looked at Frisno with excitement.

"Yes, I'm serious. Let's get married."

"What?" Roselyn exclaimed.

"Yes, let's go to the justice of the peace and get married," Frisno said.

Frisno got down on one knee and proposed. "Will you marry me?"

"We've only been dating for three months. And I need to talk to Jasmine. I never did call her back last night. I have a feeling she wants to tell me we are moving too fast," Roselyn protested.

"What about you telling me about all the Mr. Wrongs, and life is too short to keep living alone? Remember all that? When it's right, it's right. Jasmine is my friend too, but she needs to mind her business. You can call Jasmine after the honeymoon. Just say you will be my wife. Besides, we got a year to annul if it doesn't work out." Frisno smiled at Roselyn with puppy dog eyes.

"Yes! Yes! Yes!" Roselyn screamed. "I will marry you on

one condition. This has to be our secret until we can do a real wedding with all our friends and family. Believe me, Jasmine or my mother will never speak to me again if they knew I made such a big decision without them."

"All right," Frisno agreed. "Get up and get ready. We got a few hours to catch the chapel."

Frisno felt relieved that Roselyn wasn't going to tell Jasmine they were married. It was one less headache he had to worry about.

Frisno and Roselyn were married in the few hours that followed. They came back home and spent days in bed together. Frisno grew weary of hiding medicine and getting up in the middle of the night to hide his night sweats. He told Roselyn he did his best work at night, so he did a lot of paintings, but it was beginning to show on his face that he was growing tired.

Once he knew for sure that it was a good chance Roselyn was pregnant, he decided to leave. He couldn't have held on much longer. His body was tired, and he felt weaker than he ever had since his illness, even though he managed to still hide it. Roselyn just began to ask him if he was getting enough rest and perhaps he should see the doctor. He knew his time was getting limited. A few days after that conversation, which was after a few months of honeymoon bliss, Frisno left Roselyn.

Chapter Seventy-Six

Frisno looked out the hospital window. Jasmine and Evan walked in.

"I'm glad you called us. I mean, it had been so long, I thought you had written us off," Jasmine said to her friend.

"Jasmine, now you know better than that. Not hardly, hun. I was just buying my time. You know, me and Roselyn and enjoying being a man again."

"Yes. About that, did you tell her?"

"Tell her what? Come on, Jasmine. We were just friends."

"Okay, I know. Besides, Evan convinced me it wasn't my place and I didn't want any tension between us, so I didn't. And she seems so happy with you in her life."

"Okay," Frisno said, exasperated. "Well, let's get this party started, shall we?"

The nurse walked in and started to unplug the cords from all over Frisno's frail body. "The rest is up to Him."

"Thank you, Annie, girl. You've been the best."

"God bless you, Frisno."

"He better, girl. I been talking to someone lately, and I hope He been listening."

The nurse waved a soft wave and walked out.

"Why haven't you been in touch for so long? How could anyone know you were sick?"

"Evan, get her before she get started. I told you, I just needed some me time."

"But you were doing so good. What happened?"

"Honey, I have been HIV positive for years. I have lived and I have been through the good and the bad. Baby, I'm tired of fighting. The least little things get me down too easily. My body is tired."

"What about Roselyn? She been there for you?" Jasmine asked.

"Haven't seen her either in about six weeks," Frisno replied.

"Funny, she didn't tell me any different. Although her conversations are so short, I hadn't had time to ask her if you and her were still dating. I figured she didn't want to be bothered. So the last time I called her about two weeks ago was the last time I attempted to talk with her."

"When she does call you, tell her I love her and thank you," Frisno said.

"Thank you for what?" Jasmine questioned.

"I feel it in my loins; she gave me something I never had before. She gave me a gift that I will cherish forever," Frisno replied.

"What kind of gift?" Jasmine asked curiously.

"Let's just say, the morning was not my best part of the day, and with my illness, it just kept going downhill, but it was worth it."

"I don't understand, man," Evan said.

"You will, Evan. You will. I took a leap of faith, and I'm hoping for a positive outcome with the remaining persons." Frisno took a deep breath and got very quiet. Jasmine and Evan looked very confused, but decided they should focus their attention on Frisno right now.

"You okay?" Jasmine asked.

"No. What is it that I need to do to make sure I meet Jesus when I close my eyes?"

Jasmine and Evan stood over the hospital bed and looked down at Frisno. He was frail, and his looks had deteriorated quickly.

"Are you ready to have this discussion about Jesus now?" Evan asked Frisno.

"Duh, sure, what do I have to lose? All my weight is gone and my hair, so whatever Jesus got, I need it," Frisno joked wearily.

"It's not that way," Jasmine added.

"It is for me. I didn't deserve this, but I do know there is such a thing as heaven and hell, so, shoot, baby. How do I do this salvation thing?"

"Do you believe in Jesus Christ?" Evan continued.

"Child, everybody knows Jesus Christ. I just didn't want to hear what He had to say at the time," Frisno answered.

"Do you confess Him as your Lord and Savior and believe He rose from the dead and He is the Son of God and He lives today?" Evan asked Frisno.

"Yes, I believe," Frisno answered.

"Confess it with your mouth." Jasmine looked at Frisno.

"Jasmine, I said I believe, okay? I believe Jesus is the Son of the living God and He rose from the dead, for me and for you."

"Then there you go; you're heaven bound," Evan concluded.

"Good, 'cause I'm ready. Jasmine, you take care of him, you hear? And Evan, you take care of her. I love you guys," Frisno said in a whisper.

"We love you too," Jasmine and Evan said in unison.

"Tell Roselyn I'm sorry and I said thank you."

"Now what are you talking about?" Jasmine asked softly.

"Sorry for leaving her and she will explain. I would like

her to get to say goodbye, so have her come to the funeral, will you?"

"Of course we will." Jasmine leaned over his bedside and rubbed his head. Evan grabbed his hand.

Jasmine whispered to Evan while Frisno lay there resting. "I believe he is a little delusional with all this 'tell Roselyn I'm sorry, and thank you.' He probably wishes she was here."

For the next couple of hours, Frisno lay there moaning quietly as Jasmine rubbed his head. He looked up at Jasmine and motioned for Evan to come closer. "This is it, you two. I'm going home to God, and the angel who is waiting for me is the most beautiful thing I have ever seen. Almost makes me wish I could have skipped this life of mine altogether and gone straight home to God." Frisno looked dazed in the eyes but tranquil and peaceful.

Before they could get to his bedside close enough to respond, Frisno closed his eyes and then he was gone.

"He always had to have the last word." Jasmine gave a little smile and then she wept.

The day of Frisno's burial had arrived, and it was a particularly beautiful fall day. Flowers of all sorts lined the church and were laid around the casket with a beautiful picture of Frisno. The church was standing room only.

Roselyn walked around the casket. Jasmine held her close. Evan looked both dazed and stunned as they viewed Frisno's body.

Evan's thoughts seemed to pound his mind. *It could have been me.* He broke down along with the ladies, except it was more on his own accord than the death of Frisno. He felt a sense of thankfulness that he couldn't keep quiet. He began to shout, "Thank you, Lord! Thank you, Lord!" Jasmine, being his wife of many years, patted his shoulder because she already knew his story.

Roselyn looked up between her tears. "Thank you for what?" she whispered.

"That Frisno didn't suffer long."

"Who knew that pneumonia could be so deadly these days with all the medicine out?" Roselyn said in disbelief.

"I know, Roselyn, I know," Jasmine said softly. She had told the lie to respect Frisno's privacy.

Roselyn began to weep again. Jasmine found herself comforting both Roselyn and Evan.

Mia, Summer and Imani sat behind Frisno's immediate family.

"I wonder who that woman is Jasmine is comforting?" Summer said.

"Maybe it's Frisno's sister or something. She is quite shook up, it seems," Mia answered.

"I don't know. Looks like Evan is quite shook up himself."

"Y'all, it's not hard to figure out. He's been through a lot. That could have been him or Jasmine laying in that casket. God is good, you know," Imani said.

"You're right," said Summer.

Jasmine came over. "Thank you guys for coming. I will call y'all later. I am going back to Frisno's family's house for a minute."

"All right," Mia answered, "but who is that lady who is with you and Evan?"

"She is a close friend of Frisno's. She was kind of like his girlfriend," Jasmine replied.

"Girlfriend?" the ladies whispered in unison.

"Go figure. Frisno was full of surprises," Summer said.

"All right, I will see you later," Jasmine said as she walked away from the women.

Jasmine and Evan looked at Roselyn curiously as she spoke. "I am a little more emotional than usual. And I know I can't seem to stop crying, but I lost so much when Frisno left my life. He didn't return my phone calls when he got sick. He didn't stay at his apartment, and when he was there, he didn't open the door. He kept saying he didn't want me to see him that way. But I told him I had some good news, but I needed to tell him face to face. He said he already knew and it was wonderful and he would always be with me. He gave up before he even gave it a fight. One minute he's sick, and the next he's gone. It almost seemed like he was tired already. He had so much to live for. Anyways, I've been wanting to tell you, but I wanted to tell Frisno first; until he up and disappeared on me. I'm pregnant with his child."

Jasmine looked like she had seen a ghost. "Roselyn, what did you say?"

"That's right. I'm pregnant with Frisno's baby."

"When did you find that out? I mean how, when?" Jasmine asked.

"Of course, you know we were intimate. We were in love. Why do you look so surprised? Not only in love; he was my husband." Roselyn looked at Jasmine and Evan.

"What? You and Frisno got married?" Jasmine exclaimed.

"Yes, sorry we didn't invite anyone. We wanted to keep it a secret until we were able to have a real wedding."

"Have you been to the doctor?" Jasmine asked quickly.

"Jasmine, I went the first day of my skipped menstrual cycle. I had a test done at the doctor's office. They did a blood test. I'm almost eight weeks."

"I think I'm going to be sick." Jasmine ran over to a nearby pew and took a seat.

"Evan, what is wrong with her?" Roselyn asked while holding her tissue to her mouth.

"It's just so much for her at once. She would have wanted Frisno to be here for this. Her emotions and all are getting the best of her, I'm sure," Evan replied.

"Well, it is what it is. The baby is due in July."

"I should go check on my wife."

Roselyn walked behind Evan. She asked, "Jasmine, are you okay?"

"Yes, I'm okay, but by chance, have you done all your tests and things they give you for the baby when you're pregnant?"

"Yes, millions of tests, right? Just because Frisno had got pneumonia and a little weak. The baby and I are fine."

"All of your tests came back fine?"

"Yes! What the heck is wrong with you? Why the third degree?"

"I'm sorry. I'm just freaking out. Nothing is wrong. I'm good," Jasmine said, relieved. "I mean, let me play the drama queen for just a minute, will you?" They both laughed.

The day was windy and cool as Jasmine and Evan walked out of the church. Summer, Mia and Imani stood on the stoop of the church.

"I thought you all were gone," Jasmine said to them.

"Not yet," Summer said. "We heard everything from the back of the church before we left."

Jasmine looked at everyone. "Well, the funeral is done and over with. Now what? What am I going to do?"

"Jasmine, do nothing. Frisno is gone and she has been tested and it came back negative. What else can you do?" asked Summer.

"Summer, it can take years for something like this to show up. She should know to prevent it in time."

"I agree with Summer, Jasmine. I mean, to spring this on her now is a little much," said Mia.

"But to not spring it on her, is that right?" Jasmine asked everyone, looking at someone for an answer.

"Well, I feel like you should let her be happy. You said it yourself that since you've known her she's never been happier. She is healthy and the baby is healthy, and if there was anything, the test would have revealed it by now, I'm sure," Evan said.

"But it's like committing her and her unborn to death," exclaimed Jasmine.

"But what if you tell her? Isn't that committing her to death? How happy will she be thinking Frisno used her to get a baby? She then begins to question his love, his commitment. She will begin to look at the baby a different way and everything changes," Mia said.

"Mia, I hear what all you are saying, but what if—"

"Jasmine, we all know the God we serve is a God who answers prayers. All we can do is pray for her and her unborn baby. The baby will get multiple tests in the first year, and they will immediately know if something is wrong. Nothing is showing now, and if something should pop up in that short amount of time, it's still catching it early enough to prevent it from turning into AIDS," said Imani.

"I guess you're right," Jasmine said.

"I am right, and she may not have anything," Imani confirmed.

"Like I said, Jasmine, let her be happy. If something pops up, at least she will feel like it was something that happened by chance and she won't blame Frisno. Let her have her happiness and love for him and his respect. Anything can happen in life. Don't make her think he used her. After all, we don't really know what was in his heart," Evan said.

"But Evan, he said he wanted a baby," Jasmine whined.

"And he got one. It still doesn't mean he didn't love her. And it doesn't change that he did want a baby. That is not a crime," Evan protested.

"It's a crime what he did," said Jasmine.

"True, it may be a crime, but he wasn't out sleeping with women like some crazies do and committing murder. He was trying to live by leaving a piece of himself," added Mia.

"At the risk of taking someone else's life?" Jasmine shook her head.

"You're right, girl. I was just trying to lighten the situation. That was pretty messed up." Mia laughed.

They all giggled in the midst of their painful circumstances.

Imani concluded, "Only one person can lighten the situation now. Can we pray?" Imani extended her hands as the women and Evan stood in a circle and prayed.

Chapter Seventy-Seven

Imani sat alone, looking over the beautiful lawn in her yard. She felt depressed, isolated and forgotten. So many changes and battles seemed to come every day, and at this point, she not only was experiencing menopause and managing to keep it to herself, she was feeling tired. The night sweats, the hot flashes, loss of weight; it was driving her crazy. She wasn't sure what to do. She picked up the phone and called Mia.

"Mia, I think I'm going through menopause."

"You would know. What's been going on?"

"I wake up sweating like someone dunked me in some water. I've been losing weight, and I keep having these hot flashes."

"I figured that was what it was when you were at the hospital undressing and dressing."

"What do I do?"

"Don't let it control your life, Mani. It's a phase we all will go through as women."

"Easy for you to say."

"No, see, natural menopause occurs gradually when

ovaries stop producing the hormone estrogen. That causes hormonal imbalance, which can cause weight gain or weight loss. This usually happens when you're between forty-five and fifty-five, and the earliest age is usually around fifty-one. So, it's normal to feel irritable and moody."

"What can I do, Mia? I can't sleep at night and I'm tired."

"There are options like diet and exercise that work for some women when it's mild, or prescription medicine or alternative remedies. It just depends on what your symptoms are."

"I told you; night sweats, hot flashes, and loss of weight."

"All right. Then you can combat yours with just a little more exercise. I mean you don't have too much tiredness or moodiness, irritability or mood swings.

"I can give you something for the night sweats and hot flashes, that can help you get a good night's sleep and go through the day more comfortable, which can stop any progressing symptoms of menopause from coming on."

"All right, I will be in today."

After Imani went to get the medicine, she felt like she could embrace her change of life a lot better and with the knowledge that she was more aware of what was happening, so it wasn't as difficult to accept. She didn't want anymore children anyway of course, but trying to deal with not feeling so much like a young, vibrant woman anymore was a struggle. But, she decided she would just look at the bright side. She was a complete woman now who had lived her life and was embarking upon another part of life and what it had to offer. It was time to look back on the fruits of her womb and see if she had been faithful to what God had given her to do as a woman to bring others into the world. It would determine whether she was satisfied with the gift God had given her as a woman and if He too would be pleased He had entrusted her to such a major task of carrying and birthing life.

Life was beautiful in most ways—the kids, her family, her friends—but in a lot of ways, it was depleting. It was, to say the least, draining. She had given so much of herself, and it seemed life gave her so little in return. Lost grandchildren, stolen virtues, misfortunes, mishaps. Time seemed to go by too fast. Imani was empty, tired of consoling and wondered what the end result was to be. Imani was tired of holding on and gathering just enough strength to put out the next fire, and then do it all again in a matter of a season.

She was getting old and needed a little more meaning to her life. Did she share wisdom, strength, beauty and love? Was her living not in vain? Mostly, Imani was there to pick everyone else up, have a solid word or even a strong shoulder to lean on, but today she broke down in tears and they flowed like rivers as she sat quietly and alone. Was there supposed to be a climax to her life now, the moment that all moments build up to? The final breath before she could exhale? Who could she turn to now in her vulnerability? Who would she lean on and look to for encouragement?

It began to downpour, and Imani watched the rain fall from the sky. She pulled her blanket softly across her shoulders. Everything seemed peaceful and tranquil, and she suddenly realized that this very peace meant everything was finally good in her life and her family. Her life instantly seemed complete.

She was ready to embark upon another phase of her life with energy, joy and anticipation of growing wiser and stronger in the Lord. And all it took was a downpour from Heaven. The rain always indicated to her that Jesus still sits on the throne and He reigns. This is why the rain shower was the most perfect and favorite part of her life.

*   *   *

Mitchell and Braxton stood in the church and looked on proudly as Mia and Cashous christened the twins. Cashous thought it would be nice to name each one of them the godfathers of Ailjon and Angelina. They loved them so much. The rest of the family stood and looked on as well. Jasmine, Imani and Summer were named the godmothers.

Jasmine looked at Summer. "This should be the happiest day of Mia's life. She got all her men here."

"Yep, real hooka, ain't she?" Summer joked.

Mia looked at them. "Do you all know I can hear you?"

"We meant for you to hear us."

"You all can't never be quiet or stop talking," Imani chimed in.

"Imani, don't start with me today. You better tell your mama, Mike, before I take it to the streets."

"You always taking something to the street, Summer. Cashous, what in the world we got ourselves into?" Mike asked his brother-in-law.

"What you got yourself into? Jasmine, get your little brother," Mia said.

"He your twin. My husband ain't said a word; that is all I'm concerned with." Jasmine looked over at Evan, who was just minding his business.

"Probably scared to say anything," Jamal joked.

"Jamal, that ain't right," Mitchell added.

"I ain't scared. Just know when not to get into the conversation." Finally, Evan defended himself.

"If you scared, say you scared," Mitchell teased further.

"Mitchell, you crazy," said Evan.

"Braxton, we ain't going to raise no punks; might as well tell it like it is. Right, Ailjon?" Mitchell looked over at his friend.

The family continued on with their small talk until the ceremony started. Ailjon and Angelina were dressed in their white attire. Ailjon wore a little white tux with a cummerbund to match and a little tie with his little white shoes. Angelina was dressed in her lacy white dress that went all the way down past her little feet, and a white ribbon around her head. They were the cutest! As the preacher dedicated the two babies, Cashous and Mia stood proudly with their godparents around them. They handed the boy to Braxton and Mitchell, and the girl to Imani. "Make us proud," said Cashous.

Mia just smiled as she fought back the tears as the preacher spoke on the precious gifts of raising children. Imani, Jasmine and Summer got a little caught up as well as they fought back the tears.

In the midst of the tears, Summer said, "The ceremony was nice, wasn't it?"

"It was real nice," said Jasmine.

Jasmine walked over to the group, where all the ladies fumbled over the babies. "I'm hungry. Let's go get something to eat."

"No need to go anywhere. I made dinner at the house." said Imani.

"She better had," Jasmine joked.

"Okay, now I know let's go eat!" Summer exclaimed and then headed to Imani's.

"It was proved today," Jamal said to Cashous and Mia. "My children are all married, doing the right thing. Raising their children."

"Yeah, because you kids today got to learn how to do things out of the respect of the Lord, not just us older people," Imani added. "You have to have some respect for yourselves. And then raise those babies right so they can know right from wrong. Having babies is a great responsibility God entrusted you to, and you going to have to answer one day how you molded and looked over those little gifts."

Jasmine was laughing and making fun with Summer.

"Shut up, Jasmine, you the main one. Stop playing so much."

"Yes, ma'am."

Summer and Mia were laughing now.

"You kids better get serious. Life is not easy, and if you want anything in life, you going to have to work at it and work hard at it. No one is going to give you anything because everyone struggling themselves. But I tell you what; you can do anything you want to do if you put God first and trust Him. It isn't always what you want or understand. But if you hold on and hold out, God will see you through. I know what I'm talking about. Tell them, Jamal," Imani said.

"That's right. She telling you," he said, agreeing with Imani.

"It may not look like your life was meant to be, but God got a purpose for every one of His children, and one day Jamal and I will be dead and gone. You need to learn now to lean on Jesus, trust in God and keep on moving even when you don't feel like moving. Do what your heart tell you is right and raise them babies and live right. All you married now with kids, and with families. Be able to look back on your life and say 'I did good. I did the best I could with what I had' and have lots of children. That is what God could have you do and be happy. That is the most important thing. Be happy."

Mia began to sniff and she wiped her eyes.

"I knew she would be the first to get all emotional," Mike said.

Mia's sniffling turned to a slight grin at her brother's response.

"That is all right. Leave her alone, Mike. She got a lot to cry about. They tears of joy, though," Imani stated.

"They sure are," Mia confirmed.

"Say grace, Jamal. Dinner getting cold," Imani ordered.

"I thought we was just sitting here looking at the food for a minute," Evan joked.

"Evan, be quiet."

"Heavenly Father, thank You for this food," Jamal prayed. "Thank You for all the family that You have allowed to partake of this meal. Thank You for love, thank You for family. God, we thank You that we could have been all in separate places doing our own thing, but the joy of Ailjon and Angelina caused us to come this way together once again. We thank You that any one of us could have been dead and gone, but You allowed us to see another day. We thank You for the best day of our lives, because You woke us up. Thank You for allowing us to have this time together. We don't take it for granted or your love. In Jesus' name we pray. Amen."

"Let's eat!" Cashous shouted.

Chapter Seventy-Eight

Mia sat down to reflect over her life. She had been jobless, deserted, misunderstood, alone; even with family around, she was still lonely. She had felt betrayed and cheated by life when her children died and she was still angry, if she cared to admit the truth to anyone. Cheated on by man after man, abused and lost at times. It almost seemed like a constant roller-coaster. But through it all, she realized that she had made it; she was still alive. She didn't know how, but she knew that she was alive.

She had to stop and look at herself in the mirror and say it out loud—"I'm alive"—after she checked her pulse. Something felt different about today.

Cashous walked in. "What are you doing?" he asked her.

"Checking to see if I'm alive."

Cashous' heart went out to his wife, and he immediately understood.

"Oh, baby, you're alive, and you're real, and this is another day. This is a day the Lord has made for you to be glad and rejoice in it."

"I truly believe that. I just don't know if I can find happiness, if it is meant for me to be happy or I'm meant to have anything in life. Maybe I'm God's example to help someone else along the way or help people to see it's not about us. It's just that I hope God can find it in His heart to give me just one of my desires in this lifetime."

"Mia, He will because He said He would have us to have and have more abundantly. God designed it for all of us to be happy and to have the desires of our hearts."

"Can you ever tell me why my life has been so hard?"

"Can you tell me why it should have been easy? Who can you help with an easy life? You got to go through some things to have anything, Mia. No one ever achieved their goal or got anything in life without first going through something."

"Like the saying, you have to crawl before you walk?"

"Something like that."

"No, I think more like how can you know when you're up if you never fall down?"

"Okay. If you say so."

"Just feels better in my soul to say that."

"I have to go to work. Have a good day, and maybe you should get back to work."

"All right."

Mia stretched her fingers and rolled her neck around and went to get a glass of juice. She then grabbed her computer and went to work. Mia sat on her couch and typed out the last chapter of her book. She had worked hard and long. Yet, she felt she had not said what needed to be said. Life was not a fairytale; it was not easy. All her life she tried to be someone, to make something out of her life because of all the broken hearts and the pitfalls of life. She had to overcome low self-esteem, misunderstanding, loneliness, and it always seemed she was the black sheep of any gathering.

What was she to learn in all of this; what was her life to become? Mia could not find the words; she had tried, perhaps she had achieved it, or she would die trying.

She sat in front of her computer and she looked on for hours as she scrolled through her manuscript. She wondered, *Can I share this book with anyone and they read it and feel all that I feel? Can I help someone along the way to go to another place?* All she needed was a title. She sat quietly for quite a while and then it came to her suddenly and she heard God speak. Not only had God given her a title, but a message and confirmation to her life.

"Trouble Won't Last Always." Mia spoke as she typed in the title. "Amen to that!"

Reader's Group Guide

1. What lessons can be learned from Mia's search for love?

2. Do you believe Jasmine, Imani, Summer and Mia's faith became stronger because of the events in their lives?

3. Do you have lasting relationships like these women share in your life?

4. Are you encouraged, uplifted or inspired by Imani's wisdom in this story?

5. Do you think Mia's pregnancy with Drake was a result of her sinful ways, or is pregnancy a gift from God no matter the circumstances?

6. How much do you live for love of another human being or live for a loving relationship with Jesus?

7. Why do you think Mitchell went with Mia to have the abortion? Would you have done what Mia did?

8. Would you have forgiven Evan and Frisno as Jasmine did?

9. What can you take away from this story to help you become a better person?

10. Why do you think God allowed Mia to lose all her children?

11. Who was your favorite character in *Troubles Won't Last Always*?

12. Would you like to see a second part to *Troubles Won't Last Always*?